Victoria Institute

Proceedings of the Victoria Institute of Trinidad

Vol. 3

Victoria Institute

Proceedings of the Victoria Institute of Trinidad
Vol. 3

ISBN/EAN: 9783337361679

Printed in Europe, USA, Canada, Australia, Japan

Cover: Foto ©Andreas Hilbeck / pixelio.de

More available books at **www.hansebooks.com**

PROCEEDINGS

OF THE

Victoria Institute

OF

TRINIDAD.

FOUNDED   1887.

Part 3.   March 1899.

CONTENTS:

" Mirror " Office, 3, Abercromby Street, Port-of-Spain.

VICTORIA INSTITUTE,

TRINIDAD.

ANNUAL REPORTS, 1895-6.

THE Board of Management have the honour to present to the Members their Report of the working of the Victoria Institute for the year 1895.

This is the fourth Annual Report presented to the Members of the Institute, and it marks the opening of a new era, as it were, in the history of the Institution; for although the scientific work of this Institute was allowed to fall somewhat into abeyance, substantial reforms have been effected, by which it is expected that new life and energy will be given to the Institute.

At the first meeting in January, Mr. R. J. L. Guppy, the Secretary and Treasurer, tendered his resignation, but at the request of the Board he retained the office until the 14th March, when he retired with a vote of thanks for his services.

At the Annual Meeting on 21st February the following gentlemen were elected members of the Board of Management for 1895:

His Hon. Sir JOHN GOLDNEY, Kt.,
Hon. Col. WILSON, V.D., C.M.G.,
Prof. CARMODY,
Mr. TRIPP,
,, CARACCIOLO,
,, URICH,
,, POTTER.

the Government Members being :

> Hon. Dr. LOVELL,
>   „   D. B. HORSFORD,
> Mr. BOURNE,
>   „   R. J. L. GUPPY,

and the following officers were elected at the next meeting of the Board :

> His Hon. Sir John Goldney, Kt., President.
> Hon. Dr. Lovell, C.M.G., Vice-President.
> Mr. Syl. Devenish, M.A., „ „
> Mr. F. W. Urich, Hon. Secretary and Treasurer vice
>   Mr. Guppy retired, but who remains a member
>   of the Board.

In July, Mr. F. W. Urich resigned the office of Secretary and Treasurer, having received a Government appointment in Arima, and Mr. T. I. Potter was elected to replace him.

In September the Clerk, Mr. Devenish, also resigned, having obtained a better situation, and from among a number of applicants, Mrs. Latour was selected by the Board to fill the vacancy.

These are all the changes in the staff that have occurred during the year.

On the 7th February, Mr. H. C. Bourne gave notice of a motion to amend Article 17 of the Articles of Association, and on the 21st of the same month it was seconded by Dr. Lovell and carried.

The amendment is as follows :

" That Article 17 be altered by the addition of the follow-
" ing words, namely : Provided that any person who shall in the
" preceding or current year have subscribed $5 at least to any
" local society having for its objects any of the objects of the
" Victoria Institute shall be eligible for election for membership
" of the Institute without signing any written application for
" election or becoming liable for any entrance fee or subscription
" thereto, and if elected shall enjoy all rights and privileges of a
" member including eligibility for the Committee of Management :
" and shall not be required to pay any subscription so long as he
" shall continue to subscribe $5 at least per annum to such local
" society aforesaid."

This had the effect of adding at once to the Institute the whole of the then existing members of the Field Naturalists' Club who were not already members of the Institute.

It is a question for the consideration of the Board and the members generally whether a closer bond of union with the Field Naturalists' Club, such as the amalgamation of the proceedings of both institutions, and of the evenings of meetings, would not be beneficial to the Institute.

On the 27th March the following Committees were appointed by the Board :

Information and Publication.

Hon. Col. WILSON,
Prof. CARMODY,
Mr. DEVENISH,
   „   BOURNE,
   „   CARACCIOLO.

Industrial and Commercial.

Hon. Col. WILSON,
   „   D. B. HORSFORD,
Prof. CARMODY,
Mr. TRIPP,
   „   DEVENISH.

Natural History.

Hon. Dr. LOVELL,
Mr. DEVENISH,
   „   CARACCIOLO,
   „   GUPPY,
   „   POTTER.

Building and Entertainment.

Hon. Col. WILSON,
Prof. CARMODY,
Mr. DEVENISH,
   „   BOURNE,
   „   TRIPP.

The President and Secretary to be *ex Officio* Members of all Committees. Two members to form a quorum, and Committees to arrange their hours and places of meeting. Two of these Committees (the Industrial and Commercial and the Natural History Committees) made reports at the next meeting of the Board which were adopted, and some of their recommendations have been carried into effect.

In accordance with the recommendation of the Industrial Committee, Professor Carmody delivered two Lectures during the year, the first on "Commercial Products," and the second on "Short Hand as a Branch of Education," but it is to be regretted that the attendance of members and of the public was not such as these two most useful and interesting Lectures deserved.

Another recommendation was the formation of an Industrial Commercial Museum of local products and manufactures. This, though not yet effected has not been lost sight of, and it is expected that members will see the first attempt at such a museum in the very near future.

Correspondence with the Imperial Institute was advocated, but although our President is a correspondent of Sir Somers Vine, there has been little official correspondence with the Imperial Institute during this year. The publications of that institution have been regularly received, and the local Institute has been nominated the corresponding agent of the English one. It is to be hoped that matters will improve in this direction during the next year.

In accordance with the recommendation of the Natural History Committee, a drying box for preparing insect and other specimens has been prepared, and setting boards and Insect Show Cases have been imported. It is expected that the Field Naturalists' Members will now take the advantage of these facilities, and supply the necessary material to make the entomological collection as complete as possible.

The Natural History Committee also recommended the purchase of a Science Lantern.

The President, when in England in July last, ordered a fine set of apparatus which arrived in January, 1896, and the Institute may be said to be in possession of the finest Science Lantern in the island, and perhaps in the West Indies. Arrangements for the use of the Electric Light with this lantern are not yet quite complete, but it will not be long before the Board will be in a position to afford members and the public the pleasure and recreative information which are to be derived from Lantern Lectures.

On 29th October last the Board formed Art and Horticultural Sections for the purpose of encouraging and stimulating artistic talent, and the culture of flowers and ornamental plants. The first result of the formation of these Sections was an Exhibition in Art and Horticulture which was held in January, 1896, and though really a matter for next year's report it may be incidentally remarked here that their efforts were crowned with success. It is the intention of the Board to hold other and similar Exhibitions from time to time.

The financial condition of the Institute is a matter for congratulation.

The Government grant to the Institute was increased at the beginning of the year to £250 and therefore like other similar institutions in this Colony the main source of Revenue is this subsidy. The next is the revenue derived from rents and last of all is the amount derived from subscription.

The causes to which may be attributed the falling off under this last head of revenue are (1) the motion of Mr. Bourne admitting the Field Naturalists' Club (2) the late time of the year (November) when the subscriptions for 1895-6 began to be collected.

The total Revenue of the Institute for 1895 amounts to $1,482.50 net, and to this must be added a balance of $216.36 carried forward from 1894.

The total expenditure of the same period is $809.35 inclusive of the repayment to Government of the first instalment of the debt of £500 on the Building. It may not be out of place to remark here that a second instalment has also been paid on 1st January of the current year, leaving a balance of £400 due to Government.

There was therefore to the credit of the Institute on 31st December, 1895, the sum of $889.52 of which $884.03 was lodged in the Colonial Bank.

Appended is a Statement of Account and a Balance Sheet.

A list of members is also annexed.

The visitors to the Museum during 1895 amounted to 2,353. Many of the foreign visitors expressed agreeable surprise at finding such a fine collection of the fauna of the Island.

In conclusion it may be said that the Institute is now in a fair way to assume its proper position as a public Institution of this Colony, and a fitting Memorial of the Jubilee of our Gracious Sovereign whose name it bears.

THOMAS I. POTTER,   *Hon. Secretary & Treasurer.*

Victoria Museum, Port-of-Spain, 18th February, 1898.

STATEMENT OF THE RECEIPTS AND EXPENDITURE OF THE VICTORIA INSTITUTE FOR THE YEAR 1895.

RECEIPTS.	$	c	$	c		PAYMENTS.		$	c
Government Grant ...			1,200	00		Salaries	...	222	20
Reimbursements (Rents) ...	187	28				Refunded to Government	...	240	00
Subscriptions ...	67	50				Repairs	...	6	52
Art Exhibition, 1895 ...	27	72	282	50		Furniture, etc.	...	35	99
						Petty Expenses, Lighting, etc. ...	...	123	99
						Printing, Binding, etc. ...	...	180	64
			$1,482	50				$809	34

JOHN T. GOLDNEY, *President.*

THOMAS I. POTTER, *Treasurer.*

VICTORIA INSTITUTE.—BALANCE SHEET 31ST DECEMBER, 1895.

	$	c			$	c
Balance on 1st January, 1895 ...	216	36	Expenditure as above		$ 809	34
Receipts as above	1,482	50	Balance on 31st December, 1895			
			In Colonial Bank ...	$884 03		
			In Hand... ...	5 49	889	52
	$1,698	86			$1,698	86

JOHN T GOLDNEY, *President.*

THOMAS I. POTTER, *Treasurer.*

Correct according to Vouchers and Books produced.

C. W. LANGFORD.
G. CREAGH-CREAGH. } *Auditors.*

Number of Visitors to the Victoria Museum during the year 1895.

January 1st to 30th	...	...	...	...	301
February 1st to 17th	...	...	...	...	251
March 1st to 30th ...	...	...	...	...	250
April 1st to 30th ...	...	...	...	...	21g
May 1st to 31st ...	...	...	...	...	196
June 1st to 29th ...	...	...	...	...	86
July 1st to 31st ...	...	...	...	...	143
August 1st to 30th	...	...	...	...	181
September 1st to 30th	...	...	...	...	173
October 1st to 10th	...	...	...	...	60
November 1st to 30th	...	...	...	...	194
December 1st to 30th	...	...	...	...	305
			Total	...	... 2,353

ANNUAL REPORT FOR 1896.

THE Board of Management has the honour to lay before the members the following Report of the working of the Institute for the year 1896.

An earnest attempt has been made during the year to increase the usefulness of the Institution.

No change was made in the membership of the Board or of its Officers at the last Annual Meeting, which was held on the 27th of February, 1896, and the paid staff has remained the same.

Owing to the temporary absence of an unusually large number of members of the Board, on the 30th June the remaining members, acting in accordance with Section 7 of the Articles of Association, appointed the following gentlemen to act :—

Mr. B. H. STEPHENS,
  „ R. H. McCARTHY,
Dr. INCE,
Mr. J. R. LLANOS,
  „ J. R. MURRAY.

These gentlemen were of great assistance, and by their regular attendance at meetings facilitated the work of the Board.

On the 4th September the Board appointed the following Committees :—

Building and General Business Committee :

Sir JOHN GOLDNEY, President,
Hon'ble Colonel WILSON, C.M.G.,
Mr. GUPPY,
Professor CARMODY,
Mr. DEVENISH,
    ,, TRIPP.

Science, Art and Industries Committee :

Sir JOHN GOLDNEY,
Hon'ble Dr. LOVELL, C.M.G.,
Mr. H. C. BOURNE,
    ,, R. H. McCARTHY,
    ,, TRIPP,
    ,, B. H. STEPHENS,
    ,, H. CARACCIOLO,
    ,, J. R. MURRAY.

The Vice-Presidents and Mr. T. I. Potter, Hon. Secretary, being *ex officio* members of both Committees.

The latter Committee prepared and submitted to the Board a Report on the Natural History Collections and on the formation of an Industrial and Commercial Museum, which was adopted and ordered to be printed on the Proceedings of the Institute.

The Board has recently lost an elected member by the departure of Colonel Wilson from the Colony on the 4th February, 1897. In him the Institute also has lost one of its original Members, and its Chairman during its early years.

At the Annual Meeting the President referred to the proposal for amalgamating the Trinidad Public Library with the Institute. Several meetings were held to discuss the question, and at a Special General Meeting of the members of the Institute held on the 9th January, 1897, it was unanimously agreed that the amalgamation was desirable.

On the question of the best site for the United Institution, a difference of opinion exists, which has prevented further progress towards the end in view.

The chief work of the Institute for the year was the holding of small Exhibitions for the purpose of encouraging and stimulating local talent in Art and Horticulture.

As mentioned in last year's Annual Report, two of these Exhibitions were held simultaneously on the 23rd, 24th, and 25th January, and two were held in a similar manner, on 5th and 6th of June.

The last two months of the year were devoted to preparations for the Centenary Exhibition of February, 1897, a report of which will be ready shortly, but will be included in the proceedings of next year.

Reports with Appendices on the Exhibitions held during the year have been prepared and will be published in this year's proceedings.

It is sufficient to remark here, that although these Exhibitions were not successes financially, they have at least brought the Institute in closer contact with the public than hitherto, and have induced many of our young people to pay attention to Art and Horticulture.

As stated at the last Annual Meeting the Board enclosed the land belonging to the Institute with a strong iron fence. A small garden has also been laid out in front of the building and a hedge planted inside the fence.

In November it was found necessary to re-paint the front and corners of the Building.

A sum of $33.60 was spent on the roof and in erecting and keeping in repair the bamboo fence which had been put up previous to the receipt of the new iron fence.

The total cost of these additions and repairs and of keeping the Building and grounds in proper condition was $778.75.

Owing to the want of apparatus for regulating the electric current the Lantern could not for some time be used for lectures, but thanks to the assistance of the Superintendent of the Trinidad Electric Light and Power Company, this difficulty has been overcome and the Lantern is now at the service of members for the purpose of illustrating their lectures.

A number of Natural History and X ray slides also have been received for use with the Lantern.

In December the Board decided to have an evening for meetings of the members, and the last Monday of every month was fixed for this purpose.

A programme of work has been arranged, and several gentlemen have been invited to read papers at these meetings.

In June a Scientific Reading Room for the use of members was opened at the Institute.

Besides the numerous scientific books and papers received in Exchange from foreign Societies by the Institute, the following periodicals were added by the Board :—

> The Gardener's Chronicle,
>   ,, Photographic News,
>   ,, Magazine of Art.

The Hon. Dr. LOVELL, one of the Vice-Presidents, also kindly contributes the Journal of the British Medical Association.

Although a few do use the reading room, it does not receive the attention from members which it deserves.

The collection of specimens for an Industrial and Commercial Museum continues. And it is hoped that before the end of the year 1897 the Institute will have made considerable progress with this work. It is to be regretted that the funds' of the Institute do not allow larger outlay in the collecting, preparation and perservation of specimens. The Board will be relieved of considerable expense in collecting, if the Agriculturists of the Colony would co-operate with the Institute by sending specimens of their produce, in all stages, to the Institute. At the request of the Hon. Secretary, one or two sugar planters and a Life member of the Institute have sent in specimens of produce. One of our Vice-Presidents has also given the Institute a valuable collection of specimens of native timber.

The Rooms of the Institute are still in demand as a place of meeting for Societies.

The Finances of the Institute are submitted for the consideration of the members.

As the statement shows, the Receipts for the year amount to $1,726.35 inclusive of Government grant of $1,200 which if deducted, leaves $526.35 as the Receipts of the Institute from other sources. The total Receipts, though more than those of last year, are, however, less than the Expenditure by $541.74, and were it not for a large Balance to Credit from last year, there would have been a serious deficit at the end of the year. There is, however still a Balance to Credit of $341.74 to be carried forward, and there is every reason to believe that the Institute will be able to pay its way during next year if judiciously managed. As is shown above, the chief source of Revenue is the Government subsidy, and without this the Institute cannot be carried on.

The next direct Revenue to the Institute is the subscriptions of Members.

At the commencement of the last subscription year, 24th March, 1896, in addition to the members who were also members of the Field Naturalists' Club, whose subscription go to that Club, there were 27 members paying $5 per annum and 3 Associates of 10/- per annum. Since that date seven of these members have resigned or left the Colony. A second instalment of the debt to the Government was paid on 2nd January, 1896, leaving a Balance of £400 to be paid. In January, 1897, this was further reduced by £50, which makes the existing balance only £350. At the present rate of payment the Institute will be free from debt in seven years, but if it could obtain a larger support from the public, there is no reason why this debt could not be paid off within a shorter time.

Both the Revenue and Expenditure of this year are larger than those of 1895. This is owing to increased activity on the part of the Institute. Of the Expenditure a large proportion has been spent on the public, the loss on Exhibitions alone being $284.95, of which $235.70 was given away in prizes.

Some 2,600 people visited the Institute during the year. This number does not include those who visited the Exhibitions.

It is to be hoped that the public will not, in the year of Her Gracious Majesty's Diamond Jubilee, allow the Institute, the only Memorial of Her late Jubilee, which exists in the Colony, to be closed for the want of Funds.

The Accounts have been duly audited.

THOMAS I. POTTER,

Hon. Secretary.

Victoria Museum, 23rd March, 1897.

Statement of the Revenue and Expenditure of

RECEIPTS.

Grant from Government			1,200 00
Subscriptions from Members to 31st Decr...	180 00		
Receipts (Gate-money, &c.) from Exhibitions	160 75		
Reimbursements in aid (Rents, &c.) ...	185 60	526 35	

$1,726 35

Balance Sheet,

Balance on 1st January, 1896	889 52	
Receipts as above	1,726 35	

$2,615 87

Checked these Accounts for 1896, with Vouchers, and found correct.

(Signed) GEO. GOODWILLE.

" . JAMES GRAHAM TAYLOR

the Victoria Institute, for the year 1896.

PAYMENTS.

Salaries and Allowances to Staff	244 40	
Additions, Improvements and Repairs to premises }	778 75	
Furniture, Fittings and Apparatus... ...	227 57	
Expenses of Exhibitions	445 70	
Insurance Premium (3 years paid in advance)	144 00	
Printing and Stationery	52 87	
Petty Expenses (Lighting, Postage, etc.) ...	140 84	2,034 13
Refund to Government (2nd instalment)...		240 00

$2,274 13

31st December, 1896.

Expenditure as above		2,274 13
Balance on 31st December		
In Colonial Bank...	292 31	
In Hand	49 43	341 74

$2,615 87

JOHN T. GOLDNEY,

President.

THOMAS I. POTTER,

Hon. Treasurer.

(Read 31st May, 1897.)

ON A SMALL COLLECTION OF BUTTERFLIES MADE CHIEFLY IN THE TUNAPUNA VALLEY.

By FLORIAN LECHMERE GUPPY.

I exhibit a case of butterflies most of which were collected in Tunapuna Valley. Among them is a specimen of *Metamorpha dido* which is stated to be a common tropical American insect; but it is not included in Dr. Crowfoot's list of Trinidad Butterflies, hitherto the most complete. When flying, this insect might be taken for *Victorina steneles*, the Green Page. It flies very high overhead and is hard to capture. There are also in the collection some specimens of *Ageronia* and *Heliconius*. The four kinds of *Ageronia* are very remarkable and I think three of them are scarce, but I shall probably get more. In Tunapuna Valley Heliconii are very abundant. Another abundant species in that Valley is *Catagramma codomannus* (the eighty-eight.) I have found the names of some of those butterflies and I should like to identify the others. They were all caught in Tunapuna Valley except the *Helicopes* which I got at Woodbrook, and the large dark-colored butterfly near the *Nymphalis orion* in the case. This large butterfly is the only one of its kind I have seen.

Read 31st May, 1897.

SUGGESTIONS AS TO SILICEOUS AND CALCAREOUS ORGANISMS.

By R. J. LECHMERE GUPPY.

THE nature and character of organisms secreting and assimilating Silica and Lime respectively have often been before my mind. In the course of the studies and investigations I undertook some five or six years ago into the Foraminifera and Radiolaria of the cretaceo-tertiary rocks and at various other time, it has occurred to me that assimilated Lime is characteristic of animals, while assimilated Silica is characteristic of plants Hence I consider that the presence of assimilated Silica is *prima facie* evidence of the vegetable nature of the organism in which it is found while the presence of assimilated lime is *prima facie* evidence of the animal nature of any organism in which it occurs. This consequence seems to flow from the relative functions of plants and animals in relation to vital force.   The Plant absorbs the solar energy and converts it into vital force.   The Animal takes that vitality, absorbs it, uses it, and destroys it. The assimilation of Silica appears therefore to be a concomitant of the power to vitalize solar energy, while the animal not having that power is able to assimilate Lime only and not Silica.

The questions of whether Sponges are animal or vegetable was for a long time in debate—but of late years the opinion has been in favor of their animal nature.   If the suggestion I have ventured to put forward is considered to be well founded, the modern opinion will again be opened to question, and it may, after all be decided that sponges are protophytic and not protozoic. But at all events Radiolaria and their allies must be regarded as Protophytes while Foraminifera will still be classed as Protozoa.

I am inclined to think that Radiolaria perform the functions of Plants in relation to vitality, and I would further suggest that Radiolaria are the chief food of Foraminifera, at any rate in the case of the pelagic forms whether Plankton or Benthos.

While on this subject I may further suggest that the Sporozoa are merely lower forms of Annuloidea and do not properly belong to Protozoa.   Most, if not all of them are parasitic upon animals and resemble Helminthozoa (*e. g.* Flukes, &c.,) in appearance and habits.   I have on previous occasions recorded my opinion that the very numerous forms of Polycystina and Radiolaria ranged under many generic and specific names by Ehrenberg and others are really referable to a few species only.

NOTE ON THE DISCOVERY OF CORALS IN THE HARBOUR OF PORT-OF-SPAIN.

By R. J. Lechmere Guppy.

DURING the course of the dredging-operations connected with the Harbor Improvements of Port-of Spain, a number of fragments of coral have been dredged up.   The site of the discovery was

just off the old St. Vincent Jetty.   An examination of the corals
and of the associated shells has convinced me that the corals in
question are none other than true reef corals such as it is
impossible could live in such a position or indeed in any part of
the Gulf of Paria.   Moreover, the shells found associated with the
corals are without exception so far as I have observed, the same
species as are found in the Gulf and not such as would be found
associated with reef corals.

The possibility of the existence of a tertiary bed at the
bottom of some part of the Gulf has often occurred to me and I
have on a former occasion referred to such a possibility.   But the
conditions of the present coral deposit entirely preclude the
possibility of its being such a bed.   The corals have evidently
been brought here from some other place, probably from Barbados
where all the species are found abundantly.   Perhaps the lighter
or vessel in which they were being carried was swamped or cap-
sized.   At one time corals were imported here for the purpose of
being burnt into lime and it is highly probable that the deposit
now found was a cargo of such corals.

It is likely that all the massive reef corals of Barbados are
represented here, but those I have identified are the following :—

Favia ananas, Lam.   Madrepora muricata, Linn.
Astrea radians, Pall.   Manicina areolata, Linn.
Porites clavaria, Lam.

Read 31st May, 1897.

REMARKS ON SOME FOSSILS FROM THE EOCENE OF NAPARIMA.

By R. J. Lechmere Guppy.

UNFORTUNATELY for Trinidad, my collection of West
Indian Fossils has left the country, having been acquired by the
United States National Museum.   To make a collection to replace
this would be a work of time, labor and expense which I could
hardly undergo. I have, however, availed myself of all such oppor-
tunities as have occurred to me to collect Fossils.   I here exhibit a
few specimens deserving of notice. Some examples of *Echinolampas
ovumserpentis* are on the table ; and there is one specimen of

Echinolampas which differs so much from this that it would generally be regarded as a different and probably a new species, for in some of its characters it is intermediate between the eocene *Ech. ovumserpentis* and the miocene *Ech. semiorbis.* I should be inclined to refer it to the *Echinolampas antillarum* Cotteau (Descr. Echinid. tert. 1875 p. 19, pl. iii., f. 9-11) but it has more of a subcircular contour and a conical profile.

Another Fossil before you is a specimen of *Terebratula carneoides.* This is the finest I have seen of the species. It recalls somewhat *Ter. bicanaliculata,* Schlot. (Bayle and Coquand Foss. de Chili, Mem. Soc. Geol. France, 2 ser. t. 4, pl. viii., f. 17-19) and also perhaps *T. haueri,* Karst. (Kreidebildung von Sudamerika, taf. vi., f. 1.) The principal distinction between *T. carnea* of the Chalk and *T. carneoides* of the West Indian Eocene is the much larger foramen of the latter. From *T. depressa,* **Lam.** of the Chalk, *T. carneoides* is distinguishable by the absence of a Deltidium. These characters it may be admitted seem scarcely weighty enough to separate species, but they appear to be pretty constant. The cretaceous alliances of our Fossil are evidently strong, but too much weight must not be attached to this point because as pointed out by Davidson the form is represented in the living Fauna by *T. vitrea.*

T. carneoides was described by me from the Naparima Beds in quart. Journ. Geol. Soc. 1866 p. 296 pl. xix. f. 2. It was much better figured and described from the Eocene of the Island of St. Barts by Thomas Davidson in Geol. Mag. 1874, page 158 pl. viii., f. 11.

Read 31st May, 1897.

NOTES ON THE PASSAGE BETWEEN THE FORAMINIFERA BEDS AND THE RADIOLARIAN MARLS OF NAPARIMA.

BY R. J. LECHMERE GUPPY.

ON a visit I paid sometime ago (November, 1894) to the South Naparima District, my friend Mr. Ludovic de Verteuil pointed out to me what he believed to be the junction beds between the Radiolarian marls and the Foraminifera beds. On examination I was able to verify the fact. I was also able to observe evidence of the fact that a gradual transition takes place from the Foraminifera beds to the Radiolarian marls—the junction beds occupying a width of about fifty yards or so measured across the upturned edges of the beds at right angles to the strike. From a diagram kindly furnished to me by Mr. de Verteuil it appears that the line of strike of the junction beds extends so far as known from Beausejour and Plaisance through Cedar Grove, La Resource and Philipine, passing to the north-west of Dunmore Hill. This of course is quite agreeable to all former observations of the strike of the Naparima beds.

As regards physical characteristics it may be noted that the junction beds contain a larger proportion of pumice and felspathic material than any other of the rocks of the district that I have examined. Silicous casts of Globi-gerina are another feature worthy of notice in these beds. These casts of the interior of the Foraminifer are of a brilliant white bristling with what look like small spines but which are casts of the pores in the Globigerina Shell. In character generally as well as in position the junction beds are intermediate between the Foraminifera and Radiolarian beds. It is now I think proved by indisputable evidence that the passage is conformable and gradual. Previously we have not been able to assert this fact which is one of very great importance and interest from a geological point of view, and has been the source of much inquiry and discussion.

I regret not having been able to make so exhaustive an examination as I could have wished.—Among the Foraminifera I have identified the following.

Globigerina bulloides.
Biloculina depressa—one moderate example
Pleurostomella subnodosa—small and attenuate forms
              „   brevis—a few
Ellipsoidina subnodosa, Guppy
Gaudryina pupoides—two fine examples
Lagena—several species
Polymorphina horrida
Nodosaria abysorum and perhaps two other forms
Pullenia sphaeroides
Pulvinulina pauperata
Anomalina grosserugosa
       „   wullerstorfi (rare and small)

The abundance of Lagena is remarkable. Nodosaria is poorly exhibited and small forms only occur. Globigerina is fine and large—Pullenia is nowhere common to my knowledge but it is quite as abundant here as I have ever found it.

N. B.—Mr. L. de Verteuil pointed out the junction beds to me in November, 1894, and in February, 1895, I went over the ground again with him and Prof. J. B. Harrison.

(Read 31st May, 1897.)

NOTE ON A SPECIMEN OF GLOBIGERINA ROCK FROM NAPARIMA.

By R. J. Lechmere Guppy.

THIS specimen given to me for examination by Professor J. B. Harrison came from the neighbourhood of the S. Madelein Factory. It is a Globigerina Rock of blue-grey tinge containing a large proportion of mud. It shows signs of brecciation. The residue after washing contains a fair series of Foraminifera, but none of fine development—sandy forms including Trochamina, Clavulina, etc., are pretty abundant, and so is Gaudryina pupoides, but I saw none full grown. Bigenerina is common but small.

I am inclined to think that this was deposited in relatively shallow water.

APPENDIX.

I give here the names of some additional species of Foraminifera from the Microzoic Rocks of Naparima described or determined since my paper on the subject was read to the Field Naturalists' Club.

Ellipsoidina ellipsoides, Seguenza
    ,,   subnodosa, Guppy
    ,,   exponens, Brady
Stilostomella rugosa, Guppy
Frondicularia flabelliformis, Guppy
Gaudryina lobata, Guppy
    ,,   pariana, Guppy
Gonatosphaera prolata, Guppy

The two latter are from the Ditrupabed of Pointapier.

(See paper in Proc. Zool. Soc.—1894, page 647.)

ON THE WORK OF THE SCIENTIFIC ASSOCIATION OF TRINIDAD AND ON THE RELATION OF THE VICTORIA INSTITUTE TO THE FIELD NATURALISTS' CLUB AND THE PUBLIC LIBRARY.

By R. J. Lechmere Guppy.

I HEARD it said in this room by one of the most prominent members of the Field Naturalists' Club that nothing of a scientific kind had ever been done in Trinidad previous to the formation of that Club, or that if anything of the kind had been done it was now a dead letter. With regard to the last part of the remark it is no doubt true that in this Colony anything good that is done is soon forgotten. It is likely that in Europe and North America more is known among scientific men of the work of the Scientific Association of Trinidad than is known here. But all this applies as much to the work of the Field Naturalists' Club as to the work of its predecessor, the Scientific Association. As to the former assertion I shall enter upon a few particulars to show its baselessness. It is, however, difficult to estimate the value of the results of scientific papers—in their effects they resemble the "gentle dew of heaven" permeating and blessing the growths and the soil on which they alight. I shall not therefore dwell so much upon these as upon the actual results which have followed upon the publication of those papers intended to be of a purely practical character. These will be sufficient for my purpose while appealing no doubt more directly to minds which appreciate results of a strictly practical character and which are not so ready to admit the beneficial effects of a cultivation of natural knowledge not immediately or obviously tending to the production of wealth. In my paper on the Cultivation of Scientific Knowledge in Trinidad, following G. H. Lewes, I pointed out some of the benefits attending the cultivation of such knowledge and the fact that those nations and communities which neglected it perished or continued barbarous while those who cherished it flourished and became greater (See Proceedings Scientific Association, 1867, page 75).

Of the little band of men (eleven in number) who in the year 1863 joined themselves together under the designation of the Scientific Association of Trinidad with a view to the encouragement of the cultivation of natural knowledge three only remain. Of these one left us some twenty-five years ago for another Colony. Another has long ago retired altogether from active life and the third who is now before you has but little energy or physical ability left for the prosecution of study. Many others of the most prominent men in the Island who took interest more or less in, or at least wished well to, scientific pursuits afterwards joined the Association, but only a few of these still survive. Under these circumstances I have to ask your indulgence for coming before you with a very imperfect paper not upon a scientific subject but rather having reference to the means of promoting the cultivation of knowledge or the study of the causes and effects of the natural phenomena which form our surroundings.

Within these walls are stored copies of the printed Proceedings of the Scientific Association. Although it may not be possible to get a complete set of these Proceedings (the bound copy which the Association intended to preserve for its own use having long since disappeared) yet a good many of the papers are still procurable. Whilst Secretary of this Victoria Institute I got together and had bound a nearly complete copy and of most of the parts copies are still in stock. Unfortunately one part is entirely missing and this one contains the first papers published here about the Ramie Plant. In my own collection of Books I have more than one complete set of the publications of the Scientific Association.

The first series of the publications of the Scientific Association was issued irregularly. In fact I had at first great difficulty in obtaining the permission of the Association for the appearance in print of any of its Proceedings. Consequently it was only from time to time that I got some separate papers printed. Among these was one of Dr. Leotaud's entitled " Du Chocolat." Besides some two or three papers by me there were papers by Richard Hill of Jamaica on the Preparation of Meats and Meals, etc., by Dr. Mitchell on a Megassicator, and in particular one by Thomas Law, entitled " Suggestions how to establish and cultivate an Estate in Cocoa " for which there was so great a demand that the edition was soon exhausted. This paper was evidently of practical use to the Cocoa planter, though all the views propounded by the author may not have been tenable.

The first issue of publications I have now described when collected was entitled "The Transactions of the Scientific Association of Trinidad, 1863–66." It contained in all 91 pages of matter with Title and Table of Contents. Besides this there was published separately a paper by Herman Cruger "On the Meteorology of Trinidad." This contained 22 pages besides a Table and four Diagrams.

In 1866 the Association decided to print its proceedings in a more regular form and for a time the issues appeared with moderate regularity. Among the practical papers included in the first volume (446 pages including Index with Title and Contents) were contributions by Henry Mitchell on Sulphites (2 papers) on Earth Closets, on the Breeding and Rearing of Horses and on the manufacture of Sugar (2 papers) : a most important one by Dr. de Vertouil on the Town of Port-of-Spain : interesting papers by Richard Hill on Poisonous Fishes and on Fish Poisons. Mr. Prestoe's Catalogue of Plants was herein published. Great delay and trouble attended the publication of that paper. A number of other papers also appeared in this volume, some of much interest but, I have not the opportunity now to particularize them. My own contributions included several on the Natural History of the Island and one on the Trinidad Public Library which I shall refer to more particularly in the course of this paper. My paper on Dominica though not exhaustive or profound excited some little interest and there was for a time a demand for copies of the part in which it appeared. My papers on the Geology of Trinidad though crude and imperfect contain notices of phenomena of which the great economic importance will some day be recognized.

The second volume of the proceedings begun with Part IX. December, 1872. Unfortunately the publications of the Association came to an end with the twelfth part published at the end of 1881. The chief burden of carrying on the business of the Association fell upon me and owing to the increasing work of my Office, my absences from the Island, my frequent ill-health and failing energy I had to resign first the Secretaryship and afterwards the Editorship, whereon the publications ceased to appear. Papers were however read at the meetings and one or two of my own afterwards appeared in print. The most notable of these was a paper on the Water-bearing Capacities of the Rocks of Trinidad published in the Agricultural Record.

The papers on practical subjects contained in the four parts issued of the second volume of the Proceedings were (among others) Prestoe on the cultivation of Ramie ; Day on Balata Gum and on the water supply of Port-of-Spain and San fernando. Francis wrote on Casava, on Coal Deposits and on blighted Sugar Canes ; Adolph Urich on the industry of Beetroot Sugar. My contributions included one on the Geology of our Northern Hills and other papers on Natural History and one on the Town of Port-of-Spain I shall now more particularly refer to. The other papers contained in the Proceedings have had their silent influence in their appropriate way. But the results of this one are visible at every step you take in the town. The paper referred to was read by me in 1877 and an abstract of it was printed in the proceedings for the following year. My friend the late Emanuel Cipriani who was then Mayor of Port-of-Spain used his influence for the adoption of the improvements suggested by me and in consequence some of them were adopted.—So also my suggestions as to Tramways were in part, but only in part adopted. Among the improvements advocated in the paper was a better form of street gutter in fact that now universally used in Town. The paper was only printed in abstract for this reason that large and expensive diagrams would have been necessary if the paper had been printed in full ; and the means of the Scientific Association were too limited to allow of the engraving and printing of such diagrams. The improvements proposed were shown to the meeting partly by means of colored diagrams and plans and partly by means of the blackboard. So that if any one asserts that the work of the Scientific Association is a dead letter he might be answered in a way somewhat similar to that of the person who inquired for Wren's monument. As regards street gutters some of my proposals have been literally carried out and are in full operation at this moment (with the exception only of pipe drains) replacing the illshaped, wasteful and unwholesome gutters of former days by the present improved style. The old ideal was a roadway of almost semi-circular section while the gutter had two almost vertical sides of considerable height, dangerous for and unusable by foot passengers or vehicles and occupying uselessly a large portion of the roadway. The new shape of gutter section (to the originality of which I lay no claim whatever as it has long been in use in all modern Towns of any importance) presents a cross section of only slight curvature and extends the roadway from the margin of one footpath (the curbstone) to the margin of the opposite one—every inch of the roadway being thus available for the use of carriages. Practically the usable area of the roadway is doubled by the new section while the area of waterway is not diminished. Practical results of great importance have therefore enured to the public without cost to the latter as a consequence of the existence here of the Scientific

Association, though that Institution like every other designed to
benefit the people had to struggle against the bitter hostility of
the most influential classes.   The Scientific Association did not
exist for the glorification of its members—fame and glory are of
little value except to parasites and courtiers and the Scientific
Association was not composed of such.   And if greater results did
not flow from its work it was not the fault of the Association but
of those who ought to have seconded and carried out its proposals.
It is indeed much to be regretted that the improvement designed
for Port-of-Spain in the laying out of a handsome main thoroughfare through the town was utterly ignored—this might then
have been easily carried out for the Government had then lately
come into possession of Tranquillity and St. Clair, and Tragarete
Road might have been made an Avenue of which the town would
have had cause to be proud.   I know not what is meant by
calling Port-of-Spain a City, but if it is characteristic of a City
to possess a main thoroughfare like Tragarete Road then the
sooner we render ourselves unworthy of such an epithet and
more worthy of our old name of town the better it will be.

I may add as a note that an improvement I have advocated
for nearly forty years, that namely of a footwalk round the
Savanna, has been for some time past in course of construction,
but upon an extravagant and unnecessarily grand scale which
must stand in the way of the general execution of such works so
absolutely necessary to the well being and comfort of a civilized
community.

My paper on the Trinidad Public Library was read before
the Association in 1869.   I had been a member of the
Managing Committee of the Library for some years before that
and had studied Library economy practically at the British
Museum Library and at Scientific and other Libraries in London.
I acquired and studied the work of Edwards on Libraries—that
work was then unknown in Trinidad—and one result of my
Paper was that the Library obtained a copy of it.   My views
upon the subject of libraries were then the results of study and
experience, and I am still prepared to adhere with possible small
modifications to the propositions laid down in my Paper, which
contemplated the Library as the central scientific and technical
Institute of the Colony.   Some of my propositions have been
adopted and carried into effect, and in view of this again can it
be said that the work of the Association was a dead letter?
The Library is now freely open to the public which it was not
before the appearance of my Paper ; the latter was favourably
reviewed and supported by the Press, or at least by the Trinidad

Chronicle, the Editor of which at that time was a gentleman of great literary attainments and of broad and liberal and patriotic views. Subscribers only were formerly admitted to the library, as a reference to my paper will show; and it was on account of the statements and arguments in my Paper that it was opened freely to the public. But in urging the free opening of the Library I recorded my objection to the abuse of that Institution for the purpose of purveying Fiction. The true function of a public library is to afford to students means of access to works they could not otherwise obtain. One obscure and despised student who makes use of the library may, as the result of his studies, confer benefits upon the community worth pecuniarily £20,000 or £100,000. The study of science and the cultivation of knowledge always conduce to the wealth of the community though not to that of the student: but no amount of Novel reading can be beneficial to the community, though like champagne drinking it may amuse and gratify those who indulge in it. From a public and national point of view therefore a public library should be maintained for the use of the student and not of the Novel reader.

It has been alleged against me that I scarcely ever set foot in the Library. But one reason of that is that I cannot make use of the Library whose arrangement and organization is at present adapted chiefly to the supply of Fiction to those who pay a shilling a month. And I should like it to be borne in mind that in all I have put forward in this Paper I have in view the arrangements at the British Museum Reading Room (where I was for some years a Reader) and those of other Scientific and Public libraries whose arrangements are designed primarily to facilitate the student.

It has also been alleged against me that, while I find fault with the Library for purveying Novels, I take advantage of it to get novels for myself. I do not see any great force in this allegation—but I can say that I only get Novels as a subscriber and certainly not for my own use. Indeed this is one of the matters in which one has to go with the stream irrespective of one's own private views. The question as to whether Novels and Whisky are pernicious or not is one upon which opinions are much divided. But supposing that I take my share of each, it does not follow that it is right that the public money should be applied to the supply of such articles. Novels are cheap enough for all such as subscribe to the Library to buy them for themselves. By interchange (which could easily be managed by clubs or otherwise) it would be possible to secure the reading of a very large number of Novels for a very small sum. However I do not wish to insist on any of these points. None of my arguments need stand in the way of a Government grant for the supply of Fiction. I wish to leave the decision of that point in the hands of those concerned. What we want and what I am now pleading for is a really public Library maintained for the public benefit and not for the benefit of a particular class or set such as the subscribers to the present Library are. Therefore let the novels and part of the subsidy remain with the Borough Council (if it be so decided) for the maintenance of a circulating Library and let the scientific and useful portion of the collection together with the remainder of the grant go to the Victoria Institute for the formation and maintenance of a library for public and national objects.

From what I have stated you will see my object in supporting the union or amalgamation of the public Library with the Victoria Institute just as I formerly supported and advocated the union and amalgamation of the Field Naturalists' Club and the Victoria Institute. It seems a tendency of human nature to prefer division and disunion and this tendency is encouraged by those who wish to profit by disunion and division. Union is almost always for the general benefit ; but the individual frequently inclines to the view that his influence or his glory or his individual something or another will lose by union. Hence it seems to be that union like the welding of steel mostly requires heat and some force of compression or of impact from outside to perfect it. Individual action seems almost always to lead to disintegration and dissolution. The Irish Union, the Scotch Union, the American Union (twice) the Italian Union, the German Union were all effected or perfected with the aid of force. An expression of George Washington's lately quoted in a local newspaper shows that the great statesman appreciated the fact. He says " Experience has taught us that men will not adopt and carry into execution measures, the best calculated for their own good, without the intervention of coercive power."

In reference to the discussion as to where the " Challenger" Volumes should be placed, if it were a question as to where it is most for the public interest that they should be placed there could be only one answer and that is at the Public Museum (called the Victoria Institute). At no other place could they be so freely accessible to students and at the same time under proper care. The valuable scientific books stored at the Public Library are utterly uncared for and are fast going to ruin. But the way this question has been discussed shows how every Insti-

tution intended for the real benefit of the people of Trinidad is
treated. The fact is that such an Institution as ours is viewed
with hostility and jealousy by influential classes who are averse
to anything intended for the benefit of the people and who
employ their influence overt and covert in spreading ideas hostile to such Institutions. But however much man may persecute
truth his existence and welfare after all depend upon it and the
real true object of such Institutions as the Public Library and
the Victoria Institute is to keep alive the flame of truth amid
the growing fogs of error and falsehood which spread around us.
Upon the maintenance of this light of truth depends our existence and prosperity as a community—those who wish to destroy
or pervert these Institutions are those to whom the light of truth
and the welfare of humanity are hateful.

I exhibit to you copies of some of the old catalogues and
lists of the Public Library. In view of those I think it could
hardly be said by any one that the person who took the trouble
not merely to preserve and bind these catalogues but to insert in
them the leaflets containing fugitive lists of books issued from time
to time and to enter in writing in the appropriate places in the
catalogues the additions made from time to time, took no interest
in the Library. That these catalogues and lists are not
complete is due firstly to the treatment they met with at the
hands of the owner's friends and secondly to the want of uniformity in the printing and the getting up of the catalogues which
precludes their being properly bound together. This same want
of uniformity is much to be deplored in the publications of the
Victoria Institute—these being in the same way deprived of a
great part of their permanent value by being of irregular and
discordant shape and size and consequently serve only for the
ephemeral play or business of the moment and then are thrown
aside or destroyed or lost.

It is almost unnecessary for me to say that I have the very
strongest sympathy with the work of the Field Naturalists' Club
and that it was one of the great aims of the Scientific Association
to place such work on a sound and permanent basis by means of
such an Institution as the Victoria Institute, making it a popular
Institution and throwing the responsible control of it into
the hands of the promoters of natural knowledge. The constitution of the Victoria Institute was happily framed in accordance
with the requirements of such an Institution. As I shall show,
in the management of it a large measure of popular control was
infused, while securities were retained to prevent as far as possible
diversion of the public money to unworthy or unsuitable objects

When I arrived from England in 1892, I found the Institute in an anomalous condition. It had been practically swamped by the Field Naturalists' Club, a condition in which it continues more or less until this day. At that time I was not keen enough to see that this state of things was designedly brought about and continued, and I set to work to endeavour to alter it and to get the Institute freed from the shackles which bound it. In this attempt I failed signally whereupon I resigned the post of Secretary of the Institute, a post I sought and held at much sacrifice to myself solely for the purpose of getting the Institute and the Field Naturalists' Club united and the responsible control of the Institution placed in the hands of the latter. Just as it was when I was at the head of the Education Department there were secret influences at work sapping and undermining all I could do for the public advantage, and, as in that case so in this, the hostile influences were too powerful for me. The very classes I essayed to serve were the ones who became the instruments of the overthrow of the schemes devised for their benefit.

Whatever neglect or ill-treatment the Victoria Institute may meet with now or later will be the worse for all concerned. It must in any case be the Public Museum and scientific Institute of the Colony. Neglect or ill-treatment will certainly lead to impairment of its usefulness so that when the necessity for the existence of such an Institute becomes properly recognized people will say, why was such neglect and ill-treatment suffered to be? why was such and such a collection or such and such books, &c., &c., not preserved or secured or better looked after?

It is perfectly clear from the constitution designed under Sir William Robinson for the Victoria Institute that the Agricultural Department whether called Board or Society was to be a part of the Institute. But the constitution of the Victoria Institute provided in the governing body for a minimum of seven elected members to a maximum of five nominated members thus securing always a majority on the side of popular control. It is therefore essentially a popular Institution, and therefore it did not command the confidence of the Sugar Planters who consequently endeavoured to destroy or cripple the Victoria Institute and to supersede it by a body in which their influence should be paramount. Hence the establishment of the Agricultural Society endowed with £600 a year by the Government to which endowment no exception whatever has been taken while the vote of £250 to the Victoria Institute was only very narrowly passed after severely hostile criticism and the insertion of a note against the item on the estimates of the year with a view to the withdrawal of the amount from the next year's Estimates. I am of opinion that in the present state of our Agriculture the Agricultural Department should be reunited with the Victoria Institute. Nothing but a petty jealousy (whatever the excuse may be) can stand in the way of this amalgamation. Thus the Victoria Institute would be restored to the proportions designed for it as a memento of the Queen's Jubilee by Sir William Robinson, one of the foremost, perhaps I may say the principal one, of its founders. And I may note here that the course of Lectures given within these walls on Agriculture was such that every Agriculturist in the Island would have gained by attending it.

There is one point that seems to have been partially lost sight of—it is that the Victoria Institute is the custodian of the public Natural History and other Collections. In language adopted from the report for 1894 of the Natural History Society of New Brunswick (a valuable report from which we could take many hints), "These collections are not ours, they belong to the people of Trinidad and we hope that an enlightened public spirit will see that such a valuable heritage be preserved for generations to come."

The shape in which the Institute will continue to exist may be doubtful. With its present constitution it is quite capable of doing all that has been done by the Field Naturalists' Club and the Agricultural Society, nay much more, and it can only be by a jealousy carefully cultivated by those who are antagonistic to the welfare of the community that it is prevented from fulfilling all its functions. At the present moment by the Regulations of the Institute, all members of the Field Naturalists' Club are members of the Institute and all members of the Agricultural Society are entitled to all privileges of members of the Institute except that of voting. It is for the Field Naturalists' Club to say whether they will complete their union with the Institute (and this I think could be done without even a change of name.) Having done all on our part to facilitate the union it remains for them to say whether they prefer an ephemeral existence in the irresponsible position they hold or whether they will come forward and make themselves responsible masters and directors of our Scientific Institute. For my part I am for this course because it will insure popular control and interest for the Scientific Institute of the Colony which must otherwise become a purely Government concern. I am quite sure that the present incomplete and imperfect union is a source of weakness and I am also sure that a complete union would benefit all concerned and none of the arguments put forward on the side of the Separatists can really touch this point.

As an Appendix to this paper is submitted a brief account of a collection of books printed in or relating to Trinidad which may be interesting from a bibliographical point of view.

APPENDIX.

LIST OF BOOKS.

Histoire de la Trinidad—Par P. G. L. Borde. In two Parts. Paris 1876 and 1882. 8vo.

Guide to Trinidad—By J. H. Collens, Port-of-Spain 1887. 8vo.

The same—Second Edition, London 1888. 8vo.

Trinidad. By W. H. Gamble—London 1886. 8vo.

The West Indies—E. B. Underhill—London 1862. 8 vo.

The Caribbean Confederation—By C. S. Salmon. London N. D. 8vo.

The Colonial Policy of Lord John Russell's Administration. By Saul Grey—London 1853.

Warner Arrindell—By E. L. Joseph, London 1838.

The English in the West Indies. By J. A. Froude, London 1888.

Geography of Trinidad and Tobago. By J. A. de Suze Port-of-Spain 1894.

Bouffonnerie. Some amusing skits (in French by Leon H. de Gannes, formerly Librarian of the Trinidad Public Library) with corrections, etc., in the Author's own handwriting. These are bound together in the same volume with (besides some scraps not relating to Trinidad) the report on the Nariva Cocal, 1866, by J. F. Rat with M. S. plan. 4to.

The Trinidad Official and Commercial Register and Almanack—Sixteen Volumes (1871, 1877-1891) bound in Russia. 8vo.

The same bound in three volumes, 1866-75, 1876-83, and 1884-89, except for the years 1869 and 1870 when the publication was issued in a smaller size and is included in this collection in the volume entitled " Trinidad Almanack 1832-70." 8vo.

The same—another set bound in two volumes containing the issues for the years 1875-84 and 1885-91. 8vo.

Trinidad Almanacks 1832-70. Contains the issues for the years 1832, 1834, 1835, 1869 and 1870. 12mo.

West Indian Almanacks—Besides some issues of the S. Thomas' Almanacks this contains Boucaud's San-Fernando Almanack for 1880, Barbados Almanack. 1848 8vo.

Letters by a free Mulatto (J. B. Philip), London 1824 8vo.

History of Trinidad—By E. L. Joseph—Port-of-Spain 1837. 12mo.

This was in the first instance published as an Appendix to Mills' Trinidad Almanac for 1838.

Observations on the present condition of the Island of Trinidad. By W. Hardin Burnley.

Evidence collected by the Sub-Committee of the Agricultural and Immigration Society in favor of Immigration. London 1842. 8vo.

Historical and Statistical view of the Island of Trinidad, etc., by Daniel Hart. (First Edition printed in London 1865). 8vo.

Trinidad, etc., By Daniel Hart—Second Edition of the above). Trinidad 1866. 8vo.

Three Essays on the Cultivation of the Sugar Cane in Trinidad—Trinidad 1848. 8vo.

Trinidad—By L. A. A. de Verteuil—London 1858. 8vo. A revised Edition of this Book was published in 1881.

Catalogues of the Trinidad Public Library, 1851-1856, 1851-1873, 1857-1862, also 1886 and 1887 and 1892. These old Catalogues are interesting as showing what Books were in the Library in the years named. The first Catalogue has two curious misprints. At p. 24 the word "Wines" is misprinted "Wives" and at p. 44 the same word is misprinted "Mines."

The Reports for the years 1886 and 1887 (in one) included lists of the Books received in those years; but unfortunately neither these nor the 1892 Catalogue can be bound together, not being uniform in size.

Proceedings of the Scientific Association of Trinidad, 1863-1869. 8vo.

Trinidad Scientific Proceedings.—This Volume contains (I.) A complete set of Proceedings of the Scientific Association so far as published. The second Volume was never completed. (II.) A complete set of the Journal of the Field Naturalists' Club from No. 1 to No. 11 inclusive, being all published up to date of binding of this Volume.

Trinidad Scientific Tracts. This volume contains besides other papers the following:—1. The Grand Old Man of San Fernando, by J. W. Alston. 2. The Geology of Barbados by Harrison and Jukes Browne.

It should be noticed of this as of some of the remaining volumes in the collection that the heterogeneous nature of the contents of the volumes is partly due to mistakes on the part of the binder who has committed several serious blunders in binding and in lettering.

Miscellaneous.—This volume contains a number of pieces mostly printed in or relating to Trinidad

Pamphlets.—The following papers contained in this volume are specially worth notice:—Macaulay—Emancipation des Esclaves. Hincks—Negro Emancipation; Trinidad Industrial Exhibition, 1852 & 1853; Papers on Education in Trinidad, 1853. There is also a paper of interest on Porto Rico by Purdie.

B

Tracts.—Among other papers this volume contains the following:—Report of the San Fernando Borough Council Committee of 1889 ; La Lepre est contagieuse; British Honour and Interest in Trinidad and Venezuela; Minor Industries,—By J. F. Chittenden ; Banana Trade —By J. H. Hart ; Impediments to the prosperity of the British West Indies. (By T. MacGrath) ; Guaranteed Mortgages, By Sir John Gorrie.

Miscellaneous Tracts—Among other papers contains :— Report of a meeting held in Brunswick Square, 4 April, 1872 ; Les Mysteres de l'Ile aux Colibris (by Tronchin.); Le Retour de l'Exile (by Tronchin) ; Lord Harris's message on Education ; Trinidad Monthly Magazine, Nos. 1, 2, 3 (all published) ; Trinidad Handbook of Everyday Law—By G. W. Greenwood ; Creole Grammar—By J. J. Thomas.

Miscellaneous Tracts.—Among a lot of papers having no reference to Trinidad there are contained in this volume several curious and interesting Tracts as for instance, "Analysis of Agricultural Phase," by Fortune ; "Tes Pere et Mere honoreras," a Play in Creole ; Water supply of San Fernando, by H. Warner ; Minutes of the Trinidad Reform Association, 1856, &c., &c.

Scientific Tracts—Vol. I.-X. These volumes contain among other and general papers a large number of papers on scientific subjects connected with the Island of Trinidad.

Naturalists' Club, 1892-96. This volume contains the remaining Publications of the Field Naturalists' Club Journal No. 6 February 1892 to No. 12 February 1896, complete to date.

History of Trinidad. By L. M. Fraser. Vol. I. (no date) 1781 to 1813. Vol. II. (1896) 1814 to 1839.

Agricultural Record. A complete set in five vols., 1889-92, 8vo. The first four vols. are each separate but vols. v. vi. and vii. (1891-92) are bound in one.

N.B.—The Student of Trinidad Literature is referred to the Bibliography contained in the Proceedings of the Scientific Association of Trinidad, vol. i. p. 48, and vol. ii. p. 27. Scattered throughout the Proceedings are notices of Scientific Memoirs relating to Trinidad and its neighbourhood.

VICTORIA INSTITUTE, TRINIDAD,

1897-1898.

PROCEEDINGS OF THE INAUGURAL MEETING

OF THE SESSION HELD AT THE

VICTORIA MUSEUM,

30th SEPTEMBER, 1897.

The Hon. H. A. Alcazar, Q.C., Mayor of Port-of-Spain, (by special request) in the Chair.

The Vice-President of the Institute (S. Devenish, M.A., stated :—

IN the absence of our worthy President, Sir John Goldney, now in Europe, it is my pleasant duty as Vice-President to welcome your Excellency and Lady Jerningham, to the Victoria Institute, of which you have graciously consented to be Patron. Opened in 1892, in commemoration of the Queen's 50 years' Jubilee, at the suggestion and under the fostering auspices of Sir William Robinson, this Institute has hitherto had a long struggling for life and popularity, and would not have lasted so long without the generous subsidy from the Government, but in spite of the interest and special efforts of its founder, it has not yet been able to show the vitality and usefulness which we had anticipated. Your Excellency must, no doubt, be aware how, owing to the well known general apathy inherent to all tropical climates, and to the regretable " Laisser aller" consequent thereon, it is difficult for Institutions of this sort to develop rapidly and throw out vigorous lasting roots. For the last 50 years, several similar scientific and artistic societies have sprung up among us, owing to the energetic initial of a few enthusiastic Colonists, but, like a megass fire, which after a bright short blazing up, soon collapses and dies out without even leaving any perceptible smouldering débris, they have all collapsed after a few years crawling on, leaving no vestiges after them. To-day, however, we earnestly cherish the hope, even after so many sad trials, that, under your sympathetic patronage, and your enlightened direction, the public will soon realize the benefits which may be expected from this Society, and that the Victoria Institute will, henceforth, cheerfully enter into a new era of popularity and usefulness, and will prove itself worthy of the patriotic and happy event to which it owes its birth, and to which have been added, the recent unique National Grand Jubilee of Her Majesty's glorious and unparalled 60 years reign over the vast British Empire.

The Chairman (Mr. Alcazar) said he had much pleasure in acceding to the request which had been conveyed to him in such graceful terms by the Vice-President. He considered it an honour to have the privilege of presiding on this interesting occasion, an occasion which he hoped would mark an epoch in the history of the Institute. He was much afraid that the general public and indeed even the members of the Institute had begun to look upon it as a sort of moribund institution, and they were daily expecting to have been called upon to assist at its funeral. It was with pleasurable surprise that instead of being called upon to assist at that gruesome ceremony, there had been issued a most interesting programme to be carried out during the coming session—a programme which would not only be interesting to the members of the Institution but a large section of the general public, as even the working men of the community were to be catered for in the form of lectures on plumbing, painting, and other kindred subjects. When they first saw the programme, they all wondered whose was the magic wand that had electrified that anemic and lifeless body, and they now knew that it was due almost exclusively to the very kind interest which His Excellency the Governor had been pleased to take in the Institute and its work. His Excellency had shown by consenting to deliver the opening address, that that interest was to assume a practical form, and he was sure that the Members of the Institute and the public were deeply grateful to His Excellency, for they felt, and the public would feel, that if His Excellency took that interest it was because he had recognized that that Institute was one which ought to exist for the good of the community at large. He hoped that in future the tickets of admission to those lectures would be more freely distributed. The Secretary had informed him that that was due principally to the

lack of room that existed at present.   If that was so, all he had
to say was that he hoped, if the Institute was launched upon the
successful career foreshadowed for it by that night's proceedings,
that before long it would have a more suitable habitat.   In fact,
he hoped that before the opening address of the next session was
delivered, they would have a lecture room which would enable
the Institute to carry out successfully its aims and objects.

His Excellency the Governor, on rising to deliver the opening address, said it was the habit in the House of Commons,
before making a speech, to reply by courtesy, to the
speech that had been made before, or at all events refer to it.
He would, therefore, with their permission, thank the Vice-President for his kind words of welcome to Lady Jerningham and
himself, and express his regret, in accordance with the Vice-
President's remarks, that Sir John Goldney, the President of the
Institute, could not be there.   Sir John Goldney took so much
interest in the Victoria Institute, that he (the Governor) had not
been an hour in the Colony, and had not had time to have
breakfast, when he (Sir John Goldney) placed in his hands every
document he could find with regard to the Institute.   After he
he had been sworn in, Sir John Goldney urged him to take up the
cause of having lectures for the public benefit, therefore to him
was due the initiation of the interest and of the benefit which
would be derived from lectures of that kind.   He entirely agreed
with the Hon'ble the Mayor in his remark that in order to make
those lectures more interesting and to be appreciated in the
Colony, there should be a larger locale, and it was quite evident
that the people to whom they appealed especially and who wished
to be instructed in a pleasant manner, were those who should
come in numbers, and be admitted as freely as possible on the nights
when there were lectures concerning themselves.   He entirely
agreed with the sentiments, and therefore he thought he might
take upon himself to say that he should certainly work with the
Institute to try and provide for that want.   Sir John Goldney
desired that he (the Governor) should be Patron, and it appeared
that the Governor was generally the Patron and after he had
told Sir John Goldney that he entirely coincided with his ideas
and his views, he was then invited by the Committee of the
Institute to become Patron and to do what he could for an
institution which they say was in a moribund condition.   He
thought at the time that a body of men, a noble band, and they
he might say, of gentlemen in this Colony who, after a toilsome
day, could go and give their leisure to expound their own knowledge of subjects, to give to the community the benefit of their
experience, who did not grudge those minutes,—those men
constituted a noble band, and they should be rewarded for their

efforts, for it was an effort in a Country like this, where the sun was so magnificent but at the same time made itself so much felt, it was a toil to come of an evening, after a fatiguing day, and deliver a lecture which, in itself, had required on their part, in order to condense it, so much labour, so much thought, so much work. When he was invited, he was reminded of some beautiful lines that were sent on one occasion by Foster, the great friend of Dickens, to Dickens in London.—

> Come with me and behold
>
> A friend with heart as gentle for distress,
>
> As resolute with fine wise thoughts, to bind
>
> The happiest, to the unhappiest of our kind.

Those were beautiful lines, which really in his opinion summed up the desire of the people who were at the head of the Institute, namely, kindness to the poor and uninstructed, and that heart which desired that mankind should be real fellowship, and which desired to impart to others knowledge which they possessed themselves, ungrudgingly and unselfishly; and therefore they might imagine that it was with great gratitude and a great sense of the honour which was conferred on him, that he accepted at once the position. But the Committee went further. Human nature was never satisfied with one requirement. He had found by long experience that when somebody had got what he wanted he immediately found something else that he wished to have as soon as possible after that. In official life, those officials who were present would bear him out. He had never given promotion to a man that did not want another promotion within six months (laughter). Well, the Committee of that Institute then asked him to give a lecture also, or at all events, to give an address. He found that a little more discomforting, for he had had no idea of giving a lecture, and with the multifarious duties which were incumbent on the governor of this Colony, he thought the subject would at all events be a difficult one to choose. He looked at the list—ably drawn up—of what was going to take place. And he found that upon every subject upon which he could personally say perhaps something, there were orators and lecturers found who knew more than he did, and to whom he would listen with much more interest than he could possibly deliver a lecture himself. He was really particularly unhappy. He did not know what to do. What subject could he choose? He thought then that perhaps he would tell them of a subject which perhaps had not been treated before, namely the tribulations of a governor (laughter.) But even there he was stopped, because he knew several people in the colony who had many tribulations. He knew the Director of Public Works had great tribulations, because there was the Chaguaramas scheme which militated against his own. He knew that the immigrants and the planters had great tribulations because a sort of still-born Ordinance had been passed which suited neither one nor the other (laughter). He knew again that the Municipality had its tribulations, because it had not been able for twenty years to meet its expenditure. When he found so many tribulations, he thought it would be indiscreet to reveal the tribulations of their governor. But the other stroke had to come. Last Tuesday he had a very able leader, a most able leader he might say, upon that Institute; and what did that leader say? That leader said that the Westminster Aquarium in London was the most successful of its kind, although primarily instituted for the purpose of giving lectures on science, because male and female crowded in every day to see performers. He (the governor) was not a performer, and he did not know how he should benefit an institution in that way. That article went further and said that unless you were a German you could not think even of interesting any one except by amusing them. Well, he was not a German, and he did not know how to amuse. But the crowning feature of the article was that, according to human nature, ladies in the tropics wanted particularly to be amused, or they would not come, and that was the reason why the Institute did not succeed. Well he must say that this staggered him to such an extent, that he thought he would not give a lecture at the Institute again, or at all events begin. But it struck him afterwards that perhaps after all even the writer of that able article might be mistaken, because ladies in this Colony, as he knew from the mouth of the Principal of the Royal College, wanted to compete with men in regard to the acquisition of scientific knowledge, and therefore he desired to see in the future, in that hall as many ladies as men listening to the interesting subjects which had been so carefully selected for their information. Well, it then remained for him to find out some particular subject. Now, the companions of the Governor were the Blue Books and the Census. They might find these very dry companions, but they are not dry. He remembered Trinidad had a motto, namely, "Unity." He remembered that in the Christian line Trinidad did mean "unity;" and he remembered that if the colony had progressed in the past and was progressing, if the colony could be favourably compared, if this colony had a future before it, that was a trinity of hopes that might form the subject of the few words he wished to address to them. In those Blue Books, which were held out to them as being so uninteresting there was a curious history of the development of Trinidad. Taking the population of the country as one which was specially indicative of a country's prosperity, or at all events of a country not receding, they would find that in thirteen years this colony had risen from 84,000 to, at the last Census of 1891—200,000, and according to the proportion of it and the rate of progression of the population, in the year 1897, namely this very year, the population of this Island must be about 250,000 inhabitants. If they compared that with the 84,000 only that existed in 1884, that was a proof that this colony was making progress, because when they were talking of population it did not mean only having a multitude of individuals in the place, it meant housing them, feeding them, it meant that they should find a means of living and all that had to be found. They naturally added to the labour market by their intelligence, by their work, by their ability. But at the same time, it was a proof that the colony was progressing. In connection with the population he might also say that there was very great hope of every lady in the Island finding a husband (laughter) because it appeared from the Census that there were 845 females to every thousand males, so that there was a margin, and ladies could even select between two and three. This showed that the Blue Books were at all events interesting. The Revenue of the Colony in 1884, which was the first year in which a regular Blue Book was published, was £476,000. It was in 1896, £618,000, namely a rise of £142,000 a year. That, he should say, was conclusive proof that the Colony was marching, namely, going on progressing. The public debt, which in 1884 was £590,000 had diminished in 1896 to £385,000 notwithstanding all the new works which had been begun and probably to which they would add this year, because there were some important works, but that the debt itself should be so small and the Revenue so good, indicated a sound position, such as he believed no other Colony could boast of, and he congratulated them upon this (applause). He could not forget that article of Sunday, which talked of human nature, and he would talk of human nature. In human nature it always happened that when one had paid a compliment to a person he always had to say something disagreeable after it, and this was the disagreeable part, namely that that the schools in 1884 were 128, and in 1896 they were only 192, an increase only of 54 in twelve years. Worse still, the number of pupils in 1884 was 24,000, and it was only 27,000 in 1896.

The cost of course, had not increased very much, from £32,000 to £38,000, but he did not think that it was to the credit of this Colony that there should be, in a population such as he had told them, that proportion of children, and that there should not be more children attending school. So far as he could see, that audience was not one that would communicate that fact, probably to the whole Colony, but they would try to do so for their own friends' sake. This Island, if it was to progress, must mind education. The Government spared no money to give proper education to the children of the natives of this island. It was their duty to look after education, and no money should be spared upon that great and noble object. Education was the means of ennobling man, of making man something, and therefore those who looked after that had to pay for education, and were willing to do so, and the others in the Colony must respond to that. He would return to the subject presently and they would see what a neighbouring island could do in the way of education.

The imports had maintained themselves at very high figures indeed for a West Indian Colony, higher in fact than in Jamaica, and exports had done the very same thing, the only difference between the exports and imports being £297,000. It was always interesting to know what exports and imports meant. The exports meant what they produced in the soil and sold outside and got money for. Imports meant that one had to buy that which could not be produced here, and he wanted to dwell upon that, because presently when they came to the second stage of comparison he would show them that in Jamaica they understood it better than we had, and we must be careful upon that point. The whole of that £297,000 had come out of their pockets. They must make no illusion upon the subject, £297,000 had been made a present of by this Colony, to Venezuela, to England, to France, to Germany, and elsewhere. It was money out of their pockets, and that money out of their pockets was money which ought to have been in the Island if they had only grown and manufactured that which had cost that amount. Imports and exports were for the Governor a sort of weather-glass which told him whether a Colony was prosperous or whether it was not; it was one which he should have his eye upon exactly in the same way as the captain of a ship had his eye upon the compass which showed the direction. As soon as the imports exceeded the exports unnecessarily, he meant of course, after making all allowance for the due oscillations between the crops of different years, but if it exceeded it too much it was a proof that the power of spending was not upon revenue but upon the capital of the Colony and therefore impoverishing it, and that was a point that ought never to be lost sight of. Well, as he should show them, it was quite satisfactory as it was at present. It was more satisfactory still when they looked at the shipping. Now, the shipping was a very interesting point. The shipping in this Island showed that in 1896, 2,817 ships, steam and sail, came into Trinidad, representing 623,000 tons of goods; that was to say, that we imported to the amount, but he found on the clearing side that there were 2,815 ships that cleared this Colony with 619,000 tons.

That was a satisfactory statement. It showed that there was only a slight extra importation, and that they exported 4,000 tons less only than what they imported. But what did these 4,000 tons represent? They represented food.

They represented that which they could grow here. The other represented the whole wants of the community, and these 4,000 tons absolutely represented nothing else but food brought into the Colony which might be grown here, and that was a point which he insisted upon because it was probable that the few remarks he had the honour of making might be reported, and he wished the whole colony to know that, since he had been here and had studied it and had seen and taken to heart the position that he had the honour to occupy among them, he believed this colony could produce far more than it did, and he intended it to produce much more. So far as the first stage, namely, the position of the colony and its progressing yearly was concerned, they would allow with him that it really was satisfactory. It was not perhaps what they might wish in their sanguine desires to be above all other colonies, but it was satisfactory as it stood. If they compared it now—he knew that comparisons were odious, and probably in Jamaica they would not be pleased with what he had to say,—but if they compared this colony with Jamaica, he said that the whole advantage lay with Trinidad. The population of Trinidad in 1896, last year, was—of course this was approximate, because he had not got the actual figures, was 216,927 upon 1,750 square miles, which was the size of this Island. Jamaica had 481,000 with a territory of little over twice the size of Trinidad, namely, 4,207 square miles; now, that meant a population of 124 to the square mile in Trinidad and 143 to the square mile in Jamaica. Of course, Jamaica had the advantage there, as it had a larger population, but it had a very much larger territory, and there are some mathematicians here who might show them that 124 to the square mile here was very superior to 143 to the square mile it was there, because that meant less crowding, more ample space, and consequently more healthy dispositions. He believed they had here 681,000 acres of land not in cultivation, whereas Jamaica was entirely cultivated and had only 121,000 acres to dispose of. The result was that if they increased here and cultivated more, they would soon get that population at the rate at which they were going, which Jamaica boasted of. The revenue then, taking the population of that country and that of Trinidad, the revenue itself was only £825,000 against £618,000 of ours, which was not at all in proportion to what it should be, because if it were in proportion the revenue of Jamaica should be over a million, and it was below. On the other hand it, Jamaica, presented a deficit in its accounts and we presented a surplus in ours. The debt of Jamaica was £1,600,000. He had shown them that here it was £385,000, and the people of Trinidad altogether per head of the population—which was a bad calculation because it was not everybody who paid but he meant for summary purposes like this, taking it per head of the population, they had a burden of £5 1s. to our £4 9s. ; that was to say, that if they divided the expenditure of the government plus the debt of the country by the number of the people they had per head what it cost the Colony to keep up its administration and to progress, and that was a difference of 12s in our favour. But then came the point at which Jamaica led altogether, that was to say, in the question of schools. There were 930 schools in Jamaica as against 192 in Trinidad ; there were 99,000 pupils as against 27,000 in Trinidad, and they cost £45,000 against our £38,000. Now, that meant that every school here cost the Colony £200 and every scholar £1 8s., whereas in Jamaica every school cost £40 and every scholar only 9s. a head. That was the point which he commended to their notice. It was a very important point. It showed that there was a screw loose somewhere, and when there was a screw loose, they must discover where the screw was loose and endeavour to the best of their ability to make it firm again and to put that in order. The shipping again, in Trinidad and Jamaica, compared most favourably. In Jamaica they had more steamers than we had here. That was quite evident, as there was the open sea all round Jamaica, and here they had got the gulf which was like a lake and where there was not sufficient depth of water and hence big steamers could not come into the gulf as they would otherwise do. The question then arose whether it was not desirable or possible, or whether it would not be to the advantage of the Colony to find some place where big steamers would come without injuring a part of the interests that were centred in Port-of-Spain.

Those were questions that arose from a cursory look at those Blue Books which were supposed to be so dry that nobody wished to read them. But he thought he had said enough in the single remark that there were 681,000 acres of land still uncultivated, to show them that this Island, steadily progressing as it was, provided its finances were properly and judiciously administered, and advancing in every branch except the educational branch, he thought he had shown them enough to make it clear that there was still a margin of progress. It was the idea in this community that people would take an interest only in the illustrations which might there be made of some of the interesting portions of the work which they were called upon to perform. He knew that as was remarked by the Vice-President, there was a certain amount of laziness attributable mostly to the climate, and which was very natural in its way, but at the same time there was in most communities a lack of progressive zeal.

There must be a desire to serve under a standard upon which the word "excelsior" was marked. He thought that this should be the aim of the poor—he was not talking of the rich—they were none of them rich in the Colonies, they all worked hard, and they were all on the same footing, and the poor man looked to those who led for guidance, and it was the great and noble object of that Institute to show them the way.

It did not mean that they wished to enforce knowledge or to press people to come to it to do them the honour of coming simply to hear those that were selected for the purpose of giving information. What they wanted, as those lines indicated, was that kindness which appealed to their hearts, to work with them for the unity of this country, to work with them to the end of progress, and to work with them for that great word which was the Christian standard, the word "excelsior" (applause).

The Governor having concluded his Address, Dr. Knox and Mr. Potter exhibited views of the human frame obtained by the Rontgen rays. One disclosed a coin lying on the chest of a man who had swallowed it. There were similar photographs of a mummy and a fish, showing the skeletons within. As a pleasing set off, came a view of the grand assemblage in front of St. Paul's Cathedral on Jubilee day, and finally a picture of Sir Hubert Jerningham prepared by Mr. Potter from one of Dr. Lovell's collection in Mauritius.

The Chairman moved a vote of thanks to those who had kindly entertained them. The Governor, he said, had infused some life into figures which were proverbially dry, and reminded them of Mr. Gladstone's budgets. Their thanks also were due to Dr. Knox and Mr. Potter for their exhibition of one of the latest scientific inventions. The proceedings terminated at 9.30.

FOODS, ETC., IMPORTED IN 1896.

		Values.		Quantities.
1. Cereals :—				
Flour	... ...	£127,000	...	30,500,000 lbs.
Bread	... ...	18,000	...	2,200,000 ,,
Rice	... ...	113,000	...	20,500,000 ,,
Dholl	... ...	9,500	...	2,500,000 ,,
		£267,500		
2. Liquors :—				
Spirits	... ...	£ 31,000*	...	30,000 gls.
Rum	... ...	106,000	...	250,000 ,,
Wine	... ...	41,000*	...	217,000 ,,
Malt	... ...	44,000*	...	180,000 ,,
		£222,000		
3. Meat and Fish :—				
Meat	...	£ 70,000	...	6,400,000 lbs.
Oxen	... ...	43,000	...	3,800,000 ,,
Other Stock	...	8,000	...	900,000 ,,
Fish	... ...	60,000	...	8,000,000 ,,
		£181,000		
4. Milk Products and Fats :—				
Butter	... ...	£ 24,500	...	650,000 lbs.
Cheese	... ...	7,000	...	248,000 ,,
Milk	... ...	7,000	...	—
Ghee	... ...	1,500*	...	—
Lard	... ...	21,500	...	1,340,000 ,,
Olive Oil	...	14,000	...	450,000 ,,
Oleomargarine	...	3,000*	...	150,000 ,,
		£ 78,500		
5. Medicines :—	...	...	£ 10,000	
6. Sugar and Beverages :—				
Sugar	... ...	6,000	...	600,000 lbs.
Tea	... ...	2,500	...	60,000 ,,
Cocoa	... ...	—	...	?
Coffee	... ...	—	...	?
		£ 8,500		
7. Miscellaneous :—				
Vegetables	...	£ 30,000		
Peas	... ...	8,000		
Fruit	...	2,000		
Unclassified	...	20,000		
		£ 60,000		
	Total ...	£827,500		

* Averages.

N.B.—Duties not included except in the case of Spirituous Liquors (No. 2.)

(Read before the Victoria Institute, 28th October, 1897.)

FOOD ADULTERATION.

———

By PROFESSOR CARMODY, F.C.S., &c.

YOU are all very well aware that a great many things are adulterated or imitated at the present time. Never before, in the history of the world, has adulteration been so extensively practised. Purchasers are, in their own interests, compelled to exercise the most extreme caution in buying any article. Diamonds may be nothing but glass; rubies and pearls and other precious stones may be the work of some skilled chemist; gold and silver articles may be composed largely of baser metals (in this town there is a gang of vagabonds who sell brass for gold); electroplated goods are not the substantial, durable articles of former years, and they contain the smallest possible quantity of gold or silver that can entitle them to be sold as electroplate; silk is no longer the pure product of the old-fashioned silk-worm; velvets, woollen and linen goods are made largely from cotton and other fibres, and so close is the imitation that only experts can distinguish; even the leather in our boots may never have been the natural envelope of any known species of animal.

In other directions, we find stained pitch pine or deal doing duty for mahogany, oak, or walnut; steel cutting-instruments that refuse to cut anything much harder than butter; ivory imitations that are made out of camphor and guncotton; carpets, and pictures, and china, that are but poor copies of their prototypes; horsehair mattresses that are innocent of horsehair; costly feather-beds that are made with second hand feathers; and cheap watches and clocks that are but poor temporisers.

Unfortunate even is the man who claims the sole right to some successful commercial venture, whether it be a remedy for some ailment, a popular food or drink, a clever invention, or even a good book, song, or play. The remainder of his life must be devoted to prosecuting imitators and plagiarists. I could extend the above list very considerably; but I have said enough to show you that there are good grounds for the widespread commercial mistrust that exists at the present time.

In none of the cases I have mentioned does the Government of a country particularly interfere with the ordinary law of contract between buyer and seller. It is only in connection with Food Adulteration that special laws are enacted. And the reason for this is not far to seek. The question of Food Adulteration is so intimately connected with the health of the community, and this in its turn with national prosperity and progress, that the Governments of all civilised countries have found it necessary to take steps for the prevention of practices fraught with consequences so serious and certain. After careful enquiry, it was established, that many articles of food were so tampered with as to be injurious to health, and it was resolved that nothing short of active Government interference could secure for the public that protection which was necessary for their health and prosperity. Food Adulteration was regarded as a national enemy to be subdued by imperial forces. But the Governments did not confine their operations to adulterations injurious to health, they decided also to protect the public against fraudulent adulterations.

For these two classes of adulteration they provided different kinds of punishment. Deleterious adulterations were punished by imprisonment, without the option of a fine for second offences; fraudulent adulterations were punishable by fines only. And the result of the severe punishment in the one case is, that adulterations injurious to health are now comparatively rare and harmless.

Fines for fraudulent adulterations have not proved a sufficient deterrent; and they never will so long as the profits are greater than the fines.

Having said so much by way of introduction, I think I may with advantage say a few words on the early history of adulteration.

The first case of which we have any record, occurred about two and a half centuries before Christ. Hiero, King of Syracuse, sent a certain weight of gold to be made into a crown by the Court Jeweller of those days. The crown was duly returned and weighed; but the King had grave doubts, and consulted Archimedes, who although a great mathematician was not much skilled in analysis. However, he gave up all his time and thoughts to the subjects; and one day, as he was entering his bath, an idea occurred to him which he at once saw would solve this difficult problem. So delighted was he with his idea, that he forgot to dress himself, and ran home through the streets to try his test on the crown. It succeeded; and we may assume that the brass seller on that occasion was not let off with a fine.

About two hundred years later we hear of lime, an important article among the Romans, being adulterated with red lead; and, in the first century of the Christian era, of opium being adulterated with gum and the milky juices of other plants; Pliny writes of bread adulterated with earth, soft to the touch, sweet to the taste and obtained from a hill called Leucogee, near Naples; and again states that, not even the rich Roman millionaires, could buy the natural wines of Falerno, for they were adulterated in the cellars. We hear also of the appointment in Athens of a special inspector to stop the adulteration of wine; but whether the recorders were at rest, or adulterators ceased from troubling, nothing more is heard of them till about the 11th century, since which time they have been particularly active. An Act for the assize of bread was passed in the 4th year, of the reign of King John; bakers, brewers, pepperers and vintners were all looked after, and ale-tasters were appointed in the 15th century. The adulteration of wine was so extensively practised in England in the 16th and 17th centuries, that Addison thus writes in the TATLER "these subtle philosophers are daily employed in the transmutation of liquors, and by the powers of magical drugs and incantations raise under the streets of London the choicest products of the hills and valleys of France; they squeeze Bordeaux out of the sloe, and draw champagne from an apple."

In France, from very early times (13th century) we find regulations for the general supervision and inspection of provisions, flour, bread, wine, butter and drugs, until finally in 1802 Boards of Health were permanently established in Paris. Similar steps were taken in Germany; but the punishments were usually more severe.

With many of these punishments, the punishments of the present day compare favourably indeed. In Nurembourg, in 1444, a man was burnt with his false saffron, and a year later, two men and a woman were buried alive there for the same offence. In other parts of Germany, the bread adulterator was placed in a basket at the end of a long pole, and ducked repeatedly in a muddy pool. One wine adulterator was led out of the city, with hands bound and a rope round his neck; two others were branded and otherwise severely punished; a man and his wife were pilloried on the cask in which they sold sour wine sweetened with roasted pears, each being compelled to wear a necklace of the pears. But this was mild as compared with the punishment inflicted in 1482 on a falsifier of wine at Biebrich. He was condemned to drink six quarts of his own wine. It killed him. In France, in 1525, a bread adulterator was led from prison through

the streets of Paris with only one garment on, his head and feet
bare, small loaves hung round his neck, and a large lighted wax
candle in his hand, and at each of the principal churches and
public places had to ask mercy and pardon of God, the King
and of Justice for his fault. In 1718, a man who had caused
the death of one person, and the illness of others by the use of
some poisonous plant in wine, and his wife who sold the wine,
were condemned to be led by two sergeants for one day through
the streets of Berghein, carrying sandwich boards with the words
"frelateurs de vin" printed thereon, to pay a fine of 130 livres,
and 30 livres extra "pour faire prier Dieu pour le repos de l'ame
du defunt."

One novel form of wine adulteration occurred in recent
years and is worthy of mention. A particular brand of champagne secured a high reputation at Wurtemburg on account of
its unusual exhilarating effects. Suspicion was at length aroused,
and Liebig, who analysed it, found it was charged with one
volume of Carbonic acid gas, and two volumes of laughing gas.

I mentioned above that Archimedes did not seem to be an
expert analyst; but the method he adopted was a great discovery
and is still used by us. Some other tests used (even as late as
the 16th century) for detecting adulteration have not so
secured the admiration of posterity. Here is Dr. Blyth's
description of the one adopted by the ale-tasters. The ale was
spilt on a wooden seat, and on the wet place the tasters sat
attired in leathern breeches, then common enough. If sugar had
been added to the beer, the taster became so adherent, that
rising was difficult; but if sugar had not been added, it was then
considered that the dried extract had no adhesive property."

I will not detain you with history any longer, but will
merely add that in 1860 the first general Food and Drugs Act
was passed in England; other nations passed similar Acts, and
we in Trinidad adopted it in 1880, and further modified it
in 1895.

I will now invite your attention to the consideration of the
question of our own food supply. You will better be able to
judge of its importance by a glance at these Tables of values and
quantities of the principal imported food supplies we consumed
last year. To estimate the total cost to the consumer, of our
annual food supply, you must add to this the import duties, the
merchants' profits and the value of the food produced locally.
I regret that I am unable to make any estimate of the local
production except in the case of Rum. To whatever extent
these imported foods are adulterated, the people of this Colony

must correspondingly suffer in pocket, if not in health ; for you
can readily understand that the profits of adulteration go to the
actual adulterator. So far as I know there are only three forms
of purely local adulteration practised extensively, viz. :-- adulteration of milk, rum, and vinegar. If you desire to know the
extent and nature of the adulterants that are said to be used in
these imported articles, I would recommend you to read the
sensational paragraphs that appear in the newspapers from time
to time. Food adulteration, and bacteriology, and more recently
skeleton photography, have been as great a godsend to current
literature in general, as a Director of Public Works and a
General Manager of Railways are to the local press. Nothing
could be easier for me than to follow in this beaten track, to
play the role of alarmist, and to provide you with a literary
feast composed of a description of the most gruesome dishes. I
might invite you to an imaginary early coffee, and provide you
at six in the morning with the following menu :—Bread,
bleached with alum and guaranteed indigestible by a suitable
addition of plaster of Paris ; Butter consisting of Oleomargarine
and other greases; Jams and Jellies made from turnips,
seaweeds, glucose and gelatine and tinted with aniline dyes to
any desired shade ; Honey made of glucose and molasses ; Tea
made of exhausted leaves dipped in a solution of catechu gum
and then dyed with Prussian Blue ; Coffee made from chicory or
burnt corn ; Cocoa (if you prefer the imported mixture to the
genuine native article) composed of starch and sugar and with
not more than 10% of real Cocoa lest the fat in it should interfere with your digestion ; Milk guaranteed to contain not less
than 25% of dirty water, or (if tinned) possibly deprived of a
large proportion of its natural fat ; Demerara crystals which
consist of the detested Beet sugar disguised by aniline dyes.
And to relieve you of any further anxiety, I would give this
additional guarantee that all the Butter, Jam, Jelly, Honey, and
Milk consumed on the premises are warranted to contain
Salicylic and Boric acids in such quantity that, if you should
happen to die soon after, you are already partially embalmed. I
might invite you to dinner in the evening, but I am afraid you
would not accept the invitation after your experiences of the
morning, and I will not hurt your feelings with a description of
the contents of the dinner table. I will read you instead an
amusing satire on this subject from the pen of a German writer.

"There were four flies and, as it happened, they were
hungry one morning. The first joyfully alighted on a sausage of
singularly appetizing appearance, and made a hearty meal ; but
he speedily died of intestinal inflammation, for the sausage was
dyed with aniline. The second fly breakfasted upon flour, and

c

forthwith succumbed to contraction of the stomach, owing to the inordinate quantity of alum with which the flour had been adulterated. The third fly was slaking his thirst in the contents of a milk jug, when violent spasms suddenly convulsed his frame, and he soon gave up the ghost, a victim to chalk adulteration. Seeing this, the fourth fly, muttering to himself the sooner it's over, the sooner to sleep, alighted upon a moistened sheet of paper exhibiting the counterfeit presentment of a death's head above the inscription "Fly Poison." Fearlessly applying the tip of his proboscis to this device, the fourth fly drank to his heart's content, growing more vigorous and cheerful at every mouthful, although expecting each would be the last. He did not die, but on the contrary thrived and waxed fat, for even the fly pad was adulterated."

This is what you will find in the newspapers, and they are but highly coloured word pictures of actual facts. I will endeavour to place before you this evening the facts, so far as they relate to us locally, without the artistic colouring.

I will deal with this Table in the order of the values of the different classes of foods.

SECTION I.—CEREALS.

First in order of values are the cereal foods; they represent roughly one-third of the total value, and I am glad to say that there is no serious adulteration of a fraudulent character. The presence of alum in flour or bread is now of rare occurrence.

SECTION II.—SPIRITUOUS LIQUORS.

Next in value come intoxicating beverages, and with these I have thought it advisable to include rum of local manufacture. Rum is adulterated with water below the legal limit of strength. Some persons think this is an advantage from a moral point of view; but rum is a stimulant, and only an intoxicant when taken in excess. Of the brandy imported, I fear there is much that is not genuine; but for reasons, which I will explain later on, this is not often tested. The whisky imported is genuine, but much of it consists of grain spirit not sufficiently matured. It is a popular drink, and there is certain to be a large demand for any brand that maintains its standard of quality. We import large quantities of wine, as might be expected in a community into which the French element enters so largely. Claret imported is excessively acid, and answerable in my opinion for many of the digestive disorders, so common among us. Moreover, these wines contain insufficient alcohol to preserve them in this climate, and the deficiency is counterbalanced by the use of Salicylic acid. This course is adopted only in order that they may be admitted at a lower rate of duty.

Champagne and other expensive wines, are rarely examined. Some, which have come under my notice, are of very indifferent quality.

Malt liquors consist of Stout and Beer imported in bottle or in cask. The extent to which stout is consumed here is remarkable. It is said to agree better than beer with persons regularly using it. The only form of adulteration which has come under my notice is the substitution of inferior draught porter for the bottled brands of recognised good quality. A prosecution under the Merchandise Marks Act took place a short time ago for the purpose of preventing this ; a small fine was imposed, but public attention was forcibly directed to the fraud, and this may account for the considerable falling off (22,000 as compared with 35,000 gallons) noticeable last year in the importation of malt liquors in wood.

Our drink bill comes to approximately 20/- per head of the population.

SECTION III.—MEAT AND FISH.

The next important item is Meat and Fish. There is no adulteration of these to record ; although salt fish is suspected to be sometimes unwholesome.

SECTION IV.—MILK, MILK PRODUCTS, AND FATS.

We next come to Milk, Milk Products and Fats. We import £7,000 worth of milk, and this speaks badly for our local milk supply. Some brands of imported milk are of good quality, others are but skimmed milk and therefore deprived of much of their nutriment. I may here conveniently refer to our local milk supply. Milk as you know gives us our first acquaintance with the wickedness of the food adulterator. We come into the world with a very small stock of experience, and a very profound belief in the integrity of that great human race of which we have recently been admitted a member. We take with implicit confidence whatever food is given to us, and from time immemorial we learn that milk has been prescribed as the proper and natural food for infants. But we very soon discover the iniquities practised upon us. The capacity of our stomachs allows of the consumption of only a very limited quantity of food, and even this limited quantity is deprived of its natural amount of nutrition by the addition of water, not always of the purest. Is it any wonder then, that our natural instincts cause us to rebel against the time-honoured bottle? we feel, that, in addition to all the ills that flesh is heir to, we are imbibing the seeds of constitutional destruction in the countless microbes contained in dirty water, or at least that we are certain to grow up so debilitated as to be unable to resist the insidious attacks of ordinary diseases. Those who have taken the trouble to read my annual reports know that this is no fancifully drawn picture. The average number of adulterated samples is about 40%, and the average amount of water added is about 25%. The amount of fines recovered from milk sellers in 1896 was £128.

I have before drawn attention to the serious question of our milk supply being entirely in the hands of the poorest and least educated of our population. The temptation to adulterate is consequently very great. We have no general dairy in Port-of-Spain under the management of persons whose names would be a guarantee of quality; and until this happens, I do not think that our milk supply can be in a satisfactory condition. It is true that by a vigorous working of the law, we are gradually diminishing the extent and amount of milk adulteration; but even when we succeed, there is still the important question of clean cows, and clean dairy utensils. I hope the suggestion of the establishment of a large dairy in Port-of-Spain will be seriously considered and discussed at this meeting.

Butter is a large item in our imports, 650,000 lb. valued at £24,500. A few years ago, Oleomargarine was openly sold here as butter, and at the price of butter. Now this form of adulteration is almost unknown, although we still import 1lb. of Oleomargarine for every 4lb. of butter. At the present time, the chief drawback in our butter supply is the reduced proportion of butter fat, and the correspondingly high proportion of water and salt. Butter being a manufactured article, the proportion of salt and water may be largely increased at the expense of the fat. The latter is the only costly ingredient, and therefore it has been found necessary to limit the amount of salt and water that may be added. In England 80% of fat is the limit allowed; but the average amount in commercial butters is above 85%. Here on account of our hotter climate, the limit has been lowered to 75% to allow if necessary, of the addition of an extra 5% of salt for preserving purposes. Some of the butters imported here were found to contain 65-67 per cent. of butter, a few contained less than 60. Experience has shown us that 11-13 per cent. of salt, and an average of 12 per cent. of water, represent the proportions present in butters of fair commercial quality but the proportion of salt migh advantageously be reduced. We have found as much as 27 per cent. of salt, and 20 per cent. of water in some samples ; and it therefore became necessary to draw the line somewhere. We have drawn it at 75% of butter fat, which we consider a fair commercial standard for ordinary butter sold in firkins. Ghee is melted butter to all intents and purposes. It is consumed only by East Indians, and contains neither water nor salt. The amount imported last year (4,000lbs.) was much below the average. This points to probably adulteration. In 1891, the importation amounted to 160,000 lbs.

The £7,000 worth of cheese imported here is, so far as we have examined it, genuine. In some places it is much adulterated by being made from skimmed milk or from skimmed milk and lard or oleomargarine and sold under the name of filled cheese.

Lard is imported here in very large quantities. In 1896 we consumed 1,340,000 lbs. which cost us £21,500. The most serious adulteration in connection with this article occurred a year or so ago, when a mixture containing one-third of its weight of water was imported. Genuine lard contains only a fraction of a per cent. of water. If this mixture had not been detected, the adulterator would have made £7,000 a year from this island alone.

Olive oil is with us an important article. Here again is evidence of a large French population. 50,000 gallons of a value of £14,000 is our annual consumption. · No article of commerce is more largely adulterated than olive oil. The pure oil sells at a high price ; and the addition of many cheaper oils which admit of being used as adulterants,—is difficult to detect. Of these, cotton seed oil is most commonly used—the price of which is about 2/- a gallon as compared with 6/- a gallon for olive oil. There is here a large margin of profit for the unscrupulous adulterator who does not hesitate to sell cotton seed oil as "sublime" olive oil.

To oleomargarine, when sold as such, there can be no objection either from a commercial or health point of view. So closely does it resemble butter in its appearance that it has frequently been sold as butter. Indeed it is said that at a recent Exhibition a sample of oleomargarine obtained the first prize in the butter section. If the judges were experts, as they should have been, this seems impossible ; for the two can be readily distinguished.

A great many unfair statements have been made about oleomargarine. It has been said, for instance, that it is made from river mud ; but it is usually manufactured with the greatest care and attention, from beef fat which is first melted partially, the liquid portion separated, cooled, and then churned with milk to give it a flavour. As a rule it contains 85 per cent. of fat, and only 15 per cent. of water and salt. It keeps well in this climate with 7½ per cent. of salt. Compared with butter it is of course very deficient in flavour.

SECTION V.—MEDICINES.

Medicines which amount in value to £10,000 a year call for no special notice.

SECTION VI.—SUGAR AND BEVERAGES.

We consume refined sugar to the value of £6,000 a year. For a sugar producing colony this is a large amount.

The only adulteration of sugar worthy of consideration affects us as sugar producers rather than as sugar consumers. This consists in the substitution of beet crystals, coloured with an aniline dye for the well known Demerara crystals. It is undoubtedly a fraud; and, although convictions under the Food and Drugs Act have been obtained in many parts of England, in my opinion it is a question which should be dealt with under the Merchandise Marks Act, and dealt with severely. It shows us, however, that our struggling industries can be, to some extent, protected by the proper working of Food Laws in other countries.

But although sugar itself is not much adulterated, it is not infrequently replaced in preserves such as jams and jellies by a kind of sugar made artificially from starch. The use of such substitutes diminishes the natural demand for cane sugar. I might remark here, although it is not strictly relevant, that a large manufacturer of aerated waters stated some time ago that he found it impossible to use beet sugar for his syrups, because when made into aerated water this syrup always developed a mouldy flavour. This is disinterested testimony of some value to cane-sugar producers.

I will only say of tea that the quality of much that is imported could be materially improved by judicious buying. I am not aware of any serious adulteration.

We do import coffee, but why we do so, and to what extent, I am unable to give you any information.

We also import cacao, but only I presume such special preparations as Cocoatina, Van Houten's, Cadbury's and Epps's.

Like sugar, the question of the adulteration of cacao will interest you more as producers than as consumers; and it is to this colony a most important question; for the demand for cacao would be much greater, if adulteration had not been practised to the extraordinary—I might even say shameful—extent it is at present. What words are too strong to describe the sale as cacao of a mixture of starch and sugar with only 8 per cent. of real cacao? Most of the mixtures sold contain not more than 25 per cent. of cacao, and the best brands do not go above 50 per cent. Of the so-called pure cocoas I shall have something to say later on.

The great naturalist, Linnæus, was of opinion that cacao was a food fit for the gods, our modern teachers tell us that it is not fit food even for man. They tell us that nature made a huge mistake in putting so much fat into the cacao bean, that we must dilute this enormous proportion of fat with starch and sugar, or express it from the bean, before we can prepare a presentable beverage. In the long run, however, we shall probably find that nature made no mistake, and that the blame rests with ourselves because we have not discovered the proper way to use it. It has often struck me as a very singular fact that the people of tropical countries drink, and I suppose have drunk for centuries, pure cacao with all its fat, without feeling any the worse for it; and yet in cold climates, where fat, which is a heat giver, would be a very desirable constituent of food, the people complain that pure cacao disagrees with them on account of the large quantity of fat it contains. And yet these people will consume at a meal a great deal more fat, in the form of butter or bacon, than is contained in the strongest cup of cacao. I think that we should hear fewer complaints of this sort, if it were generally understood that milk, and not water, is the proper liquid to use in preparing the infusion. Another point in support of the view that cacao fat is not the indigestible substance it is said to be, is that children do consume larger quantities of cacao fat in the form of chocolate creams than is contained in a cup of cacao, and yet they suffer no ill-effects. Indeed, chocolate creams are generally recommended as the healthiest kind of sweets by the very people who condemn pure cacao as a beverage. Whether it be false teaching or not, adulterators take full advantage of the popular belief, and infinite pains to ensure that the mixtures they sell shall not contain hurtful quantities of cacao. A well-known analyst, of large experience. stated a short time ago that the cacao mixtures commonly consumed in England contained on an average 15 per cent. of cacao. That this extensive adulteration works incalculable injury to the cacao producer, it is impossible to deny. The sale of so-called pure cocoas, and cocoa essences is less detrimental to the interests of cacao producers. So called pure cocoas contain no added starch or sugar, but consist of cacao from which half the fat has been extracted.

It would not be possible to sell these as pure cocoas, cocoa extracts, or cocoa essences, if it were not for the popular belief that cacao, containing the whole of its natural fat, is indigestible. Cacao, among foods, occupies a very anomalous position in consequence. If a milk seller rob his milk of its natural fat he is heavily fined; or if butter, cheese, or oilmeal is sold containing less than the normal proportions of fat, it is a serious offence. But with cacao, the manufacturer can say that he expressed the fat in the interests of public health. He has only to print "public health" in large capitals, and he may then pose as a public benefactor. This is how it works out in plain figures to his own advantage. He buys the cacao at about sixpence a pound, he expresses from this a quarter of a pound of fat which he sells for medical uses at the rate of one shilling a pound, and then he disposes of the *impoverished* residue—which he calls an extract or an essence—at the handsome rate of from 2/6 to 3/- a pound. Instead of being an essence, it is a thing deprived of part of its essence; instead of being an extract, it is the residue of an extract. (Read labels.)

As long as the profits are so considerable, manufacturers will probably foster the belief that cacao fat is indigestible.

SECTION VII.—MISCELLANEOUS.

This section is not likely to be adulterated for fraudulent purposes. It is very remarkable that £30,000 should be spent annually in vegetables.

A special form of adulteration remains to be noticed—the sale of pyroligneous acid for vinegar. It is extensively practised locally. Acetic acid is imported here, and then diluted to the ordinary strength of vinegar. The price of wood vinegar is about twopence a gallon, the price of ordinary vinegar about eight pence. It is therefore a fraudulent adulteration. The two vinegars are very different—wood vinegar is destitute of flavour, the fermented vinegars have a peculiar and agreeable aroma.

I have now exhausted the subject of fraudulent adulteration and will briefly refer to adulterations injurious to health. Of these, milk containing impure water is a dangerous type, about which it is not necessary for me to say much. Tinned peas are often coloured with sulphate of copper. This is a very serious adulterant. All copper salts are active poisons; and the poisoning cases that occurred here at the Masonic banquet some years ago were distinctly traceable to preserved peas. I would strongly recommend people to be extremely cautious in the consumption of highly coloured preserved peas. It is an extraordinary fact that they are not allowed to be sold in the country where they are largely manufactured. and are prepared only for exportation. This remark applies also to wines containing salicylic acid, and is a great blot in the Food Laws of the countries which allow so objectionable a practice.

We largely consume ærated waters, and as these may accidentally contain lead and antimony they are deserving of notice. Lead is a cumulative poison, and small doses taken regularly may cause serious mischief, or may even prove fatal. The lead is derived from the pipes of the machinery, and the antimony from the rubber rings used in the bottles. Some manufacturers use silver pipes to prevent the dangerous lead contamination.

Another form of deleterious adulteration is the use of preservatives in perishable foods or drinks. In defence of their use, it is urged that they are present only in a very small quantity, less than would be given in medicinal doses.

But it becomes a very serious matter indeed when you are regularly and unconsciously consuming even infinitesimal doses in various articles of food. Your preserved milk and peas, your jams and wines, and your butter may each contain salicylic acid. The use of salicylic acid is absolutely prohibited in foods or drinks sold in France, Germany, Holland, Italy and Spain. In England its use is not prohibited unless it is present in excessive quantities.

I have enumerated the points of greatest importance in connection with food adulteration. I will now briefly recapitulate the directions in which food adulteration laws have proved beneficial :—

1. They protect the purchaser against fraudulent adulteration—the principle being that the purchaser has a right to be supplied with the article he asks and pays for.

2. They protect the public health from injurious adulterants.

3. They protect indirectly the honest trader from unfair competition ;

4. And indirectly also the manufactures and agricultural industries of a nation.

The practical working of these laws is essentially democratic in its character. If you read the annual reports of any Analyst, you will find that the principal part of his work consists in examining the foods largely consumed by the poorer classes, and that very few analyses are made of the expensive wines, brandies and foods of the wealthy. Provision is made for such analysis, but those who can afford the luxury of expensive beverages and foods are expected to pay for any analysis they may desire to have made.

But as very few articles are adulterated in this colony, both rich and poor are equally at the mercy of the foreign manufacturer. Among these are firms of high reputation who supply the same quality of goods to the wildest savage that they supply to the most civilized gourmêt; but I am sorry to say there are others among them who prepare an inferior quality for export, who think anything good enough for people abroad, and who afford abundant justification for the oft-repeated remark— that the West Indies is one of the dustbins for the disposal of the refuse food of more civilized countries. And if we think ill of these unscrupulous merchants, what can we think of the Governments that allow certain articles to be exported which they declare unfit for consumption by their own people. France, Germany, Spain, Italy, Holland, allow foods and wines containing salicylic and boric acids to be exported, while they absolutely prohibit the sale of such articles at home. Even England allows tea to be exported which the Customs' authorities declare unfit for home consumption. The Governments of these countries act on the principle that every nation must protect itself. Many countries abroad have no food laws, and the people of these countries are consequently without the means of protection. These are the countries where the food adulterator makes his happy hunting grounds. Here, and in most English Colonies, our food laws are based on, and are very similar to, the law in force in England. This fact must be known to the merchants who supply us with adulterated foods as they still continue to send them, and I can only suppose that they do so on the assumption that the Analysts we employ use tests as primitive and antiquated as that used by the ale-taster with the leathern breeches.

The lecturer closed his remarks by an expression of his opinion that the various Governments should not permit goods to be manufactured for export which would be considered unfit for home consumption, a state of things commonly done at present.

Speaking of milk adulteration the lecturer gave the following account of a case of added water. A milk vendor had added 30 per cent. of water to his milk, and on the Analyst being called, he informed the Magistrate there was 30 per cent. of added water.

"And what is the percentage of water, naturally present in milk?" asked the S.J.P. *88 per cent.* the Analyst replied : *What,* says the S.J.P., *88 per cent. plus 30=118 per cent. water!   Why, that is 18 per cent. more water than is found in water itself.   I dismiss the case!* (*Laughter.*)

At the close of the lecture, His Excellency called upon several gentlemen present to offer any remarks they thought desirable.

Mr. Wilson, President of the Chamber of Commerce, expressed his appreciation of the lecture, and of the fearless manner in which Professor Carmody had handled his subject.   It was his opinion, as President of the Chamber of Commerce, that such a lecture would be of enormous advantage to the colony at large, especially the portion relating to cocoa and sugar.   As to the adulteration of olive oil, he remarked that the question was discussed by the Chamber six or eight months ago, when the general opinion was that the addition of cotton seed oil was an advantage, giving the olive oil that nutty flavour so much admired in France ; in consequence of which opinion he wished, though he scarcely expected to be successful, to induce the Legislature to introduce an act, allowing this particular adulteration, upon condition that the bottles be marked "*not pure olive oil.*"

Mr. Randolph Rust said he had come to be instructed and amused, and he had been both instructed and amused by the lecture, and did not expect to have to speak, but he wished to draw attention to the common and serious adulteration of *Condensed Milk*, in spite of its asserted *purity*.   He agreed that it was the "only true and natural food for infants," and argued that for that very reason it was essential to guard against its adulteration.

Mr. Hamel Smith did not like the ugly word adulteration. It was the common practice for the public to lay the crime on the manufacturer, and as he was not a manufacturer, he trusted that those present would believe in his complete disinterestedness. He thought it very unfair to expose the manufacturers of cocoa in the way the lecturer had, for it must be remembered that all they did was to adapt themselves to the public taste, and so long as Englishmen expected to get a good cup of cocoa by pouring boiling water upon a grated powder, so long would they dislike pure cocoa.   They should learn to thoroughly boil it in *milk*, and then they would be surprised at the result.   He also desired to say a few words as to *keg butter*.   In this hot climate it is necessary to have plenty of salt and brine to preserve the butter, and this extra salt is not charged for as butter by the

manufacturers. He admitted that the article was made very
near the limit of the standard, which, however, he considered
rather high, but contended that the addition of salt was an
advantage, as it saved the cooks from adding so much to the
food. (*Laughter.*)

Mr. J. H. Hart considered the lecture to have been in the
nature of a piece of education, and was very much pleased with
it. As to cocoa, he had been able to invent a means of extract-
ing the fat of cocoa to a more complete extent than even Messrs.
Cadbury of London, who had, now, adopted a modification of
his plan, which was a great success. But he did not think it
was beneficial to extract the fat, in which point he quite agreed
with the lecturer.

Read November, 1897.

TRINIDAD AS AN AGRICULTURAL COLONY.

By RENE DE VERTEUIL.

TRINIDAD has been up to now eminently an agricultural
colony, and were its great value as the emporium of the
trade between Europe and Western and Southern Venezuela
realized, its commercial progress would contribute incontestably
to our agricultural advancement.

Unlike the majority of the other West Indies, this island
is not only a sugar colony, for the importance of its cacao production promises within a very short time to be its support in the
struggle for existence which unprotected cane sugar producers
are now undergoing. The adaptability of its soil and climate to
produce the chief tropical staples will cause it to be always an
agricultural colony, yet the efforts of those who desire to raise
its commercial status deserve all encouragement, for that would
be labouring likewise towards its agricultural development.

Much lies indeed in these few words "agricultural development," but it is a task which cannot be successfully undertaken
without the union of all classes. There should be no conflict,
especially between those cultivating the soil of the same country,
for that just interference and assistance which government in a
new country like this is called upon to bring to the support of
private initiative can be more profitably secured by combined
perseverance and determination.

The two great staples of the colony, sugar and cacao, must go hand in hand, as indeed they have done up to this time, and the cacao planters have shewn by their generous acceptance of a larger proportion of immigration expenses that they do not merely sympathize with the sugar planters in their difficulties, but have been ready to lend effective help, according to their resources. It is a natural consequence that if in an agricultural country the chief staple goes to ruin, the other agricultural industries will have to assume the burdens it bore, and if sympathy were cast aside, self protection demands a closer union between the agricultural and commercial interests of the colony when peril threatens any of them.

It has been said by some, rather with a light heart, that the collapse of the sugar industry, and its extinction in a few years would not affect this island to any great extent. This can hardly be the opinion of those knowing our conditions who have given a thought to that possibility, and who have before them the condition of the Leeward Islands, St. Vincent, St. Lucia and Tobago. It is no easy matter to build up other industries in the place of sugar, which to-day represents invested capital to the amount of two-and-a-half million pounds sterling, and which, even now in a day of extreme depression, pays out in wages to the labouring classes about £350,000 yearly, with £250,000 more in salaries to managers, overseers, engineers, and in purchase of supplies locally. Strict economy has been obligatory to prolong existence in the hopes of better times, or until some combination can be effected which will fill up the gap created by the decay of the main industry.

Up to the end of the Seventies sugar was indeed the main-stay of Trinidad. Prices ruled at £18 per ton for muscovadoes, which are this year worth under £7, and molasses fetched 12 to 16 cents a gallon, whereas now 3 cents is the extreme value.

It is suggested that had we then possessed the factories which now produce the best class of sugars, our position might be stronger to-day. Yet British Guiana which had been in advance of us by many years in the line of progress, with many advantages over us, is to-day no better off than we are, a proof clear enough that even with all improvements in manufacture, and a full yield of cane in the field, however able to fight its own battle on equal terms with other producing countries, West Indian sugar cannot compete first against bounties given by European beet producing countries which possess not only the advantages of science, but proximity to markets, cheap fuel and other necessaries for manufacture on the spot, nor again with American sugars enjoying protection to the extent of the full value we get for our produce.

The great energy and perseverance shewn by Trinidad sugar planters since the crisis began in 1884 does not appear to have been appreciated, and yet its effect has been beneficial upon all agricultural classes. Economy has been taught not only to those directly concerned in sugar, but it has spread to the other industries as well. We have witnessed those engaged in coconuts suffering likewise from an unexpected fall in prices, and seeing how pluckily their sugar brethren had put their shoulders to the wheel, they imitated them by introducing improved machinery for the production of oil, trusting to progress to save themselves. This has been done at great cost of capital, and it is discouraging to find such intelligent efforts threatened again with failure.

The cacao planters too had their moment of anxiety during the last eighteen months, and if matters have brightened up latterly, how long will these improved prices last, for with very little produce to sell, growers have reaped but very partially the benefits of the recovery. Fortunately they too have not given way to discouragement, and to meet the fall in values each one has tried to improve his cultivation and his preparation. The condition of cacao planters is however still one of anxiety, for how many are still mortgaged on the value of properties when cacao was selling at 80/- and 90/- the cwt. This is the chief danger in store, and it is only with the help of cheap money repayable on long terms that danger will be averted. The Land Mortgage Bank now in contemplation would bring about that desideratum, and do more for the advancement of the colony than high prices lasting over many years. If we ask Government to lend its guarantee in order that we may obtain cheaper capital to reduce our present mortgages, we offer with the security of our properties that energy and spirit which have elicited from the Royal Commissioners the opinion that we possess the necessary resources to enable us to tide over the present depression.

No one acquainted with Trinidad can endorse the reproach made by these gentlemen when they state that "cane cultivation unfits the people, or at any rate gives them no training for the management or cultivation of the soil for any other purpose than that of growing sugar cane." Have not some of the finest cacao properties been formed by our peasantry who had no other training but what they obtained during their stay on sugar estates? Cannot the good class of our East Indians shew as fine plots of cacao as those planted by the immigrants who came over from Venezuela, given equal conditions of soil, and when that soil is inferior, or requires energy to cultivate it, whom do we find upon it but the Indian trained on a sugar estate, or the negro laborer who in his younger days knew no other work but what his cutlass and his spade secured him on the cane plantations? Have not the Barbadians the justly earned reputation of being splendid growers of ground provisions, and raisers of poultry and small stock, but yet they had no training for that branch of industry, merely what they got in the cane fields? The cacao plantations of Grenada have likewise been established by those same laborers who learnt field work in the cane fields of their own island, and in those of Trinidad. Have fresh Africans been introduced in Jamaica to start and keep up the fruit trade which has obtained for that island along with Trinidad the honour of being considered strong enough to tide over the sugar crises without extraneous help? I think it is rather that same class which received its first training on the sugar plantations, and left them when they became independent, and the industry ceased to be remunerative. Our experience here is that training on a sugar estate is the best to secure discipline not only amongst labourers, but for the young men whose calling is outside of Government or Merchants' offices.

That sugar is still necessary to the progress of the Colony the great majority of those who consider impartially the position must admit, and a supreme effort in favour of maintaining it deserves the co-operation of all. Is it too much to expect the Imperial Government to join us? The commercial principles of the Mother Country are a bar, it is said, to the imposition of countervailing duties on bounty fed sugar imported in British markets. Yet would the advocates of the free breakfast table accept that bounties on wheat be given by the United States, Prussia, Argentina, which would give cheaper bread to the poor, but annihilate the cereal production of Great Britain? I cannot say, but I do know that the importation of live stock is virtually prohibited from foreign countries under the pretence of preserving British herds and flocks from disease, though it is well known that the various breeds of cattle, sheep and pigs of the European continent are as free from disease as those of the British Isles. Must we also see in the duty of 4d. per gallon or 33 per cent. ad valorem on ordinary qualities, imposed on colonial rum, a measure to protect the British public from the injurious effects of that spirit, and to preserve to it the beneficial influence of Scotch and Irish Whiskies?

However, whether we receive aid from the Home Government, or are left to ourselves, we must still struggle and we must therefore consider what means we have at our disposal to face the near future. Cane cultivation is attractive to the peasantry, and if many have retired from the estates recently, it is on account of the facility to get employment on the Roads and on the Public Works which have recently been executed. Unlike the pockets of planters, the Treasury has been full, and Government have always paid higher wages than private enterprize. Nevertheless, there has been a great attraction offered to laborers, especially to the negroes, in Cane farming, and the earnestness with which the majority have taken to the industry shews it to be a remunerative one, even when the cultivation of the planters is carried on at a loss. The principle of Cane farming brings about the division of labor, and is undoubtedly sound. Division of labor implies division of risks, and in a threatened industry requiring such considerable recurring outlay as sugar, this becomes effective relief.

Our Factories are fitted out with all modern improvements, and can increase their output if work is carried on night and day as in the Beet Factories. Equipped as they are, they can adopt all new methods without difficulty, and maintain their present excellence. But no one will deny that our cultivation has not kept pace with our manufacture and that it can be improved. The reason for this is that the planters have failed to secure a sufficiency of labor to cultivate as they should. Estates have kept up a larger cultivation than they had labor to maintain, with the result that disappointment has always come with unfavourable seasons. It is not correct to say that there is plenty of labor available, if planters had the means to pay for it. In British Guiana, the proportion of indentured labor is, I believe, as 32 to 25 in Trinidad for the same extent of cultivation, but there appear to be four free laborers willing to work in the sister colony to every one here. Surely if at Demerara a planter can obtain advances to pay four laborers when he requires them, his colleague in Trinidad can likewise, for he has had those advances to transform his manufacturing plant as his neighbor in the other colony did before him. The quality of sugar produced in Trinidad is to-day equal to that produced in British Guiana, and fetches the same price. If we had the same available labor we would get not only the same return of canes per acre, but probably exceed it, as our soil has many natural advantages.

Our sugar crops have not increased since 1870, it will be said, and yet our Indian population has doubled. It must however be borne in mind that the estimated cultivated acreage of land in 1871 was 83,841 acres, whereas in 1896 it was 198,000. In the first period not only the greater majority of the immigrants worked mainly on the sugar estates, but we had in addition a plentiful and useful supply of labor from Grenada and the Grenadines who did the cane cutting on the different estates at 20 and 25 cents per task, manned the boiling houses, and before returning home, relieved the cane fields. The rapid alienation of Crown lands began about 1870, and not many years afterwards, when with the extension of cacao cultivation a considerable rise took place in the value of the product, not only the coolies, as their term of indenture expired on the sugar estates became purchasers of Crown land, or were granted free tracts in commutation of return passages, but they withdrew a large number of their comrades from the plantations to assist them in their enterprises. This policy assisted the opening up of the country, and contributed to the rapid progress made by the colony, but deprived the sugar planters of their best laborers. Moreover about the same period Grenada took largely to planting cacao, and the laborers who used to come over here remained at home with the improved conditions caused by the new industry. Thus at the same time the sources of creole and coolie labor were considerably affected, and the stream of indentured immigration had to be kept up as regularly as in the days of prices, and will in all probability be necessary so long as cane cultivation is carried on. There is no doubt that the labouring population available to the sugar estates at present is not industrious. The greater number are content with the wages of two or three days a week, and can live comfortably so long as sickness does not overtake them, and then they are liberally provided for in the public hospitals.

Cane farming so far as we see at present not only cannot help to do away with coolie immigration, but will necessitate its continuance should prices improve sufficiently to continue the sugar industry. A large proportion of the present floating agricultural population will in that case take to cane farming, and starting with modest means and a small cultivation they will as soon as successful increase their sphere, and the family that could amongst its members cultivate three acres will require labor, just as the more important grower or planter, when he has increased his holding to ten acres and more.

The small peasant proprietors or renters are not the only ones who will be benefited by cane farming. The success of the division of labor and of risks will be better attained with large growers owning from say 100 to 500 acres. It is a manifest advantage to the factory to receive a large and regular supply of cane from five or six growers than from forty or fifty small ones, whose deliveries may not be as regular as must be to ensure the mills being regularly supplied.

The cultivation of the cane carried on apart from the manufacture of sugar ought to improve, for the grower will have all facility to till the soil at the proper time, and to give it full attention and care during the dry season when under present circumstances it is next to impossible for the manager of a factory growing its total supply of cane to do so, as his attention must be bestowed chiefly on the manufacture, and the main part of his labor in gathering the crop. Let the cultivation, even if it be in the same ownership, be in the hands of men unconnected with the work of the factory, and attention will be profitably given to the necessary trials and experiments to bring about an increased yield. We require special attention to the application of manures and selection of plants. Although it is the duty of the Agricultural Chemist to prepare the former, his formula will be eagerly experimented upon by all growers of intelligence—and the scientific Botanist will always find customers to take a supply of plants from him if he succeeds in raising varieties in any way superior to those now commonly cultivated.

Cane farming will again lead to the growing of provisions and the raising of stock, and after a time supply the country with meat and vegetables, upon which we now depend on our neighbours.

I had the honor to suggest to the Royal Commissioners when giving evidence before them the advantages that would follow the settlement by small farmers of the cane and other lands now thrown out of cultivation. They did not press the subject, but as I see they recommend some such scheme for the other islands, it is evident that elsewhere their attention was more strongly drawn to the point.

It ought not to be difficult to secure these uncultivated lands at a fair price, and it would be better were Government to purchase these lands and distribute them to coolies in commutation of return passages, rather than locate time expired immigrants on Crown lands, as has been done in the past. No one can deny that the coolie settlements proved a signal failure in nearly every case. The causes are clear. In certain districts the settlements were in unhealthy localities, in others, the lands, though Crown, were very poor and unprofitable, in others again, want of means of communication left the people too isolated. Want of supervision after the people were located, want of roads to get out their produce led to discouragement, and they lost the discipline and industrious habits they had acquired on the estates. They ceased gradually to work on the neighbouring plantations, upon which it was thought they would have continued to labor, and finally attracted to their holdings former comrades, both free and indentured, thus creating the spirit of desertion, now so prevalent. This unsatisfactory state of things could hardly have arisen had these settlements been laid out along established metalled roads, and in already settled centres.

The soil of the abandoned sugar estates will certainly give better results than those obtained in most of the old settlements. The land has been laid out for cultivation, drained in the majority of the estates, and been lying fallow for many years, and with tillage and manure will yield excellent returns. The small cultivator will work indifferent lands more successfully probably than large and wealthy owners. He loves tilling his land, and will sometimes get wonderful results. He counts his day's work for nothing, and does for himself double the work and produces a much better result than if he worked for hire. Cane farming will under these conditions be successfully carried on, being in proximity to factories. Provisions of every kind, live stock, poultry, &c., will be raised readily and disposed of on account of easy communication with the best markets. These facilities cannot be obtained on Crown lands, where health is exposed, living more difficult, social and moral advantages altogether wanting. If all the money expended in laying out the early settlements, the cost to the colony in hospitals and accessories caused by the injudicious location of the people, and the final abandonment by many of their holdings be taken into account, the thirty shillings which the acre of Crown land is valued at have been supplemented three or four times over. The colony has in addition witnessed the fruitless labor and deaths of many industrious people.

The purchase of these now idle lands could likewise be facilitated to others, if Banks in aid of agriculturists were established, through which advances would be made, repayable in instalments. A large amount of the funds which now go into the Savings Bank could be more profitably invested in agricultural institutions of credit, protected by a Government guarantee of interest. Depositors would get more than the 3 per cent. which are paid in the Savings Banks, as soon as the Institutions would be in working order, and such as would be entitled to borrow from them, advances at the rate of 6 per cent. People's banks would save the small proprietors here as they have done in Europe. I fail, however, to see how they are to be started without Government aid in the beginning. Philanthropic Mayors, the clergy and large proprietors started and managed these Banks in Europe. Here our Rural Mayors are the Wardens, who are servants of the State. Our clergy seldom remain in the same district long enough to place themselves at the head of such institutions, and, with very few exceptions not being natives of the country, take less interest in its material welfare, whilst our large land owners are differently situated to landlords in Europe.

There are also two classes of peasant proprietors in this country, one of which has grown up out of its own merit and labour, the holdings of which may rightly be said to have been purchased at the sweat of their brows. Amongst these will be found the pioneers of our cocoa industry, men who would have been comparatively wealthy to-day, had they not been handicapped by heavy interest, to which they consented partly through necessity, partly through ignorance. They can use their arms well, but they are seldom men of business. Some unfortunately have suffered in consequence of the confidence they reposed in the merchants with whom they dealt.

There is however another class, less worthy of sympathy. They acquire land more to evade regular work than to advance in the social scale. They are proprietors in name, and beyond the payment of taxes when that can without inconvenience be done, contribute but little to the welfare of the island. They are not uncommonly, if not themselves, at all events through their relatives whom they refuse to support, a charge on the hospitals and charitable institutions of the country. This class is most common among the East Indians. It could be reformed, I think, if subject to control, and under Government supervision, who by facilitating the purchase of lands to them on certain conditions in already established districts, would reserve the right to exact that these holdings were cultivated in useful products. Agricultural Instructors appointed to supervise and guide these people would probably obtain results that would make many of them valuable agriculturists, and a peasantry really useful to the country. Partial though I be to a peasant proprietary, I think it highly sentimental to suppose that our agricultural prosperity can be increased, nay maintained, by the preponderance of this class It is an important factor undoubtedly towards the development of the island, but not the main factor of its progress.

It is generally conceded, I believe, that the French peasantry is a model of energy, thrift and patriotism. We all know the part it took in the payment of the war indemnity imposed upon France by Germany after the disastrous war of 1870. Yet has the present power of France and its material prosperity been obtained by the preponderance of its small proprietors? The most enlightened peasantry cannot be more than the arms of the country, but what will be the arms if the body be without its head? The fable will tell you.

May I ask our officials who draw their income from the revenue of the colony whether they think that a peasant proprietary can save Trinidad in the event of a collapse of the large sugar and cacao proprietors?

CACAO.

If we follow the condition of the country during the last fourteen or fifteen years, we find that the cacao industry has doubled its production within that period, and it is to its present importance that we are better off than our neighbours. Its rapid extension dates from the administration of Sir Arthur Gordon, who in 1869 suppressed squatting and threw open the Crown lands of the colony. The position of squatters, whose cultivation was chiefly cacao in the richest lands of the interior, was legalized, and their holdings extended rapidly as roads were established. The present district of Montserrat stands out as a brilliant result of that wise Governor's policy. The agglomeration of several small properties formed the splendid plantations so much admired to-day. The former proprietors, after selling out, betook themselves further in the interior to begin afresh and to form the nucleus of future large properties, avoiding the approaching civilization.

In 1869 the lands extending behind the Couva and Pointe-à-Pierre sugar estates were in high woods. Twenty-five years later the stretch of cacao plantations had extended twelve miles or more eastward, and formed, as it were, one vast plantation interrupted merely by the Burnley group of sugar estates, from Caura and the heights of Arouca to Poole and Savana Grande. The opening up of a younger district soon followed, extending from the left bank of the Caroni, and comprising the valleys of the Tumpuna, Talparo, Cumuto, Cunape and Sangre Grande in almost uninterrupted cultivation to Tamana on the south, Manzanilla on the east, and the vegas of the Oropuche to the north and north-east. With the opening of the Sangre Grande and Caparo Valley railway extensions, before many years will have elapsed the stretch of cacao just described will meet with and disappear in the plantations of Montserrat.

In 1869 the estimated cacao crop of the island was about six million lbs., and possibly in it was included a portion from Grenada, as the small production of that island at that time was in great part sent over here for export to Europe. That quantity has now been increased four fold, and with the large extent of new cultivation, it is easy to predict a continued increase in the future, even allowing for a falling off from the old plantations. It is wise under these circumstances to make serious trials of new industries, for we must not expose ourselves after avoiding being wrecked on sugar to be engulfed in a cacao crisis of over-production. Indeed the collapse would be still more serious than that we are threatened with to-day. For the cacao industry is connected chiefly with the old families of the island, many of whom entered upon the new venture after the sugar estates which they owned had been taken away from them, and with the interests of a middle class who have successfully risen above the rank of peasant proprietors. The gains of these two classes are spent in the island, and they form along with their labours, and the small planters, the chief local *clientèle* of our dry goods merchants.

The value of our cacao exports is fast approaching that of sugar, and with the rise in prices of the former staple it promises to take the lead for the first time this year. Unless the very desirable improvement in the sugar market takes place, that lead is likely to be kept for the future. Being therefore at present the chief factor of the agricultural prosperity of the country cacao has a right to equal attention with sugar. This product has been cultivated in Trinidad from its earliest days, and it would appear that a very superior quality was grown, known as the criollo (a few stray trees are said to be still growing in the woods about Manzanilla) but we read in Borde's interesting History of Trinidad that some time last century the trees ceased to bear fruit, and many died out. He adds that only one estate in the whole island which was said to be planted with forastero, a more hardy though inferior variety, escaped the blight, or whatever it was, and bore as plentifully as usual. The result was that forastero was introduced, and is still the chief variety in cultivation. There are many strains of it caused in great part by hybridisation. Selection of plants for raising new plantations is being attended to, and the best seeds of the favourite qualities are chosen for propagation, fruit from strong and healthy trees 20 to 40 years of age being chosen by the more observing planters. Besides the propagation of the best home varieties, seed is introduced from other districts where the best results are known to have been obtained. Frequently fruit is imported from Venezuela, especially the Trujillano, the best known variety of forastero, and laid out in separate plots for the purposes of comparison. Mr. Hart introduced some plants from Nicaragua some years ago and his available supply was quickly taken up by planters, many being unable to secure a single plant. I have nine plants growing in good vega soil, but they are not very forward. They appear to be delicate and their growth is decidedly slower than that of any of our varieties, or of those imported from Venezuela. I doubt whether they will be useful, except as hybridisers to our local and Venezuelan kinds.

It may be said that there are two qualities of cacao introduced in Trinidad, estate and conuquero cacao. The preparation of the latter leaves much to be desired though it receives some further treatment in merchant's stores before shipment, and it will probably continue defective until central drying houses are established, in which the raw beans purchased from the small growers could be cured on improved methods.

Greater care is being given to the preparation of the article than ever before, and estate marks are being brought to a level. The twenty or thirty shillings difference that existed between San Antonio and Soconusco and other brands is now reduced to three and four shillings, and several other estates are obtaining the same price as these two favorite marks. Indeed it is not certain that the difference which now exists between the several estate marks is not due to greater garbling, by which two qualities are prepared, the inferior selling at much reduced value, rather than to intrinsic superiority. Owners of estates pay great attention to fermentation, and year after year we find modifications introduced with the object of attaining excellence.

Artificial drying has also been introduced, not always with success, I fear, but out of the numerous trials made, a sure and economic method will probably be discovered. So far the best dryer has been King Sol, and it is only when he refuses to shine that science is allowed a trial. A full extent of drying space is an absolute necessity, and we seldom hear of weathered cocoa on estates where there is plenty of drying space. It is the same as in the days of muscovado, when the planter with most megass houses and the best supply of megass made the best sugar and molasses.

Greater attention has also been paid to the cultivation of late. This was a natural consequence of owners undertaking the management of their properties in person. Overseers with some knowledge are employed in lieu of uneducated peons or drivers, and there is now a tendency to take over overseers and managers who have served on sugar estates. From their habit of dealing with labourers and from general experience obtained in connection with engineers, tradesmen, hospital management, they are likely to become a valuable acquisition.

The best economy we can aim at is that which will tend to increase the yield of the cacao tree. It is altogether too small, only 4 to 7½ cwt. per acre and it is only the great cheapness with which an estate can be worked that makes it a profitable investment. The prosperity of the cacao industry must therefore be considerably affected by the collapse of sugar, unable as it will be to assume any great part of the charges indirectly borne by sugar, and this is a point well worthy of the attention of Government as it is of our planters.

Grenada at the present time is dependent mainly on cacao, a paying industry from the time it became of any importance, and yet we hear that there is more distress there than in Trinidad. Are we certain that it will be different with us should sugar fail altogether? Our security depends much indeed on what new industries we can implant successfully, especially such as will thrive on old cane lands, and as this must be a question of time our welfare demands that the sugar industry should live till we discover those alternative products which can replace it. Should the tide turn once more in favour of sugar much will have been gained with the new industries introduced, and though it may not again hold the pride of place, Trinidad is certain of greater prosperity if sugar continues to be one of its chief exports, for the large spending power of that industry must not only be a great agricultural resource, but an impetus to the general trade of the colony.

COCONUTS.—Conclusion.

I will not say much on the coconut industry, though it holds the third rank in the agriculture of the island. It comes more properly under the head of subsidiary industries, and this paper is already too long to enter upon that question. Mr. Hart will address you on that subject, and no one can do so with greater authority.   •

Yet a product which has grown from an export of 2,300,000 nuts in 1871 to 14,000,000 in 1894 deserves notice in treating of the agriculture of the island. Now that oil is manufactured in large quantities and consumed entirely in the colony, the importance of the trade cannot be gauged merely by its exports. The excellent food for stock contained in the meal, after oil has been extracted is another valuable product, much sought after, and the demand for it is considerably in excess of the production, although its use is not yet general on estates. The total acreage in coconuts is 14,000 acres, about one-third of the acreage reaped yearly in cane.

To sum up. It appears to me that every effort must be made to maintain the sugar industry in Trinidad, until such time at least, as sound subsidiary products will have been established to replace it. What are those products, and in what space of time will they be capable of answering the object for which they will be introduced ? I confess, although the subject has had my consideration for several years, I feel discouraged at the difficulty. Cane-farming I am a strong advocate of, because it can assist the sugar industry most effectively, and because it will be the means of extending a useful peasantry, offering a guarantee of stability, as it will establish, in addition to cane, those minor products which we now import from Venezuela and the neighbouring islands.

I fear it will be no easy task to prepare Agricultural Banks to assist in making advances on growing crops. It will be less difficult to start them with cane farmers when advances made to them will be endorsed by the factories reaping their canes, thus giving full security to the Bank and facilitating its work.

Although cacao appears destined to take the leading part in the agriculture of the island, it is not probable, indeed it is not desirable, that it should have that preponderance over other exports that sugar had in the past.

I admit I am haunted by over production, and my alarm has some reason, for in 1871 with an acreage of 16,500, we exported cacao estimated to be worth £120,000, whereas in 1896 we exported from 94,500 acres a value of only £452,000 ! I am aware that a certain proportion of that increased acreage consists of trees not yet bearing, and of trees just beginning to bear, still the fall in prices of the last two years points that we must not trust any more in values of the past. We can face the risk of over production only if we obtain a larger yield from our trees, but not if it is caused by an unchecked increase of cultivation.

We must arm ourselves with agricultural education to meet further depreciation in value. It is a question which has the attention of the Agricultural Society, and we know that we will find a powerful and trusty ally in His Excellency the Governor,

A committee of the society has been appointed to consider the best method of teaching the elements of agriculture in our primary schools, and I have no doubt assistance will be forthcoming from the Laboratory and the Botanical Gardens in the persons of the active and capable heads of these institutions.

The moment has also come when special scholarships are required to be granted to students of agriculture, open not only to the pupils of the two colleges, but to all natives of the island to enable them to pursue a technical course of studies in Europe and America, for it is only with the aid of young men with sound theoretical training, that we can expect to progress scientifically with existing industries, and to hope to establish new ones with reasonable chances of success.

The Chairman said they had all listened to a most admirable and able paper upon the agricultural capabilities of this colony, and he trusted that it would be followed by an interesting discussion. He called upon several gentlemen to come forward.

Mr. J. H. Hart said that to tell them all in which he agreed with Mr. de Verteuil would take ten minutes, but to tell them all in which he disagreed with him could not be done in so short a time. The one point in which he agreed was on the benefits which these meetings had in ventilating questions and placing before the people the views of different sections of the community. Agreement or disagreement was sometimes a matter of mere personal opinion. He did not wish to enter into a discussion because he had to read a paper on the same subject and would be trenching on his own ground. He therefore left it to other speakers and should say what he had to say on the subject of agriculture at a future meeting.

Mr. Russell Murray said he agreed with a great deal of what had fallen from Mr. de Verteuil but at the same time he disagreed with a great deal that had been said in past discussions on the cocoa industry. He failed to see in what way cocoa had deteriorated. Most planters knew that the younger the tree was, the smaller the bean. During Mr. Hart's residence in the colony there had been a very large increase in the cultivation of cocoa, and the result of the increase had been a larger proportion of smaller beans, but in the next five years the size of bean would have improved immensely. Whether the same bean was made to produce higher grades or lower grades, as might be demanded in the market, was only a question of preparation, not so much a question of deterioration of the quality of the bean. He thought he ought to bring up the question of the fruit trade. If they read the report of the Royal Commission they would find it stated that the people of this island did not come forward. That was to a large extent true. Another reason of failure stated by the Commissioners was that the steamers were not what they should be. Leaving the period when it ceased, in 1893, he would refer to the time when it was begun by him two years ago. At that time one of the estates was shipping to their people in New York and he (Mr. Murray) was shipping to his own brokers, and it was a curious fact that he got double the price others were getting. He got very fair paying prices, and the fruit arrived in excellent condition. It was stated in the Royal Commissioners' Report that the voyage to England was too long. He had to give that statement a most emphatic denial. Probably it would be news to most persons that during this season, since April, he (Mr. Murray) had shipped something like 16,000 cases of fruit, and that these fruit now entered the London market. He should say that a great deal of the encouragement he had got lately had come from the Royal Mail Company and he was thankful to a gentleman in the room for getting that company to assist him in exporting fruit to England throughout the season. There was capital wanted, if it was to be done on a larger scale, and the large companies at home and in America would handle any quantity. At the present moment he had requisitions from England for over 500 cases of oranges every packet. If he were to ask any gentleman here to finance this venture he would say no. If it were cocoa or sugar, the answer would be "oh yes," but when it came to fruit the answer was "oh, no." There were only one or two firms here who were doing it at present; they were doing everything they could, and he was confident in saying that the fruit trade would develop, if two or three or half a dozen men with capital would put their shoulders to the wheel and push it along. During the last six months the much maligned Government Railway had done everything to assist him, by placing vans at his disposal and giving special instructions regarding the conveyance of fruit, and had made it possible to bring fruit to town and ship it at reasonable costs and charges. During the past five years he had been steadily working out the lecturer's idea of having central drying factories for cocoa. Very few persons knew that there was a factory built on his property for the drying of cocoa in bulk for the market, by which large quantities could be prepared, all of the same grade. But the factory could not be worked because the Government was standing in the way. He had applied in the usual way to the Magistrate of the district to grant him a license to purchase even ordinary cocoa, but the answer was "oh, no, you are not in a place where there are twenty houses, you cannot get it." Everyone of the Magistrates said it was a splendid idea. The people could not dry their cocoa in January last year because the rain was pouring in torrents. A neighbour of his had 10 or 15 bags of cocoa lying in his cocoa house, but he (Mr. Murray) could not take it over because he would have been fined £50 for doing so. The Attorney-General said the Ordinance might be amended. He did not see why they should not buy produce, just as the sugar planters bought canes from the cane farmers. His machine could dry 500 bags of cocoa in 18 hours. He hoped this meeting would urge His Excellency to have this matter remedied in some form or other. It was said that the buying of green produce in the country was going to open a wide gate to prædial larceny This meant that if a planter left a few pods on his trees because he could not dry them, they would disappear, but if there was a central factory in each district the small cocoa proprietor would at once take what were on the trees and deliver them to be dried, irrespective of the weather. He would meet the Attorney-General and the members of Council by suggesting that they should limit the quantity bought to 250 lbs., which was ordinary weight of a barrel of cocoa. The poor man might carry a little less than a barrel to the factory and run the risk of being arrested for stealing cocoa, but it was impossible for him to convey that quantity along the road without being seen.

Mr. Ernest Clarke did not believe that cocoa had in any way deteriorated. Ten years ago the Conuquero, planted indis criminately, not knowing that it would be better to select good pods, but now he was fully aware of the pod he was to select for planting, and this had been going on for some years. Mr. de Verteuil said it would be advisable, with Government aid, to locate labourers on sugar estate lands that had been abandoned. He (Mr. Clarke) would like to ask whether it was not a fact that in every case it was the least productive land that had been abandoned, and, if that was the case, would it be fair to put the labourer on such worthless land as that; would it not be better to put him on more productive land and give him a better chance? Was it a fact that there was not sufficient labour to cope with the demand on sugar estates, or was it not really the fact that there was not sufficient demand on the sugar estates to cope with the labour that they already had? He asked this because in his experience when work was slack on sugar estates he had known labourers that had been employed at certain parts of the year on sugar estates, to go almost hopelessly roving about the country in search of a day's work. He should be very happy to get some information on the subject.

Mr. P. Abel—I shall say very little on the subject. I have spent thirty years looking for a working man and I have failed to find him. (Laughter).

Mr R. H. McCarthy referring to the imposition of the sur charge of 4d. a gallon on West Indian Rum in England, said we complained that Great Britain taxed our rum in order to protect her whisky, but in order to protect West Indian rum we imposed a duty on British whisky of 10/6 per gallon. Mr. de Verteuil might find that an agricultural bank was not a panacea for all loss on cocoa and sugar. He had not been a colonist long enough to follow the question out in all its bearings but it appeared to him to be a new way of paying old debts, which he had no doubt would bring trade into Frederick street, and which in the face of a recent circular, a great many officials would be glad of. (Laughter.) Some people thought it a great reproach to Trinidad that vegetables were imported, but if Trinidad should get her vegetables cheaper from Venezuela, why should she grow them? Now she got vegetables from places where wages were very low, and he thought Mr. Abel would tell them that wages were very high here. It was not consistent to nurse fresh industries and to nurse sugar in such a way as to require more labour. Take 500 labourers away from the sugar estates and they would have to replace them by 500 coolies. It seemed to him they were on the horns of a dilemma. Either the cultivation of minor industries was wrong, or immigration was wrong. If they had a superfluous population to cultivate minor industries, why bring immigrants from India.

Professor Carmody said that some of Mr. Russell Murray's experiences should receive attention, but the easiest way for him to get his factory into legal condition would be to build twenty houses in its immediate neighbourhood, and as the Ordinance did not define what a house was, he might build them as cheaply as he liked. Most of them were agreed that minor industries should be encouraged in every possible way. Although it was an advantage to get vegetables from other countries in exchange for the goods that we had here, there was no doubt that the first object of every country should be to provide as much food as possible for its inhabitants. All that was necessary was to induce the labourers we had at present to work six days a week instead of two, and if they gave them inducements he was sure they would be quite willing to work. Everybody knew that the negro labourer was very willing to work when he saw a fair recompense for his labour. He did not think sufficient importance was attached to tillage in Trinidad. In regard to cocoa cultivation there was practically no tillage necessary, but with regard to sugar it must strike everybody who had experience in other countries that there was an extraordinary want of tillage. Mr. de Verteuil had explained that at the time when that should be carried on the manager was taken up with manufacturing operations. The proper time for tillage was at the approach of the dry season. They would get more work by the use of mechanical appliances. There was also a want of farming. There was no cattle-rearing, no manure producing. They might economise by the introduction of more than the one industry. There was too much reliance on artificial manure. Farm-yard manure was a boon. Any planter who depended on artificial manure to too great an extent would suffer from it in the long run. The colony should guard itself against the adulteration of cocoa. If the adulteration was reduced the consumption would increase three-fold, and there would be no fear of over-production. Agricultural education was necessary, so that people should understand the principle underlying the work they did and how much could be saved by doing things at the proper time and in the proper way. They could not hope to gain much from the ordinary work that was carried on at present.

The Governor in the course of his remarks said he congratulated Mr. Russell Murray on the fact, of which they had heard for the first time, that there was in the Colony the most perfect factory for drying cocoa that they had ever known. He wanted to discover that factory. Mr. Murray had said "Twenty houses should I have around me, but I will not build them; let the government build them and then my factory will benefit the Colony." The government was not going to build them, but the Government would look at the Ordinance and try if it was possible to relieve that factory which was going to do good to the Colony. He had also seen how loyally served the Governor was by those who were heads of departments; he had listened with the greatest pleasure to the Collector of Customs, who was not going to let one penny off the importation of goods from outside if it was to be at the cost of the money which he would show as revenue; still, Mr. McCarthy was intelligent and liberal, and in discussions of this kind he would find that if they could produce that which they were buying from outside, the country might be richer inside than it was at the present moment. They had heard conundrums without number, which showed how useful these discussions would be in the future. He came, like themselves, to listen, and they had been fully satisfied and fully instructed, and he hoped that the lecture would be reported in full, that they might all have a chance of reading and digesting that which was of paramount importance to the Colony and which had been so ably developed by Mr. de Verteuil.

Mr. Fenwick said that as far as cocoa was concerned he would offer no opinion. He might claim to have been the originator of cane farming in this Colony. He was instigated thereto some fifteen years ago, by Mr. Nevile Lubbock, who while on a visit here was very much struck with the advantages which would be derived by the encouragement of such an industry, from the various blocks of land that he saw, of land leased out to some Barbadian immigrants, and it was at Mr. Lubbock's request that he gave every possible encouragement to a number of settlers about the district of Guaracara. Very many people were under the impression that cane farming was really to be the saving of the sugar industry, if anything at all would save it, and many theories had been built upon the subject, but he thought that if the question was looked into closely from a practical point of view it would be seen that it was utterly absurd to suppose that cane farming alone could ever save the sugar industry. It would be a valuable auxiliary at all times and was already a most valuable aid, but, to begin with, no sugar estate of any size, which had been established perhaps at great cost, which had on it machinery to the value of many thousands of pounds, could ever dream of depending entirely on a supply of canes from small and independent growers. It would be the height of madness to do so, nor could they ever depend upon a regular supply to keep that machinery steadily at work and they would all easily understand that, with machinery such as was required on large sugar estates, the only possible means of working with economy was to keep it in constant and regular work. It was also contended that the supply of canes from farmers would relieve the planter of the greater part of his work of cultivation and therefore enormously reduce his demand for labour, and more was made of that point than of almost any other, because they said, instead of introducing a number of immigrants from India every year, all you want to do is to give out your fields to cane-farmers; but to give out your fields to cane-farmers or to ask cane-farmers to grow the canes on your own lands was, to use a legal term, changing the venue for the growing of those canes and changing the employment of labour in the colony, the mere fact of their growing canes did not reduce the quantity of labour required to produce those canes; therefore as long as the whole cane cultivation was maintained at its present rate, so long would there be the demand that there was to-day for labour. That demand has been constant for years, had never yet been sufficiently supplied, and he was sorry to say there seemed to be little hope of its being supplied for some years to come. They had been urged by the Commissioners to set about establishing the labourers as peasant proprietors as quickly as they possibly could, in view of the ruin which they seem to have come to the conclusion was inevitable, so far as sugar cultivation was concerned, and they had also been reproached for having done nothing towards encouraging the establishment of minor industries. It would take a long time to go fully and properly into such a subject, but he (Mr. Fenwick) wished to point out this, that by no possible means would they ever induce the labouring classes to establish minor industries on their own initiative. Even with all possible encouragement from the Government or elsewhere, in no country had such a thing ever yet been done. The only way in which so-called minor industries were established was when the initiative was taken by the large proprietors. The labouring classes were accustomed to work perhaps the greater part of their lives upon estates growing sugar or cocoa. That particular kind of work became to them a second nature, and it was impossible when those men came to acquire sufficient funds to purchase lands of their own, or to send their sons out to work, those people naturally applied themselves to the particular work which they had been born and brought up to, and it was almost impossible for them to take to any other. When a Creole or Venezuelan labourer cultivated a portion of land he took naturally to either sugar or cocoa. The Indian coolie when he came here naturally took to rice or maize. It was true that the Barbadian labourer would, when he cultivated land put out a portion of it in vegetables, but there again they saw the effect of the large proprietor, because in Barbados it had always been the custom for a large portion of each sugar estate to be planted with ground provisions. The only way in which minor industries could be established in Trinidad would be by the application of capital by large landed proprietors. If the sugar industry was to be ruined where was that capital to come from? Not from those men who were ruined, undoubtedly. If they had not got capital to carry on sugar estates they certainly would not have capital to establish minor industries. The same remark might be applied to the question of fruit-growing, and the reason why our people did not take to fruit cultivation was simply because they had never been brought up to it, had never seen it done, and did not know how to go about it, and the fruit trade here would never be properly established until men with capital came forward and established large estates. In course of years those estates would employ perhaps thousands of labourers who might be sent out with sufficient means to purchase lands of their own, and then perhaps these men would establish the cultivation they had been accustomed to, and that was why the fruit trade had been developed in Jamaica. With regard to the Cocoa Ordinance, he and a great many of other people differed from Mr. Russell Murray's opinion. The establishment of a central drying house would have immediate effect of opening the door to prædial larceny and give direct encouragement to it. The cocoa contractors who were mostly responsible for the greater part of the prædial larceny in the cocoa growing districts, held their contracts for a period of years and when their cocoa came into bearing, their contracts had probably not more than twelve months to run, and it would be a pity for such a very slight advantage, to amend the Ordinance in the manner suggested. In conclusion, their thanks were due to Mr. de Verteuil for his most interesting and admirable paper.

Mr. de Verteuil said he was amply satisfied that there had been a discussion which would be for the good of the Colony In speaking of the labour difficulty he presumed Mr. Ernest Clarke alluded to this time of the year or a little later, when those labourers would not accept the work offered to them. Mr. Clarke had not said whether he offered those people work and whether they would have accepted it. With regard to Mr. McCarthy's remark about the protection of rum, he said that England was altogether a free trade country and should receive everything exactly on the same footing. With regard to Mr. McCarthy's objection to having both immigration and minor industries he said it must be remembered that we had a population that would only work two or three days in the week, and that was why the sugar industry was bound to depend on indentured labour.

TO THE EDITOR OF THE "PORT-OF-SPAIN GAZETTE."

Dear Sir,—At the lecture on Thursday evening Mr. Fenwick stated it to be an interesting fact that the Minor Industries in Jamaica would not have thriven had it not been for the larger proprietors taking them up. Now the facts are just the reverse. The minor industries of Jamaica were from the outset, and still remain so the work of the Jamaica peasant ; and it is only within the last few years when capitalists awoke to the paying character of the business, that large areas have been planted. It has been shewn over and over again that the peasantry who are now settled on abandoned estates pay more taxes than the estates formerly paid when in working order while not asking as many concessions or privileges from the State. Sir Henry W. Norman has more than once called the small proprietors the backbone of the colony, for in the words of general Justice they constitute the *medium shots which are the strength of an army.* The first class shots waiting to "pick off the plums"—while third class shots are "no use at all."

The latter are labourers, who landless and houseless are no use at all, in pursuit of minor industries, but once raise them into the second class and they can be depended upon to develop minor industries.

PROGRESS.

E

Hugo Hoffmann, Esq., in the Chair.

The following Paper was read :—

TRINIDAD AS A COMMERCIAL CENTRE.

By Robert Henry McCarthy, Collector of Customs.

COMMERCE may be briefly defined as the exchange of superfluities; and the merchant is the medium between the producer and the consumer. In its early stages commerce was the simplest form of barter, one man giving some of what he had too much of, to another man in exchange for something which he had to spare. As society became more complex the trader arose, and with every step in civilisation his importance has increased.

Long before Columbus discovered the Western Continent; before the invention of the mariner's compass enabled ships to steer across pathless oceans; while yet maritime explorers hugged the shore, and cast anchor at night, the trading spirit had carried men to the limits of the then known world. Solomon sent his ships from the Red Sea down the east coast of Africa; before the birth of Christ Phœnician traders had reached India on the one side and Britain on the other; Europe from end to end, and I might probably add Asia, was habitually travelled by pedlars or packmen before the 10th century. Coming nearer to our own time, the wealth of the trading republics of Italy, the Free Towns of Germany, of Venice and Genoa, whose argosies covered every known sea, aroused the wonder and the cupidity of monarchs whose sole wealth lay in agriculture.

Reflection on these facts reminds us of one feature of commercial prosperity, namely, its fleeting character—the readiness with which it can rise and fall, affording in that respect a striking contrast to agriculture. Lombardy, Tuscany, and Flanders have times beyond number been devastated by war, but they are still the richest agricultural districts in Europe. On the other hand, internal commotion or fiscal oppression has permanently destroyed the commercial greatness of Ghent and Bruges and of the Italian cities, and for centuries that of Antwerp; the glory of Venice faded almost insensibly; and of many of the wealthy Hanseatic towns the very sites are unknown. We are all familiar with the rapid rise of Hong Kong and the rapid fall of St. Thomas. The removal, therefore, of commerce from one country to another is an operation with which history is familiar. The explanation is obvious—it is movable wealth, which will not bear constraint. The moral is, I think, equally obvious—it is that commerce requires to be studied and assiduously nursed.

No community—no individual is independent of, or indifferent to, the affairs of his neighbour. Similarly, all branches of industry are more or less interdependent. The agriculturist provides food and raw material for the manufacturer and trader; and they supply him with a market for his produce. Traders, too, here as in every community, have a large stake in the land, and everywhere they are among the most enterprising and enlightened agriculturists. But a trading community can flourish without any direct aid from agriculture. Hamburg and Antwerp would still be wealthy if the adjacent country were for a hundred miles inland a desert; and a very large proportion of the prosperity of the great English ports has no connection with English agriculture. Such places are, in their commercial aspect, merely centres for distribution,—forwarding agencies, so to speak; and in that capacity they have no goods of their own; they only handle those of other communities. Yet in the many ramifications of their business a host of people are employed, and through them a stream of wealth pours in to aid the producing part of the community.

Broadly speaking, all industries have a healthy influence, but there are some peculiar to foreign trade. It breeds an intelligent and progressive class, and it has worked wonders in spreading intellectual as well as material riches. John Stuart Mill mentions one advantage it confers which I prefer to describe in his own words, and upon which I desire to lay especial stress:—"Another consideration," he says "is applicable to an early stage of industrial development. A people may be in a quiescent, indolent, uncultivated state, with all their tastes either fully satisfied or entirely undeveloped and they may fail to put forth the whole of their productive energies for want of any sufficient object of desire...........Foreign trade, by making them acquainted with new objects, or tempting them by the easier acquisition of things which they had not previously thought attainable, sometimes works a sort of industrial revolution in a country whose resources were previously undeveloped for want of energy and ambition in the people; inducing those who were satisfied with scanty comforts and little work to work harder for the gratification of their new tastes, and even to save and accumulate capital for the more complete satisfaction of those tastes at a future time."

The other day in that most delightful book, "Tom Cringle's Log," I came across the following reference to Jamaica in the first year of the century. "At the period I am describing, the island was in the heyday of its prosperity, and the harbour of Kingston was full of shipping." The author then tells how at the time a large part of what we call the Spanish Main trade was centred in Jamaica, and goes on: "The result of this princely traffic, more magnificent than that of Tyre, was a perfect stream of gold and silver." Alas, Alas, he says "where is all this now? The echo of the empty stores might answer, Where? Judging from the neglect of which it has been the victim in this colony, foreign trade is thought lightly of here, and I happen to know that as regards, say, the Venezuelan trade there is a widespread feeling that only a few individual traders are concerned. Now, it is one of the common-places of economics that the consuming portion of the community, not the dealers, gets the chief benefit from foreign trade, which, further, is a potent instrument in cheapening production.

A transit trade especially is held in contempt by many persons here who ought to know better. Two honourable councillors lately combined in one scornful reference asphalt and the transit trade. Let me say in passing that last year asphalt paid to the revenue about £42,000 and left in the island for wages, stores, profits, &c., about £50,000, besides enabling good steamers to run regularly to New York at low rates. Besides these gentlemen's allusion to the transit trade, an important functionary not long ago gravely wrote as follows in an official report :—"I need scarcely say that, beyond a few trifling agency fees, the Colony derives neither direct or indirect benefit from this important trade, any more than it does from that portion of our export trade which consists of goods for Venezuela, arriving here from Europe or America, and which are either transhipped in our harbour or bonded for a day or two and then re-shipped." I need scarcely say that this statement is absolutely incorrect. In the first place, economically speaking, any distinction between transit and ordinary import and export trade is fictitious. The profits of the latter may be greater, though not necessarily so; but in either case the profit is but a commission on the transaction; and in both cases shipping and labour benefit equally. At least half the business of the great European ports is merely a transit trade; that is, the goods are consigned to somebody elsewhere, and to quote my *confrère's* words, "are either transhipped in the harbour, or bonded for a day or two and then re-shipped." Tens of thousands of people in Southampton depend on the shipping trade, and a railway company lately spent there on docks some two millions sterling. But the quays of Southampton would be grass-grown were it not for her transit trade. In Plymouth at present the Corporation are seeking Parliamentary powers to borrow £600,000 to build deep water quays in the immediate hope of getting the ocean passengers to land there, and in the ultimate hope of getting the steamers to discharge their goods there in transit. I have a still stronger illustration. Hong Kong is a rock a sixtieth of the size of Trinidad, and when ceded to Britain 50 years ago it was inhabited by a handful of fishermen. It now has a trade worth 40 millions sterling annually, or ten times as much as ours; and its shipping is fifteen times as much. It has five influential local banks; it has large docks, shipping, and insurance companies; and Hong Kong firms practically control the tea and silk trades. There are factories for the manufacture of all kinds of ship stores; there are five docks and three slips, and every description of ship-repairing shops. Its population, about as numerous as ours, has a revenue rather larger than ours, without receiving one penny from Customs. This reads like a romance, but the information comes from the unromantic Colonial Office List, which volume thus explains the marvellous record of 50 years' progress; "Hong Kong produces little or nothing, but its position has made it a centre of trade." The story of Singapore is just as wonderful. Now, these are essentially ports of transit, as is Colombo, where millions sterling have been expended on harbour works.

Let me take an example on a smaller scale, but which is under our eyes. The steamer Bolivar trades fortnightly between Trinidad and Bolivar. Nine-tenths of her trade is in tranship-ment goods, without which she would have no business here; and the profit which the Colony receives from her is due to the transit trade. These are among the benefits derived;—on wages, repairs, stores, &c., there is a local expenditure of $40,000 a year, and on lighterage and labour, $15,000, or about £11,000 altogether. Then, she brings us about 1,500 passengers a year, and if we count each of these as spending on an average £10 during their stay in the island, the direct benefit to us from the Bolivar amounts to £26,000 per annum. Then, owing to easy com-munication with the Main being provided by this and other vessels in the transit trade many wealthy Venezuelans live and spend their money here. Of the indirect benefits, which are numerous, the most obvious is this :—If a steamer comes here from Europe or America with, say, 500 tons of cargo for us and 500 for Venezuela our goods pay less freight than if she had nothing for Venezuela.

I have dwelt at some length on this portion of my subject, because I believe a proper appreciation of the value of the transit trade is needed, and because I see no reason why in the course of time we should not have twenty "Bolivars" here, distributing goods within the area bounded by St. Vincent on the north and Guiana on the south.

To summarise what I have said :—By commerce and commerce alone wealthy communities have from the earliest times been created ; commercial wealth, being easily transferred, may be readily attracted or readily repelled ; commerce benefits the consumer and cheapens production ; all commerce is profitable and therefore worthy of encouragement.

Going a step further, let us glance at the various inducements and impediments to trade and see how far they operate here.

First in importance is geographical position combined with a sheltered harbour. If the place itself has not wealth the adjacent countries must have it ; or it must be on the high-road between wealthy centres. I will not enumerate instances ; it is sufficient to say that one of these two conditions applies to every great port in the world. Again, unless there be a safe and convenient harbour geographical position alone is not of much use. In position, Trinidad is exceptionally favoured, a fact that has been recognised by every authority who has spoken on the subject ; and if her harbour is not all that might be desired it is not the fault of Nature. George Canning once referred to Trinidad in the House of Commons as the future Liverpool of the Western Continent. Picton, the first British Governor of the Colony, wrote in 1798 :—" The island possesses the most extensive, —perhaps one of the best and finest,—harbours in all America, wholly free from hurricanes. It is so situated as to command the commerce of an immense continent." Lord Harris wrote to the Secretary of State in 1848 :—" I have already pointed out to Your Lordship the very great benefits which would accrue to this island if a more liberal policy could be adopted respecting the trade with other countries.............There are many reasons for hoping that Port-of-Spain may eventually become the receptacle of the trade of that vast tract of country from which the Orinoco draws it waters.........Under the fostering care of Great Britain this Colony may become not only prosperous, but may prove of vast importance in assisting to civilise the fine extensive Continent in its vicinity." Kingsley thought that under a wise policy Trinidad ought to be the commercial entrepôt of the West Indies. Froude says :—" The harbour would hold all the commercial navies of the world, and seems formed by Nature to be the depôt one day of an enormous trade." Sir William Robinson was sanguine that with liberal fiscal laws and elastic Customs regulations Trinidad would have a great future.

The chief reason, I need not say; for these glowing prophecies was the proximity of this island to the teeming riches of Venezuela, and its forming a breakwater for the great river Orinoco, and a natural storehouse for the produce of the countries which that river washes in its course of 2,000 miles, and which are separated from the ports on the Caribbean by a practically impassable chain of mountains. Almost every product of the torrid and temperate zones—vegetable and mineral—is found in Venezuela. It has rich mines, boundless supplies of coffee, cocoa, and rubber, grain of various kinds, vast plains which support innumerable cattle. But the Orinoco is also an outlet for Columbia which has four million inhabitants, and the same physical characteristics as Venezuela. The capital of Colombia, Bogota, has 84,000 inhabitants. Though some of its merchandise passes through Trinidad, it receives the bulk of its supplies by the Magdalena viâ Honda, which is about the same distance from Bogota as is Orocué on the Meta, which river is a great navigable tributary of the Orinoco, and the easiest means of reaching the whole of Eastern Columbia. The chief obstacle at present to the development of this trade is a frontier dispute between the two republics. During the last century a considerable traffic sprang up between Columbia and the lower Orinoco, but it was crushed by the jealousy and influence of the merchants of Carthagena. So you will see that the struggle between the Orinoco and the Magdalena is an old one. In both republics the same obstacles exist to their becoming two of the richest countries in the world —the need of stable government and of security for capital.

However, no government can continue to seal up such rich and extensive regions, and the day is not distant when the basin of the Orinoco will be a favourite hunting ground for the company-promoter, and its teeming wealth exploited for the benefit of mankind. Even now capital is largely employed there. Here (referring to map) is a pitch lake, whose managers get their labour and supplies in Trinidad, leaving us 850,000 a year. Here is the gold region, from which millions sterling have been drawn, to the great benefit of Trinidad, and which is certain to have an important port here at Las Tablas. Here are iron mines of extraordinary richness. Here are virtually inexhaustible supplies of balata gum. There is the tonga bean country, a valuable product which, I am told, fetches $2 a pound in New York; over this area is found the almost as valuable rubber, the only limit to whose supply is labour for collecting it. Away up here is some of the finest coffee in the world—Trujillo coffee,—which is at present exported at great expense through Maracaibo. That port exports nearly 30,000 tons of coffee a year, about 5,000 tons of which comes from this district, and there is every reason to hope that at least that much will before very long come through Trinidad. There are steamers trading from Bolivar upwards, by the Apure and Meta. An English company has now acquired these, and it is intended to increase the fleet and extend its operations. The same company is about to establish trading stations on the rivers, and there exchange imported goods for produce. Already earnest has been given by the transmission this year to London through Trinidad of about 50 tons of rubber, worth £15,000, an interesting fact in connection with the transaction being that this was the first occasion on which rubber came by the Orinoco. It has hitherto invariably gone by the Amazon. This has been the route (shewing it on the map). All enterprise of this sort must be to the advantage of Trinidad, this island being bound to be the centre of any business on the Orinoco, owing to the impossibility of large vessels passing the bar at the mouth of the river.

As everybody here knows, we already do a considerable business with Venezuela, the total for 1896, excluding bullion, being £530,000. This is independent of the goods transferred in our harbour from one vessel to another, and which, as I have shown, bring us many benefits, direct and indirect. This class of goods is now for the first time being taken into account, and I find that it amounts in value to about a million sterling yearly. But that £530,000 is rather less than it was twenty years ago, and on the whole the state of our Venezuelan trade is unsatisfactory. Why, in the year 1895, it was estimated that we exported to that country goods of the value of a million dollars, made up, eight-tenths of textiles, and the remaining two-tenths mainly of hardware. Even if the figures be not strictly accurate, the trade was certainly considerable at that period, and included the supply of districts which have long since gone elsewhere for their goods. We then sent merchandise by the Gurapiche to Barcelona, whence it was conveyed to Caracas. Now, our direct trade is virtually limited to the coast between Margarita and the Delta of the Orinoco.

Then, as now, smugglers did an important part of the trade of Venezuela and the adjacent countries. Curaçao has been a contrabandist centre ever since the Dutch got possession of it in 1634, and it was to the smuggling trade of that island that Puerto Cabello owed its foundation. In the middle of the last century, Jamaica did an immense contraband business with Cuba and Central America as far south as Carthagena; there the domain of Curaçao commenced; and Trinidad smugglers immediately after the British conquest of this island had a monopoly from Barcelona to the Delta, and they soon beat Surinam out of the Orinoco trade. The decrees of the king of Spain, backed by the thunders of the Church were powerless to stop it, and smuggling has remained unchecked because no Venezuelan statesman has had the courage to try the virtue of the mercantile maxim of small profits and quick returns by reducing the duties.

Our trade generally has not advanced as one might wish, and it is worth while to see if this has been due to any sins of omission or commission of our own. The lower prices of our agricultural produce are an important factor. It is natural, too, that the Venezuelan dealer should prefer to trade direct with Europe, and the growth of steam communication has helped him to do this. It is also certain that we have been injured by the 30 per cent. duty. I am not able to say to what extent, but I should estimate it at from 30 to 40 per cent. of our direct Venezuelan trade.

I suspect, however, that we ourselves have not been without fault. In an old book which I have been reading, written early in the century by the French Agent at Caracas, the author scolds his countrymen at San Domingo for allowing the English at Jamaica to cut them out of the Venezuelan smuggling trade. He says : "The San Domingo merchants relied on the goodness and cheapness of their merchandise, and waited patiently for the Spaniard to come to them. The English, on the contrary, sought out the Spaniard." German firms have agencies in every town of importance in Venezuela, and the country is overrun with German commercial travellers. Some gentleman present will no doubt correct me if I am wrong in saying that in spite of our long and intimate connection with Venezuela, we have not a single agency there, and our travellers do not exceed two or three. Instead of three I should have expected thirty to be employed on what the company I have mentioned proposes to do on the Orinoco—buying produce in the country districts of Venezuela and sending clothes and provision in exchange. Does not the reproach of the old French writer apply to the merchants of Trinidad :—"They rely on the goodness and cheapness of their merchandise, and wait patiently for the Spaniard to come to them." I have a theory on the subject—that our local merchants make fortunes so easily that they do not find it necessary to bestir themselves, and, as in every trade in existence, it is only keen competition and dwindling profits which will cause them to seek fresh outlets for their goods. This theory is supported by mercantile indifference to official encouragement or discouragement. Even a Crown Colony Government must be swayed by public opinion, and if mercantile interests have been neglected the lethargy of the mercantile class is alone to blame. Have they been neglected? Writing in 1886, Sir William Robinson said :—"It may be asked what has the Government of Trinidad done to extend its trade. Has it removed any restrictions affecting commerce? Has it encouraged to its utmost the free import of goods into Trinidad for transhipment to other colonies and countries?" (Evidently Sir William did not contemn the transit trade). "Has in fact any legislation of recent years taken place with a view of benefiting the labouring and poorer classes by increasing the area of trade and by cheapening the food of the people? The reply, I think, must be that Government has done little or nothing."

I have quoted several admiring comments upon the capabilities of our harbour, which would easily hold all the navies of the world, and which is yet so calm that a Thames wherry might at almost all times ride there in safety. Well, that superb harbour is for all practical purposes no better fitted for trade than when Abercromby landed here a hundred years ago; in that direction there is nothing to be seen for a whole century of British rule, and if the timid scheme now being carried out meets the aspiration of the mercantile body, I can only say that is is easily satisfied. In 1891, Lieutenant Downes, surveying officer of H.M.S. Comus, wrote :—"I doubt if there is any seaport town with any trade whatever whose harbour is so cruelly neglected." Again :—" At present no anchorage in the West Indies is so badly off for coaling facilities." Yet this is the chief shipping port in the West Indies. From what I have seen of ports in Great Britain with far less trade, I can say that the want of harbour accommodation here is not creditable to the community. It is not creditable that the tens of thousands of passengers who annually land or embark here have to travel, sometimes two miles, in open boats, under tropic sun or tropic rain, and at a heavy expense. It is not creditable that while goods are often conveyed between Europe and Trinidad for as little as 15/ a ton, their landing costs on an average half-a-crown, and if they form part of our transit trade, they are on re-shipment burdened with another half crown per ton, and they are in addition injured by exposure and the double handling. It is surprising that no demand has been made for a deepwater quay, which would enable us to conduct our trade in a manner worthy of a progressive community, or for a dock and coaling facilities.

The fact that a large vessel could not be repaired nearer than Martinique must increase freights to this locality, as owners and underwriters naturally take into consideration the risk of a breakdown and its possible consequences. Let me mention in this connection that under the Colonial Docks Act the Imperial Government can assist, and has assisted, in such works. Again at present a steamer trading here is obliged either to lose some days in going to St. Lucia for coal, or to carry enough for her return voyage. Were she able to coal here on reasonable terms, much of the space now occupied by coal would be utilised for cargo, and freight proportionally reduced. These are most important considerations in the shipping trade, and vital if we aim at making this a great distributing centre.

The exactions with which we burden our transit trade do not stop with lighterage. Sixty per cent. of our imports are dutiable, therefore the larger part of the goods coming here in transit have to be bonded; and we charge a rent on these three times as great as if they were intended for house use, and sometimes as much as the whole invoice value. I once asked an important official for an explanation of this and he replied :—"Well, you see, we get no other revenue from them, so we charge a stiff rent." The whole civilised world condemns taxation of exports, for the simple reason that it diverts trade, and loses for you other benefits. Demerara acts much more wisely in charging goods for exportation only half the ordinary rates of rent.

Customs duties are a well recognised impediment to trade. Hong Kong and Singapore could not possibly have had their great and rapid rise were they not free ports, where ships discharged and loaded without any interference whatever. There are two kinds of Customs taxes—those levied for revenue only, and those intended for the protection of local industries. I admit that under existing conditions, it would be difficult to make this a free port, but a great deal might be done in curtailing the list of dutiable articles and releasing a large proportion of our imports from revenue restrictions. In the year 1817, the Secretary of State directed that a drawback of the duties should be granted on goods exported to Venezuela. Then, as now, the chief exports were dry goods and hardware; and the Council recommended instead that these goods should be freed from duty altogether. To repeat and extend that exemption as far as practicable would in my opinion be wise. I know that some hold a multiplicity of duties to be equitable, as reaching every class of the community; but that can be done with a comparatively short tariff. In England we used to have a great number of articles subject to taxation. Here is what Sydney Smith said of the burden :—" We have taxes upon every article which enters into the mouth, or covers the back, or is placed under the foot. Taxes upon everything which it is pleasant to see, hear, taste, or smell. Taxes upon warmth, light and locomotion. Taxes on everything on earth, or under the earth, on everything that is brought from abroad or grown at home, on the sauce which pampers man's appetite, and the drug which restores him to health; on the ermine which decorates the judge and the rope which hangs the criminal; on the poor man's salt and the rich man's spice; on the brass nails of the coffin and the ribbons of the bride. The schoolboy whips his taxed top; the beardless youth manages his taxed horse with a taxed bridle on a taxed road; and the dying Englishman, pouring his medicine which has paid 7 per cent. into a spoon which has paid 15 per cent., flings himself back upon a chintz bed which has paid 22 per cent., and expires in the arms of an apothecary who has paid a licence of £100 for the privilege of putting him to death. His whole property is then taxed from 2 to 10 per cent. Besides the probate, large fees are demanded for burying him in the chancel. His virtues are handed down to posterity on taxed marble, and he will then be gathered to his fathers to be taxed no more." Of course, all that has long since been done away with, and the British Customs tariff is now simplicity itself.

Protective duties are a less warrantable interference with freedom of trade. Let me show the effect of two of our taxes of that character. We refer to European bounties as "iniquitous," but a protective duty is the same in principle, each being intended to unfairly handicap a rival producer. We charge an import duty of £11 5s. per ton on sugar, and in consequence the consumers of sugar contributed £3,000 last year to the revenue. I believe this an unwisely large sum to levy, but at least it went into the public purse. Well, there is a local sale which may be estimated at 5,000 tons. Theoretically, the price charged for this by the producer would be £11 5s. per ton more than the natural price. Let us put it down at £5, and we find that the import duty costs the consumer the £3,000 which goes to the revenue plus £25,000 which goes to the producer. Take rum, again. The Trinidad producer is content if he gets in England 8d. (10d. less 2d. freight and charges) per gallon—yet he charges 15d. here;

and as the local consumption is about 250,000 gallons a year we have £15,000 unfairly extracted from the consumers of rum. The results of protecting these two articles, then, are that the producer could sell his goods more cheaply in the Arctic regions, after paying the carriage thither, than he sells them at present at the gates of his factory ; and that in order to help one interest the purchasing power of the community is diminished by £40,000 a year. There are other protective taxes, but these, which I have selected for their importance, sufficiently illustrate my argument. The reason usually assigned for the protection of the articles named is lest Demerara rum and sugar should flood our market, but it is curious that Demerara, presumably having the same fear of Trinidad, has similar protective duties. Such duties are in essence wrong, as every man has a natural right to spend his money to the best advantage, and they are equivalent to a compulsory reduction of wages. Further, they interfere with other industries. For instance, while sugar is at its present high price in the local market a jam factory would have no chance of success. Nor is a protected industry in a dignified position. The producer is, of course, too proud to go hat in hand to the humble consumer, and say, "pity a poor producer and drop in a penny," but he persuades the Government to do it for him.

Another example of mistaken legislation which is injurious to trade is to be found in the prohibition of the importation of cocoa except from Venezuela. The idea was to prevent the reputation of Trinidad cocoa from being injured by the admixture of inferior cocoa with the superior local article. But I believe that every producer of good cocoa protects himself by a brand, so that the prohibition only protects cocoa which is not worth protecting. The Grenada or St. Vincent peasant sends us his cattle, fruit and vegetables, and takes home our goods in exchange, but not being allowed to send cocoa here, he sells it, at a disadvantage, we may assume, in his own smaller market. We thus shut out from our port, and without any compensating benefit, the cocoas of Grenada and St. Vincent, of Cayenne and Surinam, representing a very large trade. Venezuelan imports of cocoa (which we permit) have grown from nothing to £100,000 a year ; the value of Grenada cocoa exported in one year has reached £280,000 ; and Cayenne and Surinam are, though I cannot give their production, very large exporters. Beyond a doubt then, we shut out trade worth a quarter of a million sterling, and easily capable of expansion to twice that sum , so that we have probably by this step done ourselves as much harm as Venezuela does with her 30 per cent. duty, an imposition our protests against which make the heavens ring.

I have shown that the natural advantages of Trinidad for commerce are very great ; that the expansion of the neighbouring continent is certain to be enormous, and must benefit us ; and that our trade has not advanced as much as one would have expected from the promises of the past. I have shown that though this disappointing state of affairs is to some extent due to external causes, our own inertia, and our fiscal arrangements and the restrictions consequent thereon are not free from blame. Some apology is due from a stranger who ventures to criticise local customs and policy, but it may be pointed out that a stranger, free from prejudice or prepossession, is often able to take a clearer and more impartial view than those who have grown up among the conditions criticised and who have insensibly come to regard them as natural and unquestionable. I criticise only to stimulate the citizens of the colony to help her to fill the part of which she was destined by Nature. Not a great deal of imagination is needed in order to see the boundless wealth of the Orinoco pouring into her lap, to see her the market and centre of distribution for a large area, her ships crowding the gulf, a forest of masts beside her long quays, her warehouses filled with the products of Europe and both Americas ; to see the certainty of employment attracting a large population, and with reduced cost of living wages lowered and the cost of production decreased ; factories called into existence by the needs of commerce ; agriculture on a sounder, more secure footing—a Trinidad, in fact, twice as populous, twice as rich, twice as useful in the world as she is at present.

The Chairman said he felt that he was expressing the sense of the meeting in thanking Mr. McCarthy very much for his lecture. As a stranger Mr. McCarthy had put before them in a very clear way the state of their trade, and had unhesitatingly and unflinchingly exposed their shortcomings and also provided them with food for reflection on the improvements that were to be made in the future. The subject was a very grave one and should be thoroughly discussed.

Mr. A. Warner said that the new departure at the Victoria Institute was a matter on which all did not agree and it was condemned by some members of the Legislative Council, but when they heard a lecture like this they must feel that earnest efforts were being brought to bear in order to direct the attention of the people to those questions in which they were mostly concerned. There was unfortunately no method of public discussion on these very interesting questions. He did not wish to speak slightingly of the press. He supposed it did as much as one paper could do, because one paper could not discuss a thing much itself, but there was an absence of that keen discussion on vital questions which they were accustomed to see in England and other places. We must hope that things would improve as time went on, but the Victoria Institute had struck out a new career of real usefulness in this colony and he was sure they must all wish Mr. McCarthy and those gentlemen who were associated with him in having given new life to that Institution, every success. Without reflecting on the gentlemen who had delivered other lectures, he was sure everyone would agree that none of them had been more important than this particular lecture. Let them remember the situation of Trinidad on the map. He was speaking to an audience which comprised a large number of very keen men of business who appreciated a good business site and knew that in setting themselves up in trade they naturally looked for some place where roads met and there was some congregation of persons. The position of Trinidad on the map at once suggested itself as being the prime business site of all that southern portion of the western hemisphere, standing as it did right across the threshold of one of the greatest waterways of South America, and, unless they were absolutely careless and indifferent to the trade which nature meant them to have, they must carry on a huge trade in the future. For one hundred years this fact had been fully realized, and yet this colony in its relations with Venezuelan trade seemed to have been at a standstill. There was only the hope that this place would become a veritable Hong Kong of the west, and it behoved them all on such occasions to make up their minds that it was necessary for each man to do what he could to develop the trade relations of this country, and attract the commerce that came down the Orinoco. There was something in this whole question which must appeal to whatever imperial instinct there was in them. It was a great undertaking. Barbados had arrived at the zenith of its prosperity and might be said to have no future, whereas Trinidad was a country with a great future, and that should stir them up. There had unfortunately been a rupture between Venezuela and Great Britain, but they were happy to think that it was now ended and that there was an opportunity of doing something to make this great question one step forward.

Mr. Grell said he had listened with a great deal of attention to this interesting lecture, as a large part of the transit trade of this island with Venezuela passed through his hands and he had observed its increase in four years, and the great possibilities it presented for Trinidad. He wished to express his thanks to Mr. McCarthy for his readiness as Collector of Customs, in giving all the facilities he could to the furtherance of a trade which he had told them was of such great importance to this community. Mr. McCarthy had told them that their transit trade with Venezuela, far from increasing as it should have done, was less now than it was at the beginning of the century. When they considered that the commerce of Venezuela was to-day, perhaps, ten or fifteen times what it was a hundred years ago, it seemed incredible that they should be doing absolutely less trade now with Venezuela than they did then; but when Mr. McCarthy told them, as Collector of Customs, that not only had they not given facilities of transit but that their fiscal laws actually placed prohibitive measures on that trade, there was no difficulty in finding the cause why the trade had decreased. The fact that at the beginning of the century, this Colony was the depôt for the supply of foreign goods to Venezuelan ports from Caracas to Bolivar, and the fact that they had now lost the larger portion of that trade, could only be attributed to the indifference which perhaps the merchants themselves and to a certain extent the Government, had looked on what had been considered by many people to be a trade of no advantage to this island. They had allowed Venezuelan merchants to open up and take away from them a business which might otherwise have remained with them, but for the simple reason that they had not taken any steps to keep it. They had not here any dock accommodation, which was a very great factor in preserving the trade of any country that wished to make headway as a transit centre. He had brought the question of establishing a dock here once or twice to the notice of the Government, but it was treated with cold indifference and shelved. Meanwhile, the charges which goods in transit to Venezuela had to pay had caused, together with the cheapening of steam communication, a large amount of traffic to go to Barcelona and other places which years ago used to come here. The Orinoco, a large river that should be the natural water carriage of the rich products of Venezuela and Columbia, was now being rapidly developed. They got now from Meta, cocoa and coffee, which formerly used to go down the Magdalena in very small quantities, it was true, but sufficient to prove the development of the trade. Mr. McCarthy was right in saying that one of the causes why their transit trade was not more developed was that up to very recently it had been almost the unanimous opinion of those in power that Trinidad should be considered only as an Agricultural centre. In order to see the fallacy of such a policy they had only to look at the two extremes. Hong Kong, a year ago hardly existed, and St. Thomas thirty years ago had the most flourishing trade in the West Indies but had lost its transit trade. Luckily this Colony had resources which St. Thomas did not possess and which had pulled it through the hard times. The 30 per cent. duty imposed in Venezuela, while it had affected the transit trade, had not so much to do with it as the restrictions and difficulties imposed on transit trade. Mr. McCarthy had told them that that trade was floating wealth which was very easily driven away, and he quite agreed with him. The imposition of taxes however small was vexatious, and the trade would eventually find its way to other ports where it was not hampered and restricted by any petty taxation or restrictions. With regard to their Harbour improvements, he thought it would be a great thing if they had a deep-water quay at which vessels could be discharged, more especially for facilitating through trade to Venezuela. 5/ a ton which it now cost to land goods was a very great item when they considered that 15/ was the average freight paid on rough goods coming out here. 33 per cent. on goods transhipped was far too much, and if continued they would lose their transit trade. It had been said that the colony received no benefit from the transit trade, but Mr. McCarthy's figures showed how wrong that impression was. The money paid for lighterage remained in the Colony. It gave working employment and gave a profit to owners of lighters. Warehousing also gave employment to a large number of men. Every penny spent on transit goods in this colony was of direct benefit, and the more money put in circulation must necessarily benefit not only individuals but the community at large. Their thanks were due to Mr. McCarthy for having aroused public interest in one of the most important elements in Trinidad's future development.

The Very Rev. Father Hickey rose and said he would not presume to take part in the discussion but for one remark that fell from the distinguished lecturer, who said that he was "a stranger." Well, he (Father Hickey) might claim that quality with even more right. Moreover the question so ably dealt with by the lecturer, belonged to the domain of science—that of political economy—now in science, all are citizens, so that he (the speaker) was as much a Trinidadian in that respect as any-one else. He ventured to dissent from the views of the lecturer on two points. The success of a port and the advantage of a transit trade or course depended on geographical considerations, but on something else, and if the lecturer went further back he would find that in every instance the beginning of prosperity was due to the fact that in those parts people found what was wanted and went to them for it, and naturally brought things in exchange. The fact was that commercial enterprise was only barter on a larger scale. You must have something to offer as well as something to receive. You must want something and must be prepared to give something for it, and therefore he said that at the foundation of the prosperity of any port in the

world there lay first of all, the produce of the country. Develop
that and you would make your port. Produce what you can
and put your produce before the world.   A great deal had been
said about the difficulties placed in the way of trade by the
imposition of duties.   There was something more sacred than
the strange laws of the Medes and Persians, more sacred now
even than the gospel, but in his own opinion he did not think
it even should have been sacred.   He did not think that the
principle of free trade was ever a true principle in any country.
He thought that his countrymen could claim their shares in the
glories of the Empire, but they and their fellow Celts, the Scots,
were junior partners in the firm, and whilst admiring the Empire
as one of the greatest that ever appeared, he could not claim
for the Empire the exclusive possession either of all virtue or of
all knowledge, and he found that other Empires had reasons for
differing from us on that very important point and rejecting the
principle of free trade. It was all very well to talk of free
trade, but even accepting the principle of the trade in the sense
of its first apostles, Cobden and Bright, what gave them force
was pressure on the poor brought about by taxation on bread-
stuffs. But it was one thing to allow grain to enter free from
the wide fields of America, Russia and elsewhere, and it was
quite another thing to allow flour actually manufactured in
America to enter.   No man in his senses would impose a tax on
grain. If Cobden or Bright were alive at the present day and
not their small disciples, he thought they would put restrictions
where the absence of these restrictions had the effect of impoverishing the people. The importation of manufactured flour had led
to the closing of thousands of mills in the three kingdoms, and
he doubted whether cheap bread was not more than paid for by
the increased burdens thrown on the Poor Law by the stoppage
of the factories.

Mr. McCarthy expressed his thanks to the other speakers and
said he would not trouble the audience with his views on free
trade *versus* protection, feeling sure that he was as comfortable
in his faith as the Rev. gentleman was in his.

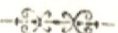

ON HARBOUR WORKS.

By H. SHELFORD BIDWELL, C.E.

Harbour Works.—The term " Harbour Works," which has been set down as the subject of the paper which I am to read to you to-night, covers a somewhat wide range; wider than could be dealt with in detail within the limits of a paper such as this.

I propose therefore to divide my subject into two heads, viz. :

(1) Harbours of Refuge ;

(2) Commercial Harbours ;

and to give a short description of works undertaken for these purposes.

Preliminaries.—Whatever may be the class of Harbour that it is desired to make, the first step is to have an accurate survey made of the proposed site, including soundings, observations of tidal and other currents, range of tides, direction and height of waves, direction and force of the most prevalent winds, and so on. It is usually desirable also to take borings at intervals over ground upon which it is intended to place any structure, in order to ascertain the composition of the bottom for some depth. I need not of course describe the method of taking soundings and borings, but perhaps a short description of tidal current observations may be interesting. For these a float or buoy of wood is made, somewhat in the shape of the feather-end of an arrow ; it is weighted at one end so as to float in an upright position and to the other end a small flag is usually attached. The observer places the float in the water at a known spot, and follows its course in his boat, fixing its position at intervals by taking angles with the compass or sextant between known objects on the shore. On the Tyne Harbour and River Works, where I was employed for some years, a very elaborate set of such observations were made every five years in order to ascertain the effect of the elongation of the Piers at the Mouth of the river upon the currents within the Harbour. There, besides 5 or 6 observers with their floats, there were lines of anchored bo... from the mouth of the River to a point some miles up the r... m, and on these were men employed in taking and recording the ...rength of the current at their respective stations ; while ...l... were stationed at the various tide-gauges along the river no... g the rise and fall of the tide. These observations continued for ...ne weeks, trips with the float being made 4 times on the flo... t le and the same on the ebb ; and as work was commenced ...on ...rs before dawn and continued till after dark we had ...on ...our floats painted with luminous paint, to enable us to ...te ...t these times.—Of course at these times it was not possible to fix the position from objects on shore, and this was only done by noting at what time and at what point any one of the above-mentioned lines of anchored boats was passed.

Tide-Gauge.—The range of tide is observed by means of tide-gauges of which the most accurate is one such as is in use here, which has a float in a tube to which the sea has access; this float actuates a pencil which marks on paper the movements of the tide, the paper uncoiling from one cylinder, moved by clockwork, and coiling itself, when marked, on another. The 1st cylinder is marked with the hours and records the time by punctures on the edge of the paper, noon of each day being registered by a special mark.

Waves and wind.—The direction and force of the waves being in all ordinary cases determined by that of the wind the observations for each go, so to speak, hand in hand. The usual method of ascertaining the prevalent winds and their force at any place is to take an observation at a fixed time every day, for as long a period as possible, of the direction and velocity of the wind at that time, noting also during the day any sudden changes that may occur. For very accurate records the anemograph is used, which registers upon a paper the direction and velocity of the wind in a manner somewhat similar to that of the tide-gauge mentioned above.

The direction of waves is of course readily observed; their height is ascertained, by lines of sights at known levels. Another feature with regard to waves that must be noted is what is known as their "fetch," *i.e*, the distance that waves may be driven by the wind before reaching the shore on which they break; thus, when we say that at such a place there is a "fetch" of so many miles we mean ordinarily the distance from that shore to the opposite shore. This affects both height and velocity.

Design.—Having obtained all the information possible the design of the Harbour is proceeded with, site for work-yard selected, and preparatory work commenced. Taking first Harbours of Refuge; these are formed by the enclosure of an area of water, more or less deep as required, within protecting moles or breakwaters, leaving an opening by which vessels may enter. A Harbour of Refuge, as its name implies, must be in such a position that vessels may enter it for shelter under any conditions of wind and sea, and on a part of the coast that is much frequented by shipping and is without any natural place of safety into which vessels may run in bad weather. There are what are called "national" harbours of refuge whose position is determined mainly by strategical considerations, a refuge from

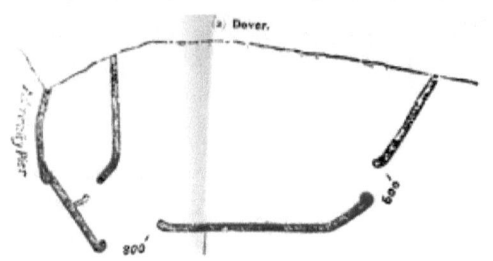
(a) Dover.

an enemy as well as from storms. These should be central for the defence of some important part of the coast and of the shipping frequenting it, and convenient for observing the movements of an enemy; they should have a large area of anchoring ground with sufficient depth for warships of large draught; and should be conveniently situated for the supply of coal, the concentration of troops and stores, and so on. For Harbours of Refuge for mercantile shipping or for fishing fleets the sites and designs must be determined by the probable local requirements, giving due regard to the factors of easiness of entrance and good sheltered anchorage at all states of the tide.

As good examples of the "national" Harbour of Refuge, that which is now being constructed at Peterhead in Scotland, and that which is shortly to be commenced at Dover, may be cited. In the former case a bay, about a mile across, is being protected by two breakwaters running towards each other in a straight line, with an entrance 600 feet wide, having a depth of 60 feet at Low Water spring tides. The area of this Harbour is 340 acres. At Dover an area of 685 acres is to be enclosed, by three breakwaters, the western arm being an extension of the existing Admiralty Pier; there will be an entrance 800 feet wide between this and the South Breakwater, then another entrance 600 feet wide, and then the eastern arm running in a straight line to the shore. Each entrance will have a depth of 42 feet at Low Water spring tides. There is also an inner pier in course of construction at present, enclosing an area of 75 acres between itself and the Admiralty Pier as a Commercial Harbour.

(1) Peterhead.

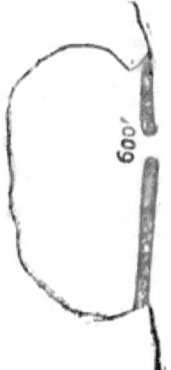

Tynemouth.—An example of a Harbour of Refuge for mercantile shipping is that at the mouth of the River Tyne, where piers have been constructed on each side of the river, mouth, converging towards each other, and having an entrance 1,300 feet wide, with a depth of about 30 feet at Low Water Spring Tides. These piers are respectively some 3,000 and 5,000 feet long, and were commenced in 1856 and completed in 1896.

(3) Tynemouth.

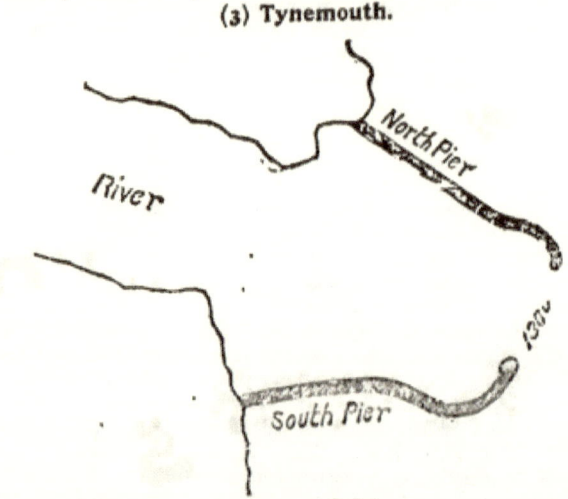

Break waters such as those mentioned are usually constructed of concrete blocks. Where the foundation is of rock, this rock is levelled off by divers, holes being drilled in the rock at any spot where necessary and charges of dynamite or similar explosive placed therein and fired; care being taken that the charges are not too heavy, lest the rock upon which it is intended to found work should be shaken and cracked. The next process is the formation of the bed upon which the lowest course of blocks is to be placed. For this there are various methods, one being to deposit one or more layers of bags of concrete; another to erect a wood-work framing, secured by bolts let into the rock and having its top edges carefully adjusted to the required level and then filling this framework with concrete in mass. A third method is to make up the irregularities of the rock surface by a layer of broken stone similar to road metal, preventing it from escaping sideways by sealing the sides with small bags of concrete. The two first-mentioned methods were both in use at Peterhead during my service there, and the third method was to be employed for levelling the top of the mound of rubble stone upon which the blocks would be founded when the rock was passed and a sand bottom reached ; this point had not been reached, however, at the time I left. Where the sand bottom occurs a foundation is made by depositing Rubble stone as mentioned. This is sometimes done from staging on to which wagons are run and their contents tipped into the sea, sometimes from Hopper-barges, and in some cases both methods are employed. The bags of concrete, the size of which varied from one ton to 20 tons, were deposited, the smaller from a special frame to which they were hooked and lowered down to the divers, who unhooked them when in place, and the larger from iron skips, of which the bottoms opened and allowed the bag to fall when over the spot in which it was desired to place it.

When this foundation is levelled the blocks are placed upon it ; at Peterhead this, and the lowering of the bags, was done by a large horizontal-armed crane, known as a "Titan," with a power of dealing with loads of 50 tons at a radius of 100 feet, the largest blocks used there being of that weight. At the Tyne the blocks were set from staging until 1883, when a crane similar to that above, to set blocks of 46 tons weight at 92 feet radius, was erected on the North Pier and a similar one on the South Pier in the following year. Several other breakwaters have also been constructed from staging, among them those at Holyhead, Portland, Table Bay, &c. Staging has certain advantages, such as the fact that work can be carried on from it at more than one spot, lines and levels for the work can be very readily given and checked, work can be carried on, so far for instance as the depositing of a rubble mound, in almost any weather. The heavy weight also of these large setting machines is apt to cause unequal settlement of the new work as it advances upon each succeeding length of it, unless the foundation is very sound, and I have seen a case where each successive length of new work was visibly broken off from the preceding length, after the crane had worked upon it for a time. Nevertheless these large machines have many advantages, such as speedy handling, &c. Blocks are also sometimes set from barges, but for this comparatively smooth water is of course necessary, and they are more frequently used in river work than in sea work proper.

The succeeding courses of blocks having been brought up to the required height the breakwater is usually finished off on the seaward side with a parapet, from 10 to 15 feet high and about the same thickness, and at regular intervals in this parapet, on the landward side are alcoves, to give shelter to persons on the road level when the sea is breaking over the parapet, as it very frequently does. The roadway is paved, and usually has one or more railway lines on it.

I have so far tried to give a slight account of some protective or refuge works. Turning now to harbours intended purely or mainly for commerce, those in England are mostly formed by the lower reaches of rivers, and their adaptation for trade consists in the construction of docks, quays, shipping places for coal, should that be one of their exports, deepening if necessary the channel, and so on.

Docks.—For a dock; the site having been selected, trenches are sunk on the lines of the enclosing walls and when excavated to the requisite depth the walls are built therein, usually of concrete blocks, backed with concrete in mass; at the same time the excavation of the interior of the dock proceeds. This is usually done by means of steam navvies, as they are called, which consist of a digging bucket capable of lifting about a cubic yard of material, on the arm of a special steam crane. A steam navvy with its 4 or 5 attendants will do the work of a gang of some 60 human navvies and at a considerably smaller cost. In constructing the Manchester ship canal, several different kinds of diggers were used, including some very large ones with an endless chain of buckets, on the principle of a dredger. The outer walls of a dock are sometimes constructed in the water on the same lines as sea-works. Docks have usually two entrances, side by side, one a tidal entrance, through which ships can enter only when the water outside is at the same level as that in the dock, and the gates of which are opened at about half flood tide, remaining open till the tide falls to this level again; the other a lock through which ships can be admitted at any time, by first raising or lowering the water in it to the level of that outside, and then going through the opposite process till the water is the same level as that in the dock.

At the dock at Coble Dene on the Tyne, afterwards called, after the Prince of Wales, who opened it, the "Albert Edward Dock," there is a tidal entrance 80 feet wide and a lock 60 feet wide and 350 feet long. The depth of water on the sill of the entrance, and inner sill of the lock is 30 feet at high water spring tides, the outer sill being 6 feet deeper. This dock has an area of 24 acres. The principal export is coal, and for this self-acting staithes or shipping places are provided, capable of shipping 1,000 tons of coal per hour. For the import trade there are 157 acres of wharf space and standage ground, with warehouses for grain, Esparto grass and general merchandize. The gates are opened and closed, and many of the quay cranes, and all the hoisting machinery in the warehouse worked, by hydraulic power. There are of course several miles of railway sidings on the wharves and standage ground, and these connect with a main line, and with several local colliery lines. There are two other docks upon the River Tyne, but I have chosen this one to give a few particulars of, as it is the last constructed. Quay and river walls if constructed in the water are, as I have said, carried on much on the lines, previously described, of sea-works. I may mention that a portion of the river quay wall at the Albert Edward Dock was constructed by means of twin barges, bearing a bridge-crane from which was hung, between the barges, the block to be set.

The making of quays and wharves may consist in building the quay wall in the water as above and afterwards reclaiming the land behind it by means of filling in, or of building it behind land which is afterwards to be removed. The actual quay is sometimes constructed of timber, but in this case it is always done, at any rate the front portion of it, in the water; the land, if any, necessary to be removed, having previously been dredged away. And this brings me to dredging. There are various types of dredgers; hopper-dredgers, which load themselves and carry away their spoil to sea; barge-loading dredgers with single or double chains of buckets; suction dredgers, which act with a powerful pump; and single-bucket and grab-dredgers. Of these the most common type is the barge-loading dredger, such as we have here at Port-of-Spain, and on works where there is much dredging to be done there will be several of these.

Where the material to be removed is earth, clay, sand, or mud, the dredging proceeds without any previous operation, but where rock is to be dealt with it is first broken up by blasting with dynamite or kindred explosives, and a common method of doing this is to place several charges upon the bottom at certain distances from each other and firing them, this breaks up the rock, forming a number of basins, as it were, adjoining each other and with the portion between each also cracked and shaken; the dredger then goes over the ground picking up the shattered material. This process is repeated till the required depth is reached. This system of blasting is known as "patch-blasting," and I have seen it used with great efficacy, charges of from 10 to 15 pounds of blasting gelatine making circular excavations in the rock of some 20 feet in diameter and 4 feet deep. There is a form of single-bucket dredger and also a suction-dredger of which the actual dredging gear is made very heavy and is used as a hammer to break up the rock. These have been used a good deal in America. In carrying away the dredged material care must be taken that it is deposited in such a position that if solid material it may not thereafter form an obstruction, or if soft may not be carried back by currents to the harbour from whence it has been removed. The spoil is sometimes used for assisting in reclaiming land.

Reclamation.—Reclamation of land, besides being accomplished by the processes previously mentioned, is also effected by warping, that is, by securing the sediment deposited by the tides, and this is done by running out groynes to check the receding tide and cause it to drop the solid matter held in suspension. When the ground has been raised as far as practicable by these means it is filled up to the height that may be desired by material deposited from the land.

Jetties.—In cases where it is not possible, or would be too costly, to make quays and wharves having sufficient depth of water alongside, and where the sea will permit with safety of vessels lying alongside a jetty, in deep water, such a jetty is sometimes constructed.

This may be either of timber or iron; in many waters, however, timber does not last a very great length of time, being attacked by boring "worms," as they are commonly called, the *Teredo navalis* being the most frequently found of these. In English waters, though the *Teredo* is found, it is not nearly so large or so destructive as the variety found in waters of warmer climates, and I have seen some piles which had been a considerable number of years in the water, which when drawn were found to be fairly sound except for a few inches from the surface. Creosoting timber protects it to a certain extent, but even this will not protect it where the worm is very voracious.

Iron jetties are constructed of girder-work supported upon piles, either screw-piles or hollow cylinders which, after being sunk to the required depth by excavating inside them, are filled with concrete.

Thus far for a general sketch of some of the work that may have to be carried out for the creation or improvement of a harbour. In conclusion a glance at the scheme of improvement that is now being carried out at Port-of-Spain. The wharf wall, starting from the corner of the Custom House, will form an angle at a point in the line of the old St. Vincent Jetty, and then be carried in the direction of a point about 150 feet southwest of the corner of the Commissariat Wharf, usually known s "Turnbull's corner." The iron jetty will run from a point 150 feet west of the old jetty 400 feet sea-ward, it will have a width of 35 feet, and have two lines of railway on it.   It was at first intended that the wharf wall should be carried as a return wall from a point 80 feet west of the new jetty back to meet the St. Vincent Wharf at its junction with the South Quay, thus forming a spur of land with the jetty projecting from it. But it was afterwards determined to continue the wall straight on as described. The total length of quay frontage being 1,400 feet. The Reclamation at the back of the wall will give an additional wharf space of rather more than 11 acres, in addition to that portion reclaimed in 1894. The wharf will have a depth of water alongside of 8 feet at low water spring tides at that portion east of the new jetty and of 10 feet from the jetty to the west end. The jetty will have at least 10 feet depth of water alongside for the whole of its length and this will probably be increased for a portion of its length.

The dredging is being carried to a depth of 8 feet below low water over that portion from the new jetty to the Queen's Jetty, from thence to the Petroleum Warehouse groyne a depth of from 6 to 7 feet has been made, while westward of the new jetty the depth is taken to 10 feet.   And here I may say something which I know is not in accordance with the general belief here, and that is that, up to the present at any rate, it is not found that the dredged area silts up.   Careful soundings have been periodically taken over the dredged ground, from which it has been ascertained that the depth to which the dredging was carried is maintained, and in no part has it been found necessary to dredge a second time.

Possible future extensions.—With regard to possible future extensions of the harbour, these will, I take it, always be to the westward; though it should be possible by warping to reclaim a considerable tract of land eastward of the petroleum warehouse groyne, extending indeed in time, if the intercepting groyne be made long enough, to the mouth of the Caroni River.   But any extensions with a view to obtaining deep water quays will be towards the Maraval mouth, and I believe that it would be practicable to make a wharf having a depth of 20 to 25 feet in front of it; dredging out to meet the deep water; or, a less costly expedient, dredging a basin of the required depth in front of the quay and a good wide channel as an approach to it.

Whether the anticipated development of trade is such as to justify the outlay upon such works it is not in my province to discuss, but I say that I see no engineering reason why Port-of-Spain should not be made a deep water harbour.

Thursday, 3rd February, 1898.

The Hon. F. LOVELL, C.M.G., Vice-President, in the Chair.

The following Paper was read :—

ON WATER WORKS FOR PORT-OF-SPAIN.

By WALSH WRIGHTSON, M.I.C.E., Director of Public Works.

WITH regard to the Port-of-Spain Water Works I daresay all of you are well acquainted with them. The works themselves are of the very simplest nature, small streams flow into small service reservoirs and thence in pipes to the town. There is no storage of water, and no filtering of it. I may perhaps be pardoned for stating that the system of water supply to Port-of-Spain is in every way unworthy of the city. The water is liable to constant and serious contamination, and of the results which may follow one has only to refer to the recent cases of typhoid fever in Maidstone and King's Lynn. In the first case it appears that the sources of supply were not protected, and they were, therefore, fouled by hop pickers from London. As there was no filtering of the water, it passing in much the same manner from the springs as the water of Port-of-Spain does from the Maraval river, the results of such fouling have been appalling. Out of a population of a little over 30,000 there have been nearly 2,000 cases of typhoid fever. Maidstone has received such a warning as will not be readily forgotten of the necessity for a pure water supply. With regard to King's Lynn there are some special features connected with it which I think may well be taken to heart by the people of this city. In 1892, I think, there was an outbreak of typhoid fever in that town. A local Government Board Inspector was sent down—you see the Government does not allow municipalities in England to do altogether as it pleases them—to make an enquiry into the causes of the outbreak. He made an exhaustive enquiry and it was pointed out that the sources of the water supply were contaminated in various ways and that the town should at once take steps to obtain a better and purer supply. The Inspector, however, preached to deaf ears. A large part of the Council backed up by a large section of the populace declared that they knew that the water was good enough, and that they would not go to the expense of constructing new works as they were rated heavily enough. Well mark the result. Another outbreak of typhoid fever has occurred. There have been over 500 cases in a small town and the loss caused to the people in the town by loss of business, owing to the epidemic, has been estimated to be more than the entire cost of new works would have been.

As you are aware the unsatisfactory condition of the water supply of this city is receiving the attention of the Government and steps are being taken both to augment the supply and to obtain the water before it has had a chance to be contaminated. Progress, as I before remarked, may appear very slow but progress is being made with the examination of the Diego Martin Valley with the object of obtaining water from it, borings aggregating many hundreds of feet have been made, the quantities of water are being measured and in due time I hope a satisfactory scheme will be evolved. To be as brief as is possible, the present lines upon which steps are being taken are as follows. It is proposed to collect at the head of the Diego Martin Valley the water flowing down the several streams by means of sinking wells or driving headings through the water bearing strata which undoubtedly lie at the head of the valley and into which the Blue Basin and Cascade streams percolate. The exact method to be adopted cannot be fixed until more definite information of the underlying strata is obtained, and borings are being made with this view. If these borings prove, and I have no doubt they will, that there is a large body of water (the borings already taken shew there is a great deal of water and the prospects are exceedingly good), a very pure supply will be available therefrom. The Diego Martin works being settled upon and completed, attention will then be directed to the Maraval river. It is intended eventually to take the water directly from the springs on Moka estate before it can be contaminated—unless, however, steps are taken for the collection of water flowing into the river below Moka there will be some diminution of the quantity obtainable from this source, for it must be self-evident that the nearer to the source of a stream water is taken the less will be its volume. The great gain, however, will be in the purity of the water as it will reach the consumer directly from the underground sources of the springs.

I should like to make it clear that it is not anticipated that more than 3,000,000 gallons per day of pure water will be obtainable in the dry season from these sources of supply. There is a mistaken impression that there is an enormous amount of water in the two rivers of Diego Martin and Maraval. This is not so. Actual measurements have been taken of the quantity and there is not, I think, any mistake.   In years like the present one there is undoubtedly a very large body of water running to waste, but during the previous two years there was very little— certainly for a whole 12 months no water to speak of passed over the dam at the Maraval Works.   The Water Works Engineer takes but small consideration of the years' maximum rainfall, he is concerned mostly with the years of minimum rainfall, because it is those in which the supply falls short.   And it is on these that he bases his calculation as to the quantity of water available.   It may be asked why the water which flows to waste during a normal wet season should not be stored in reservoirs for use in the ensuing dry season.   I am aware that a proposal was made by my predecessor to do this.   But for my part I do not think it would be a wise policy for several reasons, to attempt to do it.   My principal reason is, although there are many others, that it is very doubtful whether the site for any storage reservoir in the northern range is composed of sufficiently imper- meable strata to retain water.   A moment's consideration will shew you that hills which are so porous as to absorb rain water and to give it off, in the slow manner they now do, must be of the last material to retain water under pressure.   I feel almost certain that if a storage reservoir were built, say in Maraval, it would never fill owing to the leakage which would occur through the loose material of the hills at each side of the dam.   Storage seems to me quite out of the question.   The amount of water, therefore, which is available for the supply of Port-of-Spain is the amount discharged by the Maraval, Diego Martin and St. Ann rivers, altogether, as I said before, 3,000,000 of gallons that is not widely different to the amount which is now running through the city distribution pipes.   This quantity will, how- ever, give 50 gallons per head for 60,000 persons and is a quan- tity which with proper management will suffice for Port-of-Spain for the next quarter of a century.   If more water be wanted, a river to the east must be drawn upon and none of those west of Arima would be available.   There is, however, one river, the Oropuche, the valley of which is as yet untouched, and this river should certainly be reserved for the supply of water, not merely to this City, but possibly to all the villages along the Eastern Main Road.   Some months ago I waded down the Oropuche for several miles and I am certain that it is the finest stream in Trinidad, and I am convinced that the whole of the upper part of the valley should be reserved by the Government with the view above stated.

Mr. Chairman and gentlemen, I have detained you for a very long time and I fear that I have been somewhat tiresome. The subject is, however, a very important one.   I feel that I be left unsaid a great part of what I should have liked to have said, more particularly about the abuse of water and the methods which will sooner or later have to be adopted to put an end to it, unless indeed the people of the City deliberately make up their minds to spend ½ a million sterling in going to the Oropuche and are prepared to pay the piper in the shape of heavy water rates.

Dr. Lovell said he felt and appreciated much the honour that had been paid to him by having been called upon to take the chair, as well as to take part in the discussion on the paper which had just been read by Mr. Wrightson, and which he was sure from the importance of the question dealt with they had all, like himself, followed with the deepest interest. It was not merely a personal interest which he took in this matter, but he felt that it was but right that the department of which he was the head should always go hand in hand with the Government in all matters connected with the water supply of the Colony, because upon the purity or otherwise of that supply the health of the community mainly depended. He could assure them that it was considerably interesting to him to hear what Mr. Wrightson had said about the steps which were likely to be taken in connection with our water supply. Shortly after his arrival in the colony, he thought it his duty to draw the attention of the Government to the danger of having unprotected water-shed at St. Ann's and Maraval. Observations at the time had proved to him that they were more exposed to danger from the latter source than the former, from the fact that having had several samples of the water from that source of supply brought to him, he found that if it was allowed to lie undisturbed for only a few minutes, its impurities were plainly to be seen. The great trouble to be combatted with in England was typhoid fever, but here they had not only typhoid but malarial fever to contend against, as well as all those diseases which were consequent to a considerable extent upon an impure water supply. It was not too much to say that from 25 to 30 per cent. of the admissions into our hospitals were of this class of diseases. And he did not hesitate to say that if the water supplies of the colony were protected as they should be from the pollution to which they were at present subject, not only would the admissions into our hospitals be considerably diminished, but the large death rate which now exists would likewise be decreased, and be brought more into conformity with the death rate of England which was estimated at something like 20 per 1,000, while our ... ... 7 per thousand. With the protection of water-she ... ... drainage in Port-of-Spain he believed that the ... ... be the healthiest colony in the British Emp ...

Mr. Wrightson if he had considered the question of supplying the various villages with water by means of artesian wells as was done in Mauritius. He had had some years experience in that colony having been at the head of a similar department to this over which he presided here, and his experience was that owing to the distribution of purer water among the villagers by means of these artesian wells the death rate was considerably diminished. Port Louis had now become a very healthy town owing in a great measure to the quality of the water supplied to that town. Seeing what good it had effected by the adoption of those wells, had been the reason why he would ask Mr. Wrightson if he had considered this question. He firmly believed that if those wells were introduced here it would be far better for the villagers than their having to obtain their water supply from polluted rivers or springs. It was a subject worthy of consideration to see that the villagers got a pure supply of water as much as the town folks. As he knew that there were others who would like to take part in the discussion of this interesting question he would not detain them any longer.

Mr. Randolph Rust, who on ascending the platform took a glass of water which created some laughter, said he did not know why it was that he was called upon to address the meeting, but it was no doubt owing to his having taken for a length of time considerable interest in this question. Of course, he had always objected to meters. Now he did not mean to take up their time by making reference to what they had heard about the mode adopted by the ancients for securing a goodly supply of water, as they had heard all about that in the very interesting lecture delivered by Mr. Wrightson. He was bound to confess that his mouth watered when he heard of that splendid supply but the Government here, like those of old, had levied a contribution from the people, but they had not got the water works yet. It was not with us a question of want of water. We had plenty of water, but the question was how to conserve it. They had heard from time to time what was to be done for improving and conserving our water supply. A bridge was to be built across the Maraval river and this and that was to be done but they had not, as he said, got these water works yet. It had always been a mystery to him how they escaped from more extensive epidemics than what they had had as the water they drank was contaminated from its very source. The lecturer had told them in his lecture that the Government in England had found it necessary to send down an Inspector to King's Lynn to trace the cause which led to the outbreak of typhoid fever in that place in 1892. The Inspector visited and reported, but no steps were taken to remedy the evil that existed.

Only recently he had received a letter from a friend in King's Lynn stating that for the want of water they had had a most destructive fire there. The fact was that the water was so foul that it could not pass through the hose used by the Brigade. So that as one saw things were sometimes even worse in England than here. The lecturer had stated that in England the Government did not allow the Municipalities to do as they liked. But in this instance the Government had. Here it could not be said that there was a municipality at all. Through the action of the Government almost everything was controlled by the Government from beginning to end. They had been told that the water here ran to waste. Why should not this waste be conserved? Why should not proper reservoirs be erected for the storage of our water? They were told that the hills behind Diego Martin and Maraval were very porous. Where was the water which passed into these hills? It must be there somewhere about. Why was not the water engineers requested to tap these mountains by means of artesian wells, and he was sure if the water was there it would be found. Now as to the storage of their water. In America the reservoirs were asphalted, not concreted, and as asphalt was indigenous to Trinidad the cost of constructing a reservoir of proper dimensions for storing a large supply would be considerably lessened. He must confess that he considered the suggestion to utilize the Oropuche river and set aside its water for the future supply of the Island, was one of the best ideas ever conceived in connection with this question and it was to be hoped that the Government would carry out the suggestion. They had had experts from England to report upon their water supply; those gentlemen had been handsomely paid, but all that they had ever recommended was just as far off of being carried out as the day of the discovery of Trinidad years ago. The Water Works of Port-of-Spain were good enough, but let them ask themselves whether they could say the same with regard to San Fernando? They could not. In San Fernando the supply was exceedingly limited and the people there were by no means in as good position as those who lived in Port-of-Spain. The Borough Council of Port-of-Spain did not mean to let the consumption of water be curtailed in Port-of-Spain as the Government seemed disposed to do in San Fernando. Sometime ago the Board of Health no doubt with a view as they thought of consulting the health of the people there, ordered the closing of the various wells on Woodbrook village. He entirely disagreed with this step. The people did not use the water from the wells for drinking purposes but for washing their clothes and for watering their small gardens. For drinking they use the purer water which they obtained from the hydrants. What he failed to understand was that while so much solicitude was

·evinced on behalf of these poor people, and they were ordered to ·close their wells, the authorities allowed a certain company to dig wells around their buildings. He failed to see why a big corporation like the Electric Light Company should be favoured in preference to the poor people who lived in *Woodbrook*.

Professor Carmody said he should address himself to one part of the lecture, and that was the water supply of Trinidad. It was the habit of some persons to run down the character of the water supply of the colony. And no doubt those who had lands above the present reservoir for sale were interested in doing so, because they always found the Government a good purchaser. But from his experience of the water here as well as in England he could say with confidence that the natural condition of the water here was equal to if it did not surpass that of most of the towns in England. It was necessary to take their water supply from the upper part of the river to avoid contamination. Filter beds would be much more costly to maintain in Port-of-Spain than at Arima. Mr. Carmody then referred to the fact that for very many years he had made monthly analyses of samples of water from St. Ann's and Maraval, and it was only occasionally that any abnormal conditions were found. What he wanted to point out and draw special attention to was the polluted water in the wells. He noticed an instance where he had made an analysis of water from a well, which was in such a condition as to cause him to wonder how some of the people who drank from this well had not committed suicide. Mr. Carmody also drew attention to the milk supplied to Port-of-Spain which came principally from Peru Village where people washed, drank and cooked with water from polluted wells from which their cattle also drank. He instanced the fact that recently in one yard in that village some four or five persons were struck down with dysentery which it was proved had been caused by drinking bad water from the well.

Mr. Rust drew attention to the fact that he had alluded to Woodbrook and not to Peru Village.

Mr. Goodwille said this was a most important subject. Indeed, to his mind, it was, of all the lectures which had recently been delivered in that hall, the most important to the community, as it immediately concerned their health. He (the speaker) had never entertained any doubt as to the abundance of water that could be drawn from the sources to be found in the island, although they had always been told that they suffered from want of water. Now in his lecture Mr. Wrightson had informed them that sufficient water could be got from Oropuche to supply the wants of the whole island. This had struck him for some years past, and the question, therefore, was why had the Government not availed themselves of this abundant supply long ago. It is true they had been told that to utilize it they would have to incur an outlay of some £500,000, but why not have borrowed that sum long ago and paid the interest upon it. The people had paid a great deal more in insurance rates since the fire in 1895 than the interest upon that sum could have amounted to. He saw no difficulty in the Government's raising the amount. They were paying far more than £20,000 a year upon insurance rates, which, as everyone was aware, had risen from ¾ to 1¼ per cent. since the fire. Nothing was more likely to cause Insurance offices in England to lower their rates than the knowledge of our having an abundant supply of water. The higher rates did not affect property in the burnt district alone, but every insurable property in the island. At present the people in England were told that there was no water in Trinidad which was not true. He felt persuaded that if the Oropuche water was utilized not only would the people in Port-of-Spain benefit largely, but population in the surrounding districts of the river would increase, and again the water might be used for irrigating purposes.

Mr. Hamel Smith suggested that water be taken from the hills above Moko instead of going to Oropuche.

Dr. Laurence spoke of the absolute necessity of having a pure supply of water, if they desired improvement in the health of the community. It was only that evening that he had been informed of an undoubted case of typhoid fever which was attributable to the drinking of water from Maraval.

Mr. Wrightson replied. He said with regard to the suggestion to introduce artesian wells here, it was doubtful whether they would succeed. Levels and the conditions of the substratums had to be carefully considered. There were only two parts of this island where the conditions were suitable. And beyond the hills of Montserrat the same contamination might be met with as was now complained of at Maraval. The Government did not propose going to Moko but intended to catch the underground springs in order to get a pure supply of water. With regard to what had fallen from Mr. Rust, he could scarcely follow him through his well reasoned and thoughtful remarks, but with regard to what he had said about erecting large reservoirs for storing their surplus water, what he would say was that some time ago he found it suggested in a local newspaper that a concrete reservoir should be built capable of containing a 30 days' supply

of water. Now as the daily consumption was something like
300,000 gallons, a reservoir to contain thirty times that would
cover quite two-thirds of the area of the Queen's Park say, and
be built at an enormous cost. Regarding the use of metres he
was quite aware that there was a great objection to them. But
when the proper meter was used it was the fairest way of distributing water. In all continental countries they were used.
In Trinidad they were much required. It was not in the barrack
yards where the waste was great. No. It was in the well-to-do
quarters, in places where large baths were constantly kept filled
and the overflow of water ran out. No one wished to curtail the
supply of water, but what he wanted to arrange was that there
should always be a sufficient supply so as to avoid the locking off
which frequently occurred.

THE DOMESTIC USES OF ELECTRICITY.

By E. W. DICKENSON, Electrical Engineer.

IN the case by which Electricity can always be made to
assume that form of energy which happens to be the most useful, lies its great and ever-increasing importance. This is fully
borne out by the wonderful strides it has made during the last
25 years in its application to nearly every branch of science and
art; and the amazing manner in which it has penetrated to all
quarters of the globe, proving wherever it goes a blessing and
help to man. Trinidad folk are now quite used to it, and
partly see what it can do. They ought to be proud that they are
a long way ahead in this respect of many places in England with
better facilities, and as great, or even greater a population. It
may be said "we see what Electricity can do, but what is
Electricity, I wish we could get to know what it really is?"
I only wish Electricians knew. It is a real conundrum to
us, and can best be answered by asking what seems to be a very
simple question—"what is light?" From our infancy we have
known the difference between light and darkness, but there is
not one of us here who can say what light really is. What is
gravity? Why does the cricket-ball feel so heavy when we try
and catch a good skyer? The question seems unanswerable.
But this much we do know; we understand how to place our
wires and magnets so as to get Electricity into a convenient form

and when so formed how to make use of it. We must fully
understand that Electricity in one form or another is now and
always has been part of nature, as one of its great forces, and is
no new invention as some people erroneously suppose. We are
apt to forget that thunder and lightning were the fear of the
savage thousands of years ago. To forget that Pliny described
the peculiar Electrical properties of Amber, as being known
long before the Christian Era, and that when rubbed off having
the power of attracting certain objects to it.

＊   ＊   ＊   ＊   ＊

We must not forget that the Chinese were acquainted with
the directive properties of the magnet as early as Anno Domini
121, when they used it on their journeys by land, and that
gradually from these early times our knowledge of the subject
has been getting greater and greater, through the work of
experimenters of several countries, until we come to Queen
Elizabeth's time when the great Dr. Gilbert made a series of
fresh discoveries, which gave him the title of the founder of the
science. The brilliant experiments of Faraday, however, in
the autumn of 1831 when he discovered what is known as induc-
tion, form the real commencement of the rapid rise and development of this science, but it was not till 25 years ago, when the
knowledge of the few became that of the many, that its importance came to the front so rapidly, and its usefulness was so
clearly demonstrated. I cannot pass here without trying to
give you some idea of Faraday's discovery, for on it is based the
principles which underlie the design of all our present electrical
machinery.

＊   ＊   ＊   ＊   ＊

So you see that a length of wire and a piece of steel can,
under certain conditions, immediately produce electricity. If
there is anything useful or interesting happening in the
outside world you may be quite sure that it will not be long
before it is known in the home. When the *busy* house-wife
heard how Electricity could help her it was not long before she
sought to know more about it, and the result was that Electricity
which at first was more used out of door became firmly established
in the home, where it is daily proving more and more a necessity.
The domestic uses of Electricity may be classed under 3 heads :—

1st. Its use as Light.

2nd. Its use as Power.

3rd. Its use as Heat.

Its use as Light.—Very little beyond what is already so well known to the audience can be advanced to demonstrate the advantages of the Electric Light over those of any other illuminant. To begin with it is clean and this attribute cannot be applied to any other light within my knowledge, and is one that is sure to be appreciated by every careful house-wife. It is also convenient, as with a proper arrangement of switches, there is no dangerous and often disastrous navigation of a furnished room while endeavouring vainly to get to the matches and the unwary burglar also can be startled into semi-unconsciousness on its quiet but sudden switching on. When properly installed, the danger from fire is very small, and it has been proved repeatedly from published returns of Insurance Companies that it is the very safest kind of light. This I think must appeal especially to people living in the tropics where the houses are for the most part built of timber dried by the heat to matchwood and liable at any moment to catch fire. A very simple experiment will show you that even the burner or bulb from which the light comes is quite harmless.

*   *   *   *   *

I think many errors are made in the method of lighting our homes. The common way inartistic, though effective, of hanging the light from the ceiling cannot be commended nor the one of the light projecting from the wall at the end of a bracket, yet, this latter is preferable. In fact any method in which the bulb itself can be seen is wrong. The ideal method is by reflection, that is, the light is thrown on to the wall, ceiling, or some light but unglazed surface, and then reflected in a kind of glow throughout the room. To illustrate this I have fired a light in this manner and you will see how pleasant such an arrangement proves. The back ground can of course be altered to suit the colour of the room. The arc light similar to, but smaller than that used in the streets of Port-of-Spain can also be used like this with very good results as the unpleasant glare from one particular point is distributed over a considerable area. Another application and a very pretty one is that of decoration. A set of 20 or 30 tiny coloured electric lights among the flowers and plants of a well laid table make a very effective display not easily forgotten. We now come to the use of electricity in the home as a power, this power being supplied, if necessary, from the same wires which do the lighting. Before us we have, as you see, examples in this direction in the form of fans, both large ceiling fans and small desk fans. These are only to be felt to be appreciated in a hot climate like that of Trinidad. One of the most useful applications of electricity under this head is the telephone.

It is a very common mistake to suppose that when a telephone is spoken into that the actual sound is carried along the wires to the person who is receiving the message. When anyone speaks the surrounding air becomes agitated with very minute waves :—for example; if we throw a pebble into a quiet pool the water all round the place where the pebble touched the surface becomes covered with waves, which travel along the water in circles to the banks and there give the resisting earth several slight concussions A very similar thing occurs with the telephone. The portion of the instrument into which we speak called the transmitter is struck by the little sound waves, and so made to vibrate. These vibrations are trasformed inside the instrument into electrical currents vibrating at exactly the same rate. It is these electrical currents which flow along the wire through the streets and at the other end are received and again converted into mechanical vibrations in the ear piece where a plate vibrates in unison with the currents received. This plate transmits its vibrations to the air in sound waves again and the ear receives the message. It is not always the pleasantest thing to have in the house but it is most decidedly useful and convenient. One minute you will hear the house-wife ordering all her supplies through it and the next asking her lady friend if she left her gloves there the other evening and to proceed to talk of the latest thing in hats. But we all know the telephone more or less! The electric motor of which the fans are a small example can be arranged to pump water from a neighbouring well or pond, to mangle the clothes, clean the knives, knead the bread, churn the ice cream and to do many other things to lighten household cares. The thief is now no longer dreaded for immediately he opens the window the alarm is given by electricity some way off, say in the porter's lodge or the stables. The servants being thus aroused and the lights suddenly turned on, the unfortunate man is disposed of in a very short time. The electric bell has superseded the old form of pull bell and has been found most useful especially in the houses of colder climates where everything being well walled in, sound does not travel so easily as it does in the open houses of the tropics. Electricity is now used for alarm clocks and has the advantage of persistenly ringing until actually stopped by the person called. Even the children are not forgotten and toys driven by electricity are now made to delight their little hearts. The uses to which power may be applied in the home are very numerous and will suggest themselves to a thoughtful mind. And now having partly seen what electricity can do in the way of light and power in the house we come to one of the latest developments—that of its use as heat. It has long been known that the passage of the current through a medium resisting its flow,

causes the temperature in that medium to rise and this fact is
made use of in this particular application. If we send a sufficiently strong current through a thin piece of wire the latter
becomes red hot and if the current be increased will reach a
white heat and eventually melt. To show this I have here, &c.

*   *   *   *   *

A very striking example of the immediate result of such a
simple experiment is the cigar lighter one of which I have
here.

*   *   *   *   *

You can easily imagine if a wire similar to the one I have
experimented upon were imbedded in sand, glass, cement or
enamel and the electricity applied how very hot that surrounding material would become. This has been done and brought
to a useful purpose in the heating of dwelling houses or in the
cooking of food. It seems strange to feel as I have felt the
temperature of a room gradually increase on account of a very
unimportant-looking but ornamental plate hanging from a stand
placed in some suitable position or to have your feet warmed in
the same peculiar manner. Electricity can be used in bed as a
warmer, the hot bottle being kept up to the proper temperature
very easily as may be imagined. It is being very successfully
used in ironing clothes and when it is understood that the iron
keeps at one perfect temperature the whole of the time and that
there is no changing of irons, it will be at once seen how convenient it must be. I have here 3 irons of different shapes and
if anyone doubts the temperature they may come up after the
lecture and feel them.

*   *   *   *   *

It is now not a far cry to the kitchen and here we can see a
decided change for the better to be made by the introduction of
electricity. I do not think there is one person here who could but
wish to see the day when the dreadful kitchen, such as is often seen
in Trinidad, with its grimy coalpots and its general unsavoury
appearance is a thing of the past, and something a little more
wholesome instituted nearer or attached to the dwelling house
where the cooking of the food could be easily supervised without
the risk of indisposition on the part of the lady of the house.
Such a state of things can be attained by the use of electricity,
and I have here as examples several cooking utensils heated by
its means.

*   *   *   *   *

In spite of being boycotted by the whole army of Trinidad cooks I will endeavour to grill a chop as I think it will be the first to be cooked by electricity in Trinidad. The feeling is general that the cost is and will be to the end of the chapter so great that its adoption can only be hoped for by those of more than ample means, but I am sure that while it undoubtedly deserves to rank as a luxury, it will be well within the means of those with average incomes when the cost of current is modified. The reason why electric heating in the direction of cooking is able to compare favourably with other methods is that the heat can be applied just where it is required and there is remarkably little waste.

Mrs. Seaton says with regard to the oven : " The electric oven realizes the ideal oven which Mattieu Williams had in his mind when he wrote : "The perfect oven has yet to be invented which will give out heat from every side." It is indeed a perfect thing from a scientific point of view, for

Firstly, the food is cooked in a pure atmosphere, the heat causing no combustion.

Secondly, no ventilation is required, therefore no heat is wasted, and in roasting meat less waste of food compounds takes place. Perfect also by my own experience from the practical and domestic point of view. Clean, certain in its action, requiring less watching than any other oven, it has even before the present stage of development was reached, given me the most satisfactory results. I have never turned out better pastry than from this oven and it adapts itself to every purpose for which heat is required, more readily than any other oven I know."

In conclusion I hope that Electricity having done so much in the past will do more still for us in the future, and I am looking forward to the day when the manufactories will turn out Electrical Domestic servants, warranted not to get lazy or do what they shouldn't, as I think it is the one thing necessary now-a-days to make housekeeping bearable. I must add that my thanks are due to the Electric Light and Power Company for their kindness in allowing me the use of their current and apparatus. I regret not having been able to make the subject more interesting, but Electrical Engineers as a rule are rather doers than talkers.

Thursday, 17th March, 1898.

His Honor Sir JOHN GOLDNEY, President, in the Chair.

The following Paper was read :—

ON THE CARE OF HORSES.

By FRANK POGSON, M.R.C.V.S., &c., &c.

WHEN asked by the Management of this Institution to read a paper on the care of horses, my first thought after I had consented to do so, was " Where shall I start and where shall I stop ?" my second thought was, " Who am I going to lecture to —owners of horses or coachmen and grooms ?" After due consideration I decided to try and speak on subjects which I thought might interest both parties. I shall first speak on the subject of buying a horse. There is no one who has mixed much in general society but has found, from prince to peasant, that one of the tenderest points of a Britisher's self opinion is touched by the bare supposition that he "knows nothing about a horse; yet how few have really studied the subject closely, and how many less have possessed the opportunity of a technical acquaintance even with the leading points necessary to form a fair and just judgment of a horse's capabilities, powers and suitableness for which he is required. Next to choosing a wife, buying a horse to carry you "for better or for worse" is the affair in life that requires most deliberate circumspection. True, the former is proverbially "a lottery," but there is no reason that the latter need be, for the man who will study the subject, need not, in suiting himself with a horse, buy one with such serious defects as may make him feel he is sold again and money paid. Let me say here that any "person in search of a horse," should look rather for the good qualities, as you would in a friend or trusty servant, than mere beauty for

> " Whoe'er expects a perfect ' horse ' to see,
> Expects what never was, or is, or e'er will be."

Choosing a horse. Firstly, we will suppose that you are not over particular as to colour, and that the venerable saw, "a good horse is never of a bad colour," has its due weight with a sensible man. Grey, chestnut, roan, bay, brown, or black, there are good of all. Greys are handsome, but as they grow older and white, stain themselves so frequently by lying down that much more cleaning is necessary ; add to which, their hoofs are often white, and softer and less dense than those of blackfooted horses. To describe a good sort of horse is perhaps not difficult. A really good sort of horse cannot well be put quite out of place, he is capable of all services that can be required of him, with perhaps the reservation of racing, and even at that, he can at a push, often make a good show. We are told, and with truth, that a thin, clean, good head, and cheerful eyes, are indicative of good, and (if I may use the terms in speaking of a horse) indicative also of an amiable and generous temperament and disposition. Long oblique shoulders usually betoken freedom of action, so far as the fore parts are concerned. . A deep girth and long back ribs denote strength, as do good loins ; wide hips, freedom of action ; long good thighs and large clean hocks, show strong propelling powers. The energetic horse has generally a large eye, fine muzzle, large nostrils, small ears, thin skin, and clean limbs. The sluggard has usually a small sunken eye, in a large heavy head · the ears are large and sloping, and seldom move, the nostrils are almost always small, muzzle fleshy, ribs flat, belly pendant and the tail drooping and not unfrequently very full. With these preliminary remarks we will proceed to the examination for purchase. The best time to view a horse is early in the morning, in the stable, as if there is any tendency to swollen legs or stiffness in the joints, it will then be most apparent. The horse should always be examined from a state of rest, especially if he is being examined by a non-professional or a novice. If there are any symptons of his having been previously exercised, such as sweat about his withers or his legs, have been recently washed, it is advisable that he should be left in his stall till cool. There is more than one species of lameness, which becomes less apparent after exercise, and where there is a tendency to swollen legs, a smart trot and grooming will often fine his legs and render them clean. In examining a horse for soundness, system should be observed, otherwise defects are easily missed. The prospective buyer should, on walking into the stable, immediately note how the horse is standing, and continue to watch for the space of a few seconds, whether he stands square and evenly on all four legs. If there is any complaint in the fore feet, one will probably be "pointed," that is, extended before the other, or he will frequently alter the position of them taking one up and setting the other down ; or the hind legs will be brought under the body to relieve the fore feet of some portion of the weight. Any of these symptoms should direct your attention to the feet when you see the horse out. During these casual observations do not allow the horse to be touched or interfered with in any way. Note also during this time whether the horse cribs or windsucks ; even if he does not show those symptons whilst you are watching him, it can easily be ascertained whether or not he is addicted to those habits, by careful examination of the manger or hay-rack. Now let the groom go to the horse and turn him round, watching carefully how he turns, stiffness, especially in the hock, being better detected at this time than any other. On bringing the horse out of the stable take a general survey of him first, noticing the condition of his skin for mange, &c., whether he has any blemishes, or whether he shows any temper or stupidness. Take up your position in front of the horse about 8 feet away and notice the eyes if they are bright and clear, then look at his fore legs and notice if they are in proper position, that there are no enlargements of the fetlock, or abrasions on knees; and that the feet are the same size and stand square to the front. After taking note of any defects or irregularities; move along the near side, and note the confirmation of the ribs or loins, also the double action of the flank, indicative of broken wind. Keeping the same distance, stand behind the horse and run the eye down from the croup to the feet, noticing any defect and noting same. Follow the same course on the offside and finish where you began. This general survey finished, start again by examining the head. First examine the horse for age (about which if I have time I shall say a little later on). 2nd. Examine the tongue and molars. 3rd. Examine each nostril carefully for any suspicious discharge or inflammation. 4th. Feel the poll, for poll evil. 5th. Pass the hand along the channel of the jaw. 6th. Cough the horse. Now go to the near side, keeping your face towards horse's head with hand on the crest and passing it to withers. If the horse has a sore or a gall there he will immediately shew it by flinching. Pass your hand down the shoulder and over the shoulder joint, noticing if there are any old galls or seton marks, continue your hand down the fore arm, over the front of knee, feeling particularly for old scars or broken knees. Pass your hand over front of shank bone, and then pass it on to the fetlock and cornet when any enlargement, splint, ring bone, side bone, otherwise called ossified cartilages, ought to be felt. Now turn round, this time having your back to the horse's head and with the left hand examine the back part of the same fore leg, for sprains or tendons and ligaments, marks of speedy cut, brushing, and wind galls, &c. Now we come on to the foot, the foundation of the horse, and too much attention cannot be paid to it. Pick up the near fore foot and bend the knee to see if the front of the fetlock will touch the forearm as it ought to do if the knee is all right. While you have the foot up, stoop and see if the abdomen and groin are clear of any swelling or fistula. Now examine the hoof itself, and examine it very carefully, for the old saying "no foot no horse" is as true to-day as it was when first spoken, and I shall therefore dwell a little longer on this important part of the horse than on any other. First, we should look to the size of the hoof; a small foot is not only objectionable in itself, even though it be a natural formation, but is often a characteristic of disease. A small and upright hoof is a morbid structure. White hoofs are to be eyed with suspicion for they are really weaker and more liable to disease than the black ones. Now look if it is contracted, that is, is its circular form destroyed by narrowness of the heels? A good hoof is circular in the tread, or nearly so, measuring as much from side to side, as from toe to heel. The wall of the hoof should at all times be perfectly smooth and free from ridges, and of a shiny dark colour, and perfectly cool. The proper obliquity is an angle of forty-five degrees with the plane of the shoe. If the angle is materially less, the shoe is flat, or perhaps concave; if the angle exceeds it, the foot is contracted. *The frog.* The healthy frog is firm yet pliable and elastic. Should there be smell, or if on squeezing the frog matter exudes, there is thrush. Thrush by many people is considered of little importance, but it must be remembered if there is purulent matter there must be inflammation, and where there is inflammation, there is pain, so that, when a horse with thrush steps on to a stone he is liable to fall (owing to the sudden twinge that occurs) to the peril of the rider and the ruin of the knees. It must therefore be admitted that thrush is a serious objection especially in a riding horse. The sole should also be the subject of close inspection : in its healthy state it is inclined to be concave, but if in connection with high heels, and extraordinary concavity is present it is a sign of internal contraction. If the sole is unusually thick, and does not give way during exertion, the elasticity of the foot must be diminished. If the sole is less concave than natural, or approaching to flat, the foot is weak. Having now finished the fore limb, we will now proceed to examine the hind limb in a similar manner. In this limb the chief joint is the hock, and should always undergo a most rigid examination, as from its complicated structure and the work it has to perform it is the seat of the lameness behind in nine cases out of ten, and it would take me the whole of the evening to describe minutely the different diseases of that joint, and I shall therefore deal very briefly with the same. The first thing to look for in the hock joint is spavin. There are two kinds of spavins, bone spavin and bog spavin ; the latter can generally be easily detected, but bone spavin in its incipient stage can only be found by experienced horsemen who have been used to examining hocks frequently, and I may say here that if two veterinary surgeons disagree it is in 99 cases out of a hundred whether a horse has or has not spavin. After looking for spavin, you must look for thorough pin capped hock, curbs, and old strains. Having finished the hock, proceed to examine the shank bones and back tendons the same as in the fore limb. Having now finished the near side of the horse, return to the off side of the head and examine that side in a like manner. This examination finished the next thing to do is to examine the horse to see if he is lame. Let him at once be trotted (don't walk at first and then let him trot), and let the groom hold the rein very slack. There is no occasion to trot fast, let him go quietly at about the pace of 6 miles an hour. Let him go about fifty yards in a straight line from you and then return, careful note being taken to see if he goes level and also how he turns. Now back him to see if he is rocked or not. The horse should now be tried for his wind either by galloping or by what is termed "bulling." Next have the fore shoes taken off and carefully examine the feet for corns, false quarter, seedy thrush, pumice sole, &c., &c. If these directions be carefully followed, and you miss seeing anything wrong, it will be not because you did not look for it, but because you failed to see or feel it, when you were looking or feeling for it. We will now imagine you have satisfied yourself and got a horse ; let us now see how he should be kept. "*Grooming*"—The objects aimed at by grooming are to get rid of dust, dirt, and the superficial layers of the skin which are constantly being cast off. The neglect of grooming produces skin disease, particularly the parasitic forms caused by pediculi and acari. The process of dressing horses requires great practice, patience, and experience, the brush should be used with and cross the hair, it should be drawn firmly through the hair to ensure its penetration to the skin. Few men are willing to expend the time and energy required in grooming a horse properly ; the brush is generally applied in such a manner that the superficial and "*not*" the deep seated dirt is removed. They trust more to the curry comb than the brush, and scrape the dirt out instead of brushing it out. The legitimate use of the curry comb is to clean the brush, and no other. Cleaning the legs is an important point of grooming. In dry weather a simple brushing is sufficient, followed by hard rubbing : but in wet weather we have the element mud to contend with To brush at wet mud would be to make matters worse ; as a result of this washing is generally resorted to. Leg washing is a practice which, as generally performed, must be wholly condemned. It is not the actual washing, but the fact that the legs are invariably left damp, or even wet. Experience shows that this is a prolific source of skin affection and rheumatism. Washing horses is a practice that there is much difference of opinion about, especially in Great Britain. Some authorities condemn it altogether, saying that there is nothing to justify it, and that it is a plea for laziness. *Management of the Feet.* -The management of the feet can be comprehended in a few words. Have them picked out after work, dirt washed out, frog dried ; avoid stoppings as being unnecessary, if not harmful, let the horse be regularly" shod ; little or no interference with the foot permitted, except the removal of the month's growth ; the shoe should be made to fit the foot and not the foot to fit the shoe ; nails to be kept as low as possible, the wall on no account to be rasped, the frog to receive pressure and nothing but the loose portions removed with the knife. The results of neglect are often very troublesome and sometimes incurable. Thrush is the most common result of neglect due to not giving the frog pressure and keeping the feet clean and dry, and I can assure those here present to-night that a very large percentage of the horses in Port-of-Spain to-day are affected with that disease. Some feet are unnaturally brittle and sometimes hoof ointments are applied to prevent this. Such cases are best treated through the system ; brittle feet are often due to digestive derangement. Clean stable flooring is essential to sound and healthy feet. *Water.*—I think I may safely say that it is only within recent years that the necessity for the supply of pure water for use of both man and beast has been recognized. Before the light of scientific investigation into obscure causes of epidemic diseases was brought to bear, but little attention had been paid to the subject. The first point that naturally rises in dealing with the subject of water is the quantity required. Quoting from Veterinary Captain F. Smith who says from experiment made in India, the average amount was about $8\frac{1}{2}$ gallons daily taken as follows :

The morning water	...	...	...	...	1.9 gallons.
Mid-day		...	...	...	3.4 ,,
Evening	...	...	...	...	3.15 ,,

For myself I am of opinion that of the quantity of water to be given, the horse himself is generally the best judge. Excepting in a few cases, such as where the horse is excessively hot or exhausted, or has from any cause been kept without water for an undue length of time or where there is a tendency to purgation or diuresis the horse may be safely allowed to drink as much as he likes. It is the rule in all well managed stables that horses should be watered before being fed. If the contrary practice is followed, namely, feeding first and watering afterwards, the horse is liable to have an attack of colic or other abdominal derangements. The reason is simple enough. If the physiology of the horse's stomach be studied, it will be seen that the water does not stay there, but passes very rapidly through it on its way to the cæcum or large gut. Now suppose the horse has just been fed, the stomach is consequently full of undigested food, therefore the water passing through is liable to carry with it into the small intestines, some portion of the food before it is properly prepared for transmission.. This food, not being digested, acts as a foreign body in the small intestines, and produces irritation and consequently colic. *The principles of feeding.* The principles which guide us in the feeding of animals are determined by the anatomical arrangements of their digestive system and by the uses to which they are put. Looking at the matter from a plain practical point of view, a horse must be considered as a machine, out of which it is desired to obtain the greatest amount of work at the smallest expense and the least risk; a cow may be regarded as a milk-making and breeding machine, oxen (as a general rule) as meat making; sheep as mutton making, and pig as pork and bacon making. It is therefore necessary that food must be given to meet these several requirements; it must however in all cases be wholesome, abundant, clean, and sweet, and the hours of feeding regular, and the quantity given proportional to arrangements of the viscera of the different animals. The length of time occupied during stomach digestion in the horse is generally in proportion to the amount of nitrogen contained in the food, thus hay passes out of the stomach much more rapidly than oats. It is disadvantageous, therefore, to mix food of different degrees of digestibility for the reason that as they all pass into the intestines together, much of the matter in one food remains unacted upon by the gastric juice. The feeding of horses is or should be determined by the nature of their work. The velocity with which this is performed should regulate the bulk of food they receive. Horses performing slow work are necessarily dieted differently from those performing fast work. During fast work the stomach should practically be empty. Horses should, therefore, be fed one or two hours before they are required, and the food given should be of a concentrated character, such as oats. With slow or moderate work the same extreme care need not be exercised with regard to abstinence before going out, but even here it is wise not to allow the stomach to be too much distended with bulky food. I have seen several cases of horses dying from ruptured stomach through being worked immediately after a full feed. Regularity in feeding is a great preventative of dietetic diseases, three or if possible four, times a day should feeding be practised, in small quantities at a time. Fodder should principally be given to saddle and harness horses after their work is performed, and arranged so that something is left them to take quietly during the evening and night. Horses that work the greater part of the day must be fed as opportunity offers though regularity in this respect should, as far as possible, be maintained. Sudden changes in diet should be avoided, horses fresh from the pastures should be gradually brought on to the usual stable food. The necessity of increasing or reducing the corn ration to correspond with the work performed is another

point of practical importance. Where a reduction in diet is re
quired, bran mashes can be gradually substituted. Food of a
bad, nasty, coarse, or bulky nature is a fruitful factor in the production of that singular disease, broken wind. Animals with
narrow chests, badly " ribbed up," and of a bright mealy colour,
are notoriously 'bad doers;' they never look well, are prone to
derangement of the digestive system, purge on the slightest pro-
vocation, and are generally known amongst horsemen as washy.
A horse can live 25 days without food if sufficient water be supplied ; if no water be given he will barely live eleven days.
Different kinds of food. Oats. Oats is the grain par excellence for horses ; this has been established over and over and
over again by practical observation, and we explain the reason
of it by saying that in oats the principles necessary for nutrition
exist in the best proportioned condition. A fair analysis of
good sound oats as described by Captain F. Smith is as follows :

Moisture	...	...	...	...	11.40
Alluminoids	...	...	...	...	14.50
Fat	...	...	..	...	6.72
Carbo-hydrates	...	..	...	...	65.08
Salts	...	...		...	2.30
					100.00

Oats and other grains are essentially concentrated foods and
are readily digested. I have often been asked to describe a
good oat and the best description I can give is as follows : Good
oats should be at least 12 months old, plump and short, rattling
when poured into the manger, sweet, clean, and free from dust
and chaff, and weighing not less than 40 lbs. to the bushel of 5
lbs. to the gallon, they should have a clean and almost metallic
lustre ; the hard pressure of the nail on the oat should have
little or no impression. The smell of good oats is earthy and
the flower sweetish to the taste. The weight of oats is an indi-
cation of their value. The daily allowance of oats depends on
the work required ; race horses and hunters receive as much as
they can consume, which will average about 16 lbs. per diem.
Saddle horses 10 to 12 lbs. ; army horses 10 lbs. ; ordinary
working horses about 10 lbs. *Maize.* Maize contains less nitro-
genous matter than oats, but is very rich in fats. Maize in my
opinion should be given crushed and if possible mixed with chaff
or chop-chop so as to ensure mastication, otherwise it is likely to
produce indigestion. I am not a great believer in maize myself,
as though it generally improves the horses' condition and coats, it
reduces their energy and makes them sweat profusely when at

H

work. *Bran.* This is the envelope of wheat after grinding. Like molasses, bran has very much deteriorated in quality during the last few years, owing to the great improvement in milling machinery which leaves very little else except the bare outer skin of the wheat grain. Bran is generally given as a gentle laxative and forms also an important article of sick diet, and the practice of administering it to horses weekly, is attended with good results. The proper way to make a bran mash is to pour boiling water over the bran, and let it remain covered up till cool enough to eat. *Linseed.* Linseed is excellent for sick or debilitated horses. For animals out of condition it acts sometimes in the most surprising manner and is well known to have a good effect on the coat and skin. For ordinary purposes 1lb per diem mixed with other food will be found sufficient. In boiling linseed it should just be kept covered with water and boiled until it assumes a sticky mass; it can then be mixed with the other food. *Hay.* Good hay should be about one year old and of the well known palish greenish tint, hard and long, clean and fresh, and possessing a well known aroma and sweet taste. A great degree of difference exists in the amount of proximate principles contained in hay. This depends upon the growth, in which perhaps the soil plays the chief part; it is a well known fact that certain pastures (or the hay grown on them) are celebrated for their fattening properties whilst adjacent lands of the same formation produce grass or hay very inferior in nutritive value. It is therefore advisable if possible to purchase hay that has come from off good pasture grounds. As regards the relative value of Para grass and Guinea grass I will leave it for the meeting to discuss. Two years ago I recommended that in the contract for the supply of grass to Government animals, Guinea be stipulated for, and up to now I see no reason to change that opinion. I had intended in the first part of my lecture to explain a few of the most common tricks of English and Irish horse dealers to palm off a "wrong un" on the unwary, but on second thoughts I decided not to do so, as I thought that if I did so, some of the audience might try to practice those tricks of which they are now ignorant. In conclusion let me again remind you that when you buy a horse you want all your senses about you, and always remember that in a horse deal your best friend will let you in if he possibly can, and if he succeeds in doing so, your other friends will consider he is quite right and that you are the fool for being let in.

The discussion that followed did not bring out many fresh points. Mr. de Montbrun opened it at the request of the Chairman. The lecture, that gentleman remarked, had brought them many things they did not know; indeed, Mr. Pogson had left only one thing open; that was the washing of horses. He considered washing an animal and bathing it two very different things. He did not agree with washing horses, that was using soap and so forth, but in this climate he thought in bathing a horse the refreshment to the horse compensated for any loss of gloss to the coat ; they must however have the animal thoroughly dried afterwards. Dr. Inskip Read pointed out there must be a certain amount of dandruff in the horse. A man had this washed out; why not a horse ? Mr. Pogson retorted that this should be groomed out.

The Chairman : But you occasionally have your horses taken down to the sea.

Mr. de Montbrun said that he considered that a good practice. Mr. Reginald Smith agreed and said he knew a race horse that won for three years. It was too weak on the legs to take the ordinary exercise and was trained by swimming it in the sea at Cocorite. Mr. Bowen who followed went further. Washing a horse he said was a very good thing in this climate and he even went so far as to advocate the use of soap.

Commander Coombs pointed out that in India and other hot climates in which he had had experience the Syces gave the horses drink when they returned heated. At home they would not do this. Mr. Pogson's answer was that he would not do it himself in a hot climate, but he agreed there was enough heat in the water to take it up to the horse's temperature and avoid the ill-effects such a practice would create at home. Mr Meaden here joined in the discussion and agreed with the last part of Mr. Pogson's reply as their water was 80 or 90 degrees and Mr. O'Connor cited Captain Hayes as recommending the giving of water under such circumstances in India. Mr. Pogson here got in a professional shot at Captain Hayes. Everybody, he said, here appeared to have his book (he had it himself) but a great many of the profession considered him a quack. He was too fond of letting outsiders know too much (laughter).

Mr. Meaden said the lecturer had travelled all over the ground. He had told them how to buy a horse but what they wanted to know in these days of cycles and motor cars was how to sell one (laughter). He was on Mr. Pogson's side as regards washing and thought a hay wisp cleaned a horse perfectly. But he had not seen a groom in Trinidad who could make a proper hay wisp.

The Chairman : Nor have I.

Mr. Meaden said they bought a great deal of rubbishing grass too in Port-of-Spain. Para grass, he did not think good fodder. Guinea grass he thought essentially the better and Professor Carmody's analysis proved the weakness of Para grass's food value. Guinea grass had a very high food value. He found it grew 120 per acre; Para grass about 107 and Trinidad natural grasses (which were very poor) about 7 or 8 tons. The lecture was most interesting and instructive and he would like to hear Mr. Pogson further on the subject in another lecture.

The Chairman said in the Windward Islands they fed their ponies on maize and cane tops. Practically speaking they gave them no grass and never got hay. Whereas in the Bahamas they used Para grass and Indian corn and in the East grass and paddy. Trinidad was the only hot country in which he had seen hay used. Was it useless extravagance? In Singapore two veterinary establishments had taught the Malays perfect shoeing with the very malleable iron they had there, and they never had a horse lame.

Mr. Meaden suggested it would be a good thing if they could be taught to shoe in Trinidad in the same way. Maize as a horse food did not answer in Trinidad.

Commander Coombs asked if hay was a necessity in Trinidad and Mr. Pogson said he would merely answer by saying he never used it here himself. The only thing he had to object to in too much green grass was it was apt to prove laxative.

Mr. Clark thought the mule disposed of the argument against washing or bathing horses. He was never curry combed but was bathed two or three times a week. Mr. Bulmer asked what about molasses? Mr. Pogson replied that was a difficult question. Molasses was given in Trinidad to make the animals eat something else; bad hay or chop chop. He did not see any harm in molasses, but it must be given sparingly. He did not use it himself. In answer to Mr. de Montbrun the lecturer said he preferred Para grass to hay in Trinidad. The Chairman thanked Mr. Pogson for his very interesting lecture on behalf of himself and those present and suggested they should arrange for some lectures to grooms. They were in the hands of the grooms and though he did not wish to say a word against them they had not the knowledge to attend to horses properly. He thought some practical instructions to grooms would be a wise outcome of the lecture.

HEALTHY HOMES.

By E. Prada, Esq., M.R.C.S.

IN the programme originally drawn up for these lectures, Dr. deWolf was the person chosen to lecture on " Healthy Homes," and it is due to his departure for Europe that I stand before you here to-night. Far more pleased would I be to be sitting listening with you to the exposition of this subject by this old servant of the Colony so full of knowledge and ripe experience. Hitherto these lectures have been delivered by experts on the different subjects which they treated. I lay no claim whatever to being an expert in sanitation, and my only qualification for being here to-night is the interest which, as a citizen of Port-of-Spain and a medical man, I take in all matters which concern the health of the population. It is true that latterly any concern for the health of the people has been denied the medical profession, and men of some influence have accused us of seeing with delight the clouds of dust which sometimes rise from our streets on account of the profits which may result therefrom. But it is only ignorance that speaks in that way. The tendency of the medicine of the present day is to discover means of preventing disease. Sanitary science during the last fifty years has decreased mortality and disease, and lengthened the span of life, and it owes its origin and development to medical men. Sanitary science is not a very old science but the progress that has been made has been rapid, a fact which is well exemplified in the London of to-day as compared with the London of the last century. In those days "the streets were unpaved or paved only with rough cobble stones. There were no sidewalks. The houses projected over the road-way, and were unprovided with rain water gutters so that during a shower the rain fell from the roof to the middle of the street. The streets were filthy from constant contributions of slops and ordure from animals, and human beings, any system of scavenging being unknown. There were no underground drains, and the soil of the town was soaked with the filth of .centuries. The rooms of the poor were more like pigsties than human habitations, unventilated, and strewn with rushes which were seldom changed, and the wretched inhabitants closely packed in these miserable hovels must have been very prone to suffer from infections of all kinds." It is not to be wondered at that black death and sweating sickness, typhus and cholera found a congenial atmosphere in the London of that day. To-day London is the healthiest of the large cities of Europe, and epidemics such as those which decimated the population in the past are unknown. But, to come to our subject. The subject of " Healthy Homes" may be treated from different points of view. A member of this Institute translated it into meaning "The Housing of the Working Classes"—an important subject which has engaged the attention of Royal Commissions in England and which may engage our attention at no distant date. One correspondent calls my attention to the fact that our meat supply is not inspected and adds "No home can be healthy which is compelled to eat diseased meat for want of protection by inspection." We have been promised a medical officer of health; let us hope that the inspection of our food-supply will be one of his most important functions. It is my purpose, however, to limit these notes to a consideration of the conditions which affect the health of the dwelling, and finally to refer briefly to certain conditions which affect the health of our homes in the aggregate, viz.: the town of Port-of-Spain. There are three things which are indispensable for the health of the dwelling, viz.:—pure air, pure water, and pure soil, and the following five conditions which arise from them are those generally laid down as necessary to the healthiness of the dwelling:—1st, The site must be dry. 2nd, There must be free and efficient ventilation. 3rd, The sewage must be removed *immediately and perfectly* so that there may be no chance of contamination. 4th, A pure supply of water, and proper means of removal of water by means of which perfect cleanliness of all parts of the house can be insured. 5th, A construction of house, suitable to the climate, which shall secure perfect dryness of the foundations, walls and roof. Let us consider the first condition—*The site must be dry.* Here we must examine the nature of the soil and see what conditions will affect its dryness. And for the purpose a few definitions will be necessary. The *soil* is the decayed upper surface of rocks mingled with the remains of animal and vegetable matter. It is a fruitful source of bacteria—infusion made from garden earth even though diluted 100 times, still contains thousands of bacteria in every drop. The soil of the plain on which Port-of-Spain is built consists of sandy loam and has great water absorbing power. *Ground Air*—All soils contain air which is called the ground air which moves about freely in the soil from changing conditions of temperature or pressure:—There is a constant interchange going on between the ground air and the atmosphere. At night when the air is cool it tends to sink into the pores of the earth and the ground air which is still warm rises into the atmosphere; thus it is that in malarious districts the night air is charged with the miasm of malaria which it brings with it from the soil. When it rains the water enters the pores of the soil and drives the ground air to find an exit where it best may, and this exit is found in the places free from rain-water, viz. : under our houses, and into our bedrooms. If this air comes from a filth-sodden soil you can imagine that it is not exactly pure. *Moisture* is the water mixed with the air in the intestices of the soil. Different soils have different powers of absorbing moisture, and our soil has a strong absorbing power. In digging a surface-well we come upon water at a varying depth—this water is the *ground water* and exists under every soil. It is a large underground lake with a water level which varies according to circumstances. This water is in constant movement endeavouring to find an outlet—so that when contaminated by the soakage of a cess-pit it is not stationary, but travels about in different directions. If I have made my meaning clear you will easily see how a cesspit affects the health of a house. Its liquid contents soak into the soil of the yard and contaminate the ground water and the ground air. A shower of rain raises the level of the ground water to the surface and drives the contaminated ground air into our bedroom. This is the process by which a foul cesspit affects the health of a house through the soil. In a petition to the Legislative Council the petitioners seem to think that the soakage of the contents of a cesspit into the soil is beneficial—but as I have demonstrated the very contrary is the case. You will also understand how easily surface wells like those that exist in Woodbrook and St. James can be contaminated by the contents of the neighbouring cesspits. There is in addition in Woodbrook the possible contamination from decomposing bodies in the far too near cemetery. How can we prevent dampness and the inrush of contaminated ground air into our houses? The house must be built at a certain height above the ground, and there must be free ventilation under the flooring of the house. But the ground air may rise and enter our bedrooms through the flooring. To prevent this the site should be covered with some impermeable material which would make it perfectly dry and prevent the access of air from the ground. A thick layer of concrete or asphalt would meet the requirements—I have seldom seen this done in houses built here, but there is no doubt that it would add materially to the health of a house. To keep the soil of a yard from contaminating the air the best thing is to concrete it. Free drainage will make the soil dry. The second condition that *there must be free and efficient ventilation* is one which in the tropics is so obviously necessary that with the exception of the coolie mud-huts the most ignorant carpenter knows that a house must have as many doors and windows as it possibly can. In cold climates the ventilation of a house is a science and the position of the fireplace

relatively to the window is a question for expert consideration.
In time of sickness, however, ventilation in any shape is strongly
objected to by a good many people in Trinidad. Every door and
window is hermetically closed and every chink and crevice is
carefully packed with old linen, and woe betide the young inexperienced practitioner who dares to condemn these time honoured
practices. Our houses are generally detached so that there is
free circulation of air on all sides, and as they are seldom more
than one story high we get the full play of the sunshine. The
third condition is that the sewage be removed immediately and
perfectly so that there may be no chance of contamination. This
can only apply to the water-carriage system which is the only
one which can remove sewage immediately and perfectly. In
this town we have different ways of disposing of excrement. We
have a very imperfect sewer system ; we have the abominable
cesspits ; and we have the pail system. In spite of the imper-
fection of our sewerage system I do not hesitate to say that the
sewer district is the healthiest part of the town of Port-of-Spain.
Out of 83 cases of typhoid fever admitted into the Colonial
Hospital in the years 93-94 and 95 only 5 came from the sewer
district. Later on I shall refer to the advantages that will result
from the introduction of an efficient sewerage system. I may
call attention to one or two things in reference to our sewer
system. Two years ago there were complaints that the water
supply in the houses was at times contaminated with sewage ;
on examination it was found that this was due to the fact that
as the water pipe opened directly into the closet-basin, it was
easy for sewage to find its way into the pipe by suction,—and
an intermittent water supply favours this suction action. The
Board of Health, or some other authority, immediately ordered
the pipes to be removed from the basins and to be placed away
from the basin at a certain distance from it. The result
is that in the greater part of the sewer district very little water
find its way into these basins. An occasional pail of water may be
poured into a basin by a very energetic servant. We have escaped
the evil of the contamination of our water, but we are now being
poisoned by the sewer gas coming from these waterless water-
closets. The health authority ought to have provided, or caused
to be provided, a separate cistern, or flushing box, placed at a
certain height above the closet basin from which the closet could
be effectually flushed and cleansed. *Pails.*—Of the conser-
vative methods for the disposal of excreta the pail system is the
lesser of the two evils. It is a simple system which if carried
out with punctuality and thoroughness offers no very serious
objection. The receptacle is an iron or galvanized pan and ought
to be provided with a tight fitting lid. It ought to be removed
every day, or every second day, and the hour of removal ought to

be as early in the morning as practicable. While in the house the contents must be kept dry by charcoal-dust, ashes, or dry earth. The new pan ought to have undergone a thorough process of disinfection.

Cesspits.—With regard to cesspits it cannot be too strongly insisted on that in the vicinity of houses to retain in any receptacle, however well-constructed, a large collection of solid and liquid excrement there to undergo putrefaction with the formation of offensive gases, is a violation of every sound sanitary principle. I have already shown how the contents of a cesspit soak into the soil and find its way into the dwelling. Most of us have experienced the foul odours which pervade our atmosphere in the evenings. And there are dwellings where such smells are a constant companion! Fœcal odour, if it does not actually produce disease produces a state of depressed vitality which easily leads to disease. The model bye-laws of the local Government Board require that every cesspit should be at least 50 feet away from a dwelling and 60 to 80 feet from a well, spring or stream. Any one who has any experience of our barrack yards and even of some of our more pretentious dwellings will agree as to the urgent necessity of some such local regulation. Some time ago I attended a child suffering from typhoid fever in a yard in George street. It was the last room of a long row of rooms, and one could with one step from that room enter the foul stinking cesspit directly opposite. In a pretty little cottage recently built, and not very far from here, one of the bedrooms is not more than five or six feet from the cesspit (which by the way is shared by the next house) with the result that the occupant of that bed-room was nearly carried away by a severe attack of dysentery. These are examples of a state of things that prevails all over the town. The model bye-laws of the Local Government Board enact that the walls and floor of a cesspit should be " of good brick work in cement rendered in cement." Latterly we have heard a good deal of the opposition to the Board of Health's order in reference to the concreting of cesspits. It is obvious that it is a sound and sanitary order. But the reasons for building these new cesspits four feet above the ground are not so obvious and as far as I know this is a local innovation of doubtful value. The fourth condition that there should be a pure supply of water, and at the same time proper means for its removal from the premises leads us to a consideration of the different ways in which water is supplied to the dwelling. We get water :

    1. From wells which may be shallow, deep, or artesian.

    2. From the storing of rain water.

    3. From public water-works.

Wells.—A surface well is one which derives its water from the ground water, and is very liable to contamination from the soakage from cesspits. Such wells exist in Woodbrook and St. James, and in many yards in Port-of-Spain may be seen the pumps and the remains of the old wells which have since been filled with rubbish. That surface wells are a source of danger is proved by a reference to the historic Board street pump which being contaminated from a cholera cesspit in its immediate neighbourhood was the cause of a formidable outbreak of cholera in Soho which resulted in the death of over 600 persons. The people affected were supplied with water from this well. Deep wells do not derive their water from the ground water but go through an impermeable stratum into a water bearing layer below. An artesian well is a deep well in which the water is under sufficient hydrostatic pressure to well out at the surface. The water from these wells is very wholesome and palatable and not liable to contamination. Rain water collected from the roofs of houses and stored in large iron tanks is largely used in the country. Such water is liable to be fouled by the excrements of birds and vegetable spores. As collected in the tanks it is difficult of inspection on account of the very small openings in these tanks, which, however, allow fouling of the water by dead mice, etc. Rain water is also collected in shallow concrete cisterns which are also liable to fouling by collecting dust and insects and occasionally rats and mice. Water is supplied to Port-of-Spain mainly from the Maraval River, about which I shall have something to say later on. Its quality is generally reported by the chemical analyst as being good. I may here remark that water may be chemically pure but bacteriologically unfit for human use. With regard to quantity it has been computed by some authorities that 25 gallons per head is a sufficient quantity for purely domestic purposes :

Drinking and Cooking	...	...	...	1 gallon
Ablution and general weekly baths		...		7 ,,
Washing and laundry	...	...	...	6 ,,
Water Closets	...	...	...	...	6 ,,
Flushing and waste	...	...	...	5 ,,
				25 gallons.

In considering the amount of water per head we must take into consideration local circumstances, the habits of the community and the proportion of people using baths. Our water wants must not be judged by European standards. In this hot climate we drink more water; we bathe more frequently, and the lower classes which in England are sometimes termed the Great Un-washed, in Trinidad are fond of bathing. London has a supply of 40 gallons per head, and Glasgow of 50, and I think we ought to have at least double the supply of either of these towns. In America they are more generous with water. The city of Washington has a supply of 105 gallons per head; and New York of over 100 gallons. In any case the supply should be liberal and not niggardly and it is better to err on the side of excess than to run the risk of disease through want of water. We must however not waste water. By 1 or 2 in the morning every bath in this town is filled, and after that time every bath in the town wastes once or twice its own volume of water. If we are to have an efficient sewerage system, we require an adequate supply of water and we must begin to limit waste as much as possible. Our baths are much too large; they are not large enough to swim in, and they are too large for the ordinary purposes of a bath. A small bath that could be filled in half an hour would save a good deal of waste, and on aesthetic grounds would be a distinct improvement—it isn't unusual for four or five of the inmates of a dwelling to take their turn in bathing in the same water. I suppose that public opinion has killed the meters so that it would serve no useful purpose to waste much time over them. Meters would cause economy of water in the very class of people among whom for the general good of the community it is important that water should be freely used. With good regulation and vigilant inspection waste will be reduced to a minimum. While on the subject of water I may recommend that every household should be supplied with an efficient filter. The water as supplied to us does not undergo any process of filtration at the reservoir. The subject of filters has lately been investigated by Drs. Sims Woodhead and Cartwright who after submitting all the well-known filters to most rigorous tests came to the conclusion that the only filters which could confer protection against the communication of water borne disease were :—

1. Filter Chamberland—Système Pasteur.

2. Filtre Mallié—Theories Pasteur.

3. The Berkefeld filter.

The 5th condition—"A construction of house suitable to the climate, which shall secure perfect dryness of the foundation, walls, and roof." This comes more within the province of the architect. The concreting of the site we have already considered. A verandah or gallery on all sides of the house equalizes the temperature within. Concrete walls keep away dampness more effectually than porous bricks. As to the roof, thatch is cheap, and picturesque, but harbours vermin, insects, and damp. Galvanized sheets which are used so largely lead to excessive heat of the house in the day, and on account of the rapid evaporation to excessive cold at night. Slates are the best material for roofs. There is a good deal of opposition, and from influential quarters, against the introduction of a proper system of sewerage in this town. An enumeration of the advantages that will result from such a change will I hope show the opponents of the scheme how unreasonable is their opposition. (1.) It will do away with the cesspits, abominations which no progressive community such as ours ought to tolerate. Cesspits pollute our soil, poison our air and kill or sicken our people. (2.) The subsoil will be drained which will result in drying of the soil and freedom from dampness. Dampness of the soil is a great factor in the causation of Phthisis and other pulmonary diseases. In Port-of-Spain one out of every 9 deaths is due to Phthisis. After the introduction of sewerage works in the following towns the rate of Phthisis mortality showed the following percentage of decrease :—

Macclesfield	31 per cent.	Leicester	32 per cent.
Banbury ...	41 do.	Rugby	43 do.
Ely ...	47 do.	Salisbury	49 do.

In the reduction of the typhoid fever mortality the results were still more striking—

. Cardiff ...	40 per cent.	Banbury	48 per cent.
Merthyr Tydvil	60 do.	Croydon	65 do.
Salisbury ...	75 per cent.		

(3.) The waste waters from our houses and yards are composed of animal and vegetable substances which rapidly putrify. Sir John Simon says that "Such refuse at its worst is a very condensed form of sewage, and even at its best is such as cannot without nuisance be let loiter and soak by the wayside." With a proper sewerage system these waters would find their way into the sewers. To recapitulate. With a proper system of sewerage the waste waters and water-closet sewage will be removed *immediately* and *completely*, thus excluding all danger of disease from these sources ; our water-logged soil will be drained, rendering it dry and healthy, and our death-rate from pulmonary diseases, typhoid, etc., will be materially reduced ; our surface water will not find its way into our street gutters to produce foul odours, and pollute our air ; we shall get rid of the cesspits. The city of Munich is a good example of the good that can be effected by sewerage works. These works were completed in 1881. From 1866 to 1881 the average yearly admission to hospital of cases of typhoid fever was 594. From 1881 to 1888 it had been reduced to an average of 104 though the population had in the meanwhile increased from 152,000 to 278,000. Comparison of the death-rate before and after the introduction of sewerage works in the following towns will show the beneficial results to be derived from such works :—

Croydon	...	from	23.7	to	...	18.6
Macclesfield	...	„	29.8	„	...	23.7
Salisbury	...	„	27.5	„	...	21.9
Newport	...	„	31.8	„	...	21.5
Cardiff	...	„	33.2	„	...	22.6

So that we can reasonably expect that our present death-rate of over 31 may after the introduction of sewerage works be reduced to 21 or less.

I shall now proceed to consider certain conditions connected with the town of Port-of-Spain which must affect the health of our homes. The *Water Supply*. The stream which mainly supplies us with water is totally unprotected above the reservoir; it has a large village on its bank, with the necessary cesspits, and above that it is liable to contamination from cattle. It ought to be a source of great anxiety to this town that such a condition of things exists. A few months ago in the town of Maidstone with a death rate of only 12.4 there occurred nearly 2,000 cases of typhoid fever—1 out of every 15 of the population in that town was attacked by this disease. The cause was the contamination of the springs above the reservoir by typhoid excreta from a case among some hop-pickers who had encamped near the spring. In the Colonial Hospital not very long ago there died a young coolie who came from Maraval above the reservoir and whose disease was undoubted typhoid fever. The water after collection in the reservoir is served out to the town in the same condition as it is received. It does not undergo any process of sedimentation or filtration. As diarrhœa and dysentery are answerable for more than 1-5th of the number of deaths in Port-of-Spain (363 out of 1809) we should be careful that in any future scheme of water-works our water be delivered to our homes as pure as the present means of science can make it. 2. The *Dry River*.—A gentleman of great experience who takes a deep interest in the welfare of the town writes as follows about the Dry River, and I adopt fully his statements. "The foul sewer which runs through the city of Port-of-Spain is a standing reproach to the intelligence of the community. The absolutely ineffectual methods of cleansing adopted are ridiculous.

To see a gang of men cutting the bush on each side and burning it up—while the pools of putrid filth are respectfully left alone is a surprise to one but primarily acquainted with the rules of sanitary science." He suggests the following remedy. "This main sewer should be made into a proper concrete channel for its whole length commencing at the Belmont Bridge and doing a piece each year. In 10 years at £1,000 or £1,500 a year the work would be completed—or the money might be borrowed and the work done at once. All the gravel is there and the builder would only have to buy cement and fill it on the outside."

3.—There is a spot between Woodbrook and the sea at the back of the Electric Light Works which so far as I know bears no distinguishing name. It ought to be called the Plague Corner. I shall attempt to give you an idea of the awful conditions which are collected at this one spot—First there is the heaped up refuse of the town dumped there by the scavenging carts. With careful observation you will see that attempts have been made to destroy the rubbish by burning. Next to this seems to be a place reserved for depositing the contents of the pails. Even as I stood there at 9.30 in the morning a covered cart brought its load : the pails were emptied, slightly washed and carted away. Then came a coolie with a pail on his head. The pail had no cover. He went through the same process and went away. Just beyond the pail region the two main sewers of the town empty their contents into the shore to the apparent delight of scores of corbeaux which hover about the spot. At low tide there is a large tract of open shore ; the sewers, however, empty their contents into the edge of the shore, the solid parts deposit and bask in the hot sun, and the liquid parts form sluggish streams to the sea. Between these two sewers is a large drain with foul stinking black contents. And to end up the picture beyond all this is a mangrove swamp. I do not know what the death-rate of Woodbrook is, but it ought to be very high. Why should these conditions be allowed to exist in the immediate vicinity of a large town like this? Why can't the rubbish of the town be destroyed by an incinerator such as exists in the Colonial Hospital? The powder resulting has some value as a manure and might be made a source of profit. Why are these main sewers not prolonged into the sea so as to be below the level of the water at all states of the tide? Why isn't there a proper system for the disposal of the refuse from the pails? I was informed that pails are emptied there at all hours of the day ; that they are brought there with or without cover in carts or by coolies.

4.—The large swamps to the south-east of the town are the cause of a good deal of disease in the neighbourhood and must affect materially the health of Port-of-Spain. Let us hope that at no distant date we may be able to write as was written of an American town under the same circumstances, "Thousands of acres once nearly covered with water, swampy, and grown up and covered with reeds, brake, and coarse grass, interspersed with knolls covered with small trees and tangle wood, the favourite haunts of reptiles and muskrats sending forth over the adjacent country a noisome and pestilential miasm have become converted into dry land, rich pastures and meadows where vast herds of cattle may be seen cropping the rich luxuriant grasses."

I feel that I have treated the subject imperfectly but with limited knowledge and the short time at my disposal it could not be otherwise. I hope, however, that I have succeeded in stimulating your interest in the health conditions of your homes and of the town in which you live. Our aim should always be to attain to that ideal of civism—a healthy citizen in a healthy city..

At the request of the Chairman Mr. Guppy opened the discussion. It was, he thought, extremely desirous that sanitary improvements on the line suggested by Dr Prada should be carried out in Port-of-Spain. But they could not carry it out without money to do it with.

Dr. Lovell observed Dr. Prada had prefaced his interesting address with a regret he had to take the place of Dr. de Wolf now through ill-health on leave of absence from the Colony. But when Dr. de Wolf came to read in the papers as he undoubtedly would Dr. Prada's address he would agree that he had had a most able representative (applause) and that Dr. Prada had discharged his duty in a most satisfactory manner. For himself he had seldom listened to an address on such an important subject with so much interest, or to one so ably delivered. Dr. Prada had touched upon an innumerable number of subjects very successfully, particularly considering the necessarily limited time at his disposal, and had certain varied number of points of the greatest interest to the people here in Trinidad. Dr. Prada had dealt with the matter most ably and exhaustively, and he (the speaker) was certainly very little inclined to contest any of his arguments. There were one or two points, however, that though not so important perhaps as many Dr. Prada had mentioned, appeared to him to some extent to influence the health of their homes in Trinidad. The first was the necessity of raising the houses above the ground to provide for the circulation of air underneath and keep them dry. Then there was the question of trees. People coming to Port-of-Spain were invariably astonished how small the town looked from the

Gulf which was owing to trees having overgrown the whole city. Too many trees should not be let grow near the houses and he pointed out both these things made for disease. He pointed out that in most of the houses occupied by gentlemen from the Main in Port-of-Spain precautions were taken not only to concrete the foundations but also the yards. This was a most wise precaution as it prevented not only rain water soaking into the house but subsoil water from getting into it and the universal adoption of this precaution was well worthy of consideration. He thought Dr. Prada dealt with the sewerage question in a very happy manner, and he supported the idea of such a system. He instanced the case of Port Louis, Mauritius, as a city where the advantage of a sewerage system had been proved. The work was done by Mr. Chadwick, whose plans were very similar to those he had prepared for the drainage of Port-of-Spain and in reply to a question previously asked by the Chairman, Dr. Lovell said that Mr. Chadwick's scheme provided for the separation of storm water from sewerage water, and between the two there would be no connection. There was no storm water admitted to enter the sewerage pipes whatever. To allow this would be a very great objection indeed. Dr. Lovell went on to speak of the enormously good work done in Port-of-Spain in scavenging by the corbeaux and expressed his pleasure that these invaluable birds had not become less prevalent since their Government protection had been withdrawn.

Mr. Bourne said he had not realized as he perhaps ought to have done that the chemical analysis of water gave no information whether as to bacteriological contamination and perhaps should not have been aware of it until an actual outbreak of epidemic. He wished to know how far the human animal could have bacteria communicated to him by cattle. Very little, he supposed. And Dr. Prada he noticed only recommended one filterer, the Pasteur. Was this an adequate substitute for the boiling of water or would not the boiling of water always be a judicious precaution even where the Pasteur filter was used ?

The lecturer said contamination from cattle would be purely organic and by them he did not think any disease germ would be communicated to man. With the Pasteur filterer it was unnecessary to boil water. It was a perfect filterer and it had been tested with bacteria and most thoroughly and impartially in every way.

Mr. Nathan confessed that from being a sceptic he had become absolutely convinced of the positive necessity of a sewage system for Port-of-Spain. At first he was frightened by the knowledge that the town was perfectly saturated with fœcal matter and to make excavations for a sewage system. would undoubtedly liberate a considerable quantity of germ disease. But he proceeded to show how completely his views had been changed after a practical knowledge of the sanitary conditions of Port-of-Spain by advocating a complete sewage system. Of course the question of expense was a very difficult one to deal with but he thought they might take it as settled that a great deal of Port-of-Spain would be put in a position in which all fœcal and refuse matter would be carried away by water carriage right out to the Gulf away from the shore. Such a system was absolutely necessary to their safety.

Dr. Laurence lilted a lance at the Government, the Borough Council, the land owners and occupiers, but especially at the Government for indifference to sanitary reform and spoke of the appalling need for immediate sanitary reform in the city. Some day the Government would wake up to face a fearful epidemic.

Mr. Syl. Devenish closed the debate with observations on the sanitary building of houses which he said was greatly needed in the city.

Then the Chairman thanked Dr. Prada for his paper which he again highly praised and incidentally observed Dr. Laurence had denounced the barrack system from a sanitary point of view but it could also be denounced from a moral point of view for he found the barrack yard system responsible for a great deal of the crime of Port-of-Spain. He advocated the barrack yards being made with thoroughfares through them so that the police could pass through and so act as a deterrent to the immorality and crime that went on in them.

Read 5th May, 1898.

THE RESOURCES OF TRINIDAD.

By L. Bert de Lamarre.

IN attempting to address you on such an important subject as the Resources of Trinidad, I must ask your kind indulgence to the many defects that will no doubt be apparent to those whose knowledge of the subject is far more extended and varied, than I can possibly lay claim to. My residence here has not been of sufficient duration to enable me to study out in an entire practical way the complete resources of this magnificent Island. However, in deference to the wish of your indefatigable President (Sir John Goldney) I shall endeavour to the best of my ability to give a short sketch of what those resources are. Trinidad is essentially an agricultural country and its main industry continues to be the cultivation of the Sugar Cane. This industry has given employment to many in the past, and still does so, but unfortunately competition of Beet Sugar, largely supported by artificial means, is causing a rapid decrease of the area under cultivation. Many of us can remember the palmy days of the West Indies when "Sugar was King" and all of us know only too well the serious depression under which an industry of such vital importance to the well being of this colony now struggles for existence.

So far we look in vain to the Mother Country for that help which is required to counteract this outside competition, but there are not wanting indications that the European Bounties will eventually be abolished, and we may yet see a return of that prosperity which once prevailed.

There is considerable difficulty in the way of getting a proper system of tenant farming established, mainly on account of the facilities enjoyed by the labouring classes in this Island of existing from day to day without the trouble of exerting themselves to work, and when obliged to do so they find that cocoa and rice cultivation are preferable in a great measure to that of the sugar cane. I can understand that amongst the creoles here a preference should be shown for cocoa cultivation as they have from an early time been accustomed to it, and they will generally be found settled in larger numbers in the vicinity of cocoa estates than elsewhere. As a matter of fact in dealing with a sugar estate we are not able to count much upon creole labour, as the greater part of them find work on the cocoa estates; and those that remain for employment by the sugar planters, with few exceptions are those for whom it might be well to have a Vagrancy Act established. To be successful with the tenant farming the cultivation and manufacture of sugar must be kept separate, and distinct.

With regard to the bounties, it ought to be borne in mind that the Continental Governments of to-day have not only to keep these bounties going merely as a measure of trade emergency, but also as a political measure. The political reason of the Continental Governments in keeping up bounties is, that through their Agency they are able to employ an immense number of labourers, who in their turn give them their votes at the elections, and if the beet sugar factories were to be shut, the people employed in them, who are nearly all voters under the regime of universal suffrage, would join the opposition and vote on the socialistic side, thereby endangering the safety of the community at large. If the beet sugar factories were closed the various Governments would probably be compelled to give relief to the unemployed labour occasioned thereby, under the form of huge workhouses, or by opening up Government works, such as railways etc., etc.

It is on this account that the Government bounty givers find it so hard to abolish what at heart they have a desire to be rid of. The same state of affairs relatively exists here, created by the Government giving aid to sugar planters in the shape of imported Indian labour, but which they are now so desirous to bring to a close.

It is to be feared that if the Colonial Government reduce Planters to extremities as they are now gradually doing, they will have some day to support in some way the whole of the imported Indian labour at present existing here.

By getting rid of the existing bounties it does not follow that we shall see an immediate rise in the sugar market, but it may possibly bring about a reduction in the acreage under sugar cultivation, through the want of labour; this factor becoming more and more scarce day by day.

As a matter of fact if it were not for the Indian labourers indentured or otherwise, no single person here from Port-of-Spain to San Fernando could continue sugar cultivation.

This state of affairs it appears is not so disastrous in the Naparima district but yet it is to be supposed that there will be some day short-comings there as well, necessitating a reduction in acreage, and probably causing the closing of some factories, which had been originally started to cope with a certain output, and which will not be able to attain this on account of the deficiency of labour, or through tenant farmers not coming forward to work and plant up the land. The labour question is now as it will ever be our most difficult problem to solve, but it is to be hoped that eventually the Home Government will see its way to give relief to the Sugar Planters, to whom the Colony is indebted yearly for over half a million sterling put into circulation by them. From the foregoing it must not be gathered that if the sugar industry fails entirely that the Colony of Trinidad will be ruined, as we have here many great factors which even should the sugar industry be entirely blotted out, will gradually help it to become the most magnificent of all the West Indian Colonies, a position which it is already on a fair way to attain. At not too distant a date we shall see that the prosperity of Trinidad lies in the multiplicity of properties by the alienation of Crown lands or otherwise and the greater part of Trinidad's agricultural resources shall in time to be due to the divisibility of landed property into two main classes, those already in possession, and peasant proprietors.

The peasants or creole labourers who are willing to work will eventually form a body of small proprietors who by their numbers and the varied collection of their products, will in a few years have the command of the market.

No matter to what class they belong, these owners of small properties must necessarily become producers, who will undoubtedly form a majority and the future wealth of Trinidad will then to a great extent lie with them.

There are many errors which may perhaps retard their success and advancement as a class, such as the forgetfulness of their origin, and instead of making of their sons and daughters, good agricultural labourers (whereby they may be able to help their advancement) sending them to follow schools, where incomplete education is given which mostly results in turning out incomplete professionals and idlers instead of good agriculturalists who can plant and work their own lands. The fault here does not lie so much with the labourer, as with those who have the management of the education of the Trinidad working class, which in my opinion is based on a wrong principle; and tends to draw him away from his natural calling. In presence of the actual state of the labour question here, what the sugar planters fear is that, if we can only rely upon the Indian labour and the very small quantity of agricultural labourers, attracted from the neighbouring Islands, estates will be unable to keep up even the existing cultivation on account of the difficulty of finding labourers to work the land.

On the other hand I believe cocoa will always be prosperous, barring some unexpected diseases, as the cocoa planters do not require what a sugar planter does, and the conditions of labour are by no means the same.

All the large cocoa plantations are in the hands of gentlemen of undoubted energy and great abilities, and nothing has to be said on the future of that other main branch of our products. It is of no practical use to review an industry which is prosperous and which is increasing in value every day. Now let us pass to the minor industries called minor now, but which with time it is hoped will be developed, into major industries. In Trinidad we possess a magnificent soil, in some places, well adapted for the cultivation of orange and lime trees; some beautiful fruit are collected during the season, but a large quantity is entirely lost on account of the fruit not finding a market. If orange plantations were established here, a line of Steamers properly fitted for the purpose of carrying fruit ought to be subsidized enabling the producer to send his fruit to the American or English market.

Orange fields if established ought only to contain grafted oranges, and those of the best species, and it must be borne in mind that oranges not grafted usually bear a fruit which does not keep so well as the grafted fruit. The latter is hardier, has a better skin, bruises much less easily, and is also of a better class with more flavour and sweetness.

Grafted orange trees of about 12 months old can be brought up from Florida or Jamaica and being replanted here, will after 4 years give a good crop if well cared for, and one which will repay handsomely all cultivation expenses if shipped in a careful manner. Now in the same line of minor industries, there is the lime (*Citrus limetta*) which grows wild here and ought to have produced large quantities of lime juice for the English market, but which so far as I have been able to see has not succeeded as an industry up to now.

This non-success is due from what I have seen to the defective process employed to extract the product from the lime fruit. In the common lime of the West Indies of which the composition varies according to the solid and the altitude in which the lime is grown, the products to be extracted are as follows :—

Lime juice to be shipped as raw juice, or as cordial lime juice, or as concentrated lime juice, used in England and America to manufacture citric acid.

Essential Oil of Lime shipped to England and used by perfume manufacturers.

The extraction of lime juice in a factory especially put up for that purpose ought to have a steam three roller mill, an hydraulic press to obtain the balance of extractible juice from the pulp after leaving the mill, a still to extract the essential oil from the expressed lime juice, and lastly a battery of copper tayches to boil the juice if it is to be manufactured into concentrated lime juice. The extraction of oil can be made also by hand, worked by the Sicilian process which will make an oil of a better quality but in a smaller quantity.

The complete process to manufacture lime juice and essential oil is as follows. The limes are collected from the fields and accumulated near the mill where they are passed through the rollers, the juice being collected from the mill bed, and forwarded to the still. The pulp from the mill is forwarded to the hydraulic press which completes the extraction of the juice, and essential oil remaining in the pulp. The juice from the hydraulic press is forwarded to the still, and there mixed with the first juice as received from the mill, then the juice is boiled in the still, delivering during its ebullition some water from the juice and essential oil, after about one hour's boiling all the essential oil has passed through the condenser and is received in jars; then separated after a certain time from the water from the condensed liquid which had passed through the condenser. The juice remaining in the still is forwarded to the copper tayches where it is boiled to make concentrated lime juice. Cordials are made with the first raw juice from the mill and require special preparation. In a well equipped factory the manufacture of lime juice is a paying concern, but the first condition to success is to have enough limes and a complete well equipped factory with all the implements required. After the lime and orange industries we come to an entirely new industry for Trinidad which is that of the India Rubber. The plants furnishing rubber are legion, but as we are supposed to work for our present generation, leaving to the future the care of itself, the difficulty of forming such a plantation is the choice of the plants. We must choose accordingly a plant which is best suited to the soil in which it has to grow, the conditions of climate, having likewise to be taken into consideration.

Rubber is produced by plants which begin to give a return, some at 5 years and others between 20 and 30 years of age.

The two plants which I think answer best to the climatic conditions of Trinidad are the *Castilloa elastica* and the *Manihot glazowii*.

Castilloa elastica is not a very hardy plant but grows well on undulating lands, in the shade of hills, and where there is a considerable amount of moisture in well drained soils. Some magnificent specimens can be seen at Mr. Adrien de Verteuil's Tortuga Estate. These are on very good cocoa lands, which seem admirably adapted to the complete growth of that description of the rubber tree as they cannot stand a prolonged drought.

The other plant which I have chosen to plant on lands subject to drought and sometimes also inundated by the Caroni river and the back water caused by the Railway embankment, is the *Manihot glazowii*. I have deliberately chosen that plant, as it is a very hardy one, does not fear sun or rain and can resist a dry season of six months as it does in Ceara (North Brazil.) This description according to Sceligman, who, is a recognized authority on rubber, has proved as great a success in India as it has in Ceylon, and may therefore be very justly called the India rubber tree of the future. The principal habitat of this tree being the province of Ceara—some objections have been raised against its adoption for new plantation on account of the commercial value of the rubber obtained from it, but on looking over a late prices current I find that quotations are, for fine Para (which is supposed to be one of the best obtainable) 3/10 and for Ceara 3/2½ per lb.—not a very great difference when we take into account the different methods for preparing it for the market. I am informed that this alone causes the difference in value, and if more care were used in collecting and preparing in Ceara, its produce would fetch as good a price as that of Para.

Tobacco culture is another industry that ought to thrive here as the plant grows luxuriously on most of our soils. The trouble is, that we seem to have no one amongst us who understand anything about its manufacture. Like most other industries this requires a special knowledge and training. In order to make it successful, a plantation would have to be formed on a large scale, and properly equipped in every detail, including of course, the services of a thoroughly qualified practical expert. Another industry of which a great deal may yet be expected is the culture of Rice, and I notice it is being rapidly extended. So far all that is produced is treated for local consumption in a somewhat primitive fashion, but if the industry grows as it promises, we may yet see a rice mill in our midst, as they now have in Demerara.

It seems to me that much more provisions ought to be grown for local consumption, and from what I see in all the valleys lying near the populous districts, any industrious man, would make a very good living by turning his attention to this, and diligently cultivating the soil. Why should so much food stuffs require to be imported, when they can profitably be raised here by the people themselves?

There are other Agricultural products which might be referred to, but time does not permit. I will say nothing of the resources of Trinidad as a commercial centre, these are great from the geographical position of the island alone; and I hope some day, to see our capital the emporium of great trade with the Main land.

I am afraid, however, that if the proposed scheme of underground sewerage for Port-of-Spain is carried out, with the inevitable consequence of typhoid and other fevers, which must result in a tropical city where there is not a very large supply of water, and where germs will luxuriate in the obscurity essential to their growth and reproduction; this dream will take a long time to realize. This matter is one which greatly interests me as a Chemist, and I may possibly ask your permission to give a paper on the subject at some future date.

The mineral resources of Trinidad are so far confined to bituminous material. All of you know better than I can say the vast amount of wealth contained in the famous Pitch Lake of La Brea, and from the geological construction of the island I expect deposits of Bitumen in various forms can be found in many districts of the island, but whether in such a form as would make it profitable to work them, is a problem that still requires to be solved. A great deal more could be said regarding our underground resources, than the limits of this paper will allow.

I have very inadequately endeavoured to give you my ideas, more particularly regarding Agriculture, on which we must mainly rely, and there is no doubt, but with proper cultivation and the appliance of scientific knowledge, much more may be expected from the soil in the future than has been obtained in the past. I hope I have not wearied you and may with your permission, continue this paper at a later date.

19th May, 1893.

The following paper was read :—

ON EDUCATION IN TRINIDAD.

By R. J. Lechmere Guppy, Late Chief Inspector of Schools.

I—*General Considerations.*

I have been asked to read a paper on Education at the Victoria Institute. It is with reluctance and misgiving that I accept the task, for, as I said, when asked to read such a paper, my views and opinions on the subject are so different from those held by the most powerful classes in this community, that I fear that little good will arise out of anything I may put forward. However, I have been assured otherwise, for I had on a former occasion said that I would not mind sacrificing my ease and convenience if good arise therefrom ; but I do not feel encouraged to do so if no good is to be gained. And then again, I must ask your indulgence on the score of my health which has of late almost entirely incapacitated me from literary work of any sort. However I feel that having incurred the obligation, I must do what I can to fulfil it. And it is almost only at the last moment that I have put pen to paper to endeavour to do so. These preliminaries will I hope dispose you to receive a most imperfect and hastily gotten-up paper with that indulgence you might not otherwise find it easy to accord.

For the history of education I must refer you to encyclopedias and standard works on education. In all communities even the most rude there existed some form and means of education and in the growth of society such form or means must have assumed definite shape adapted for the bringing up of the individual in conformity with the conditions under which his life had to be passed. Certain it is that in all fully organized communities we find educational institutions to have existed. I cannot however take up your time with any further reference to these but proceed at once to the discussion of those points which immediately concern us as regards the education of the community of which we form a part. The fundamental and immutable principles on which public education must be based are so well indicated in the article on the subject in the Standard Library Cyclopedia published some sixty or seventy years ago that I cannot do better than quote it here.

"In every nation even those called uncivilized there are and necessarily must be certain practices and usages according to which children are instructed in those things which are to form the occupation of their future life, and every civilized nation (*and we may presume nations also called uncivilized*) have some general term by which they express this process of instruction. In the European languages derived from the Latin and in others that have a mixture of that language this general term is Education. It is not important to consider the more or less precise notions attached to this or any other equivalent word ; but it is enough to observe that as the language of every nation possesses such a term it is a universal truth that all nations admit that there is something which is expressed by the comprehensive term Education or by some equivalent term. But like all other general terms which have been long in use this term Education comprehends within the general meaning already assigned to it a great number of particulars which are conceived by various people in such different modes and degrees that two or more persons who agree in their general description of the term might very probably in descending into the enumeration of the particulars find themselves completely at variance with one another.

"In every society Education *(in what particular manner conceived by any particular society is of no importance to our present inquiry)* is as a general rule and must necessarily be subjected to the positive law of the society and to that assemblage of opinions customs and habits which is not inappropriately called the positive Morality of Society. This Truth is the basis of every inquiry into Education. In no country can there exist as a general rule an education whether good or bad not subordinate to the law as above explained : for if such Education did exist the form of that society or political system could not coexist with it. Education then should be in harmony with and subordinate to the political system ; it should be part of it.

"Every person has two distinct relations or classes of relations towards the State : one comprehends his duties as a citizen wherein he is or ought to be wholly subordinate to the State : the other comprehends all his functions as a producer and enjoyer of wealth wherein he has or ought to have all freedom that is not inconsistent with the proper discharge of his duties as a citizen. It is barely necessary to state this proposition in order to perceive that his Education as a citizen should be directed by the State. To suppose any other directing power any power for instance which may educate him in principles opposed to the polity of which he is to form a part is to suppose an inconsistency which in discussing any question involving principles we always intend to avoid.

"How then ought the State to exercise superintendence over the education of the citizen? It is not our purpose to attempt to answer this question which involves the consideration of some of the most difficult questions in legislation. It is sufficient if we present the question which it belongs to the civilization of the present and future ages to solve. But we may answer the question so far as this : the State having the superintendence of the citizen's education, must have the superintendence of those who direct that education in other words it must direct those who are to carry its purposes into effect. The body of teachers therefore must be formed by or at least must be under the control of the State. Unless this fundamental truth be admitted and acted on the State cannot effectually direct the education of its citizens.

"We may further recognize the principle that individual competition in education must not be destroyed. It is possible to reconcile the two principles of state control and individual competition. The state may allow no person to teach without being examined and registered : such register will show if he has been trained under the superintendence of state or not. This fact being established it may be left to individuals or associations of individuals to employ what teachers they please. In all schools founded or supported by the State it follows as a matter of course that none but teachers' trained by the State should be appointed.—*Standard Library Cyclopedia.*

So long ago as 1867 in a paper * read before a meeting of the Scientific Association at which His Excellency Sir Arthur Gordon was present I remarked on the defective state of education in this island and the absence of the means of properly developing what has been called the " tribal Conscience †. " Immense changes and improvements have taken place since then. The education system of that day though excellent in principle had been rendered utterly sterile by the influence of the dominant classes. Having failed to prevent its existence they almost entirely destroyed its usefulness. It was the influence I speak of that reduced the schools to such a condition that it was possible to write a report on them such as that of Sir Patrick Keenan. Though even then anyone who chooses to read between the lines of that report can see how much better (bad as they were) the Government schools were than their

---

* Proceedings Scientific Association Trinidad 1867 Page 92.

† I have not been able to find a better term than this. Those unacquainted with it can consult Clifford's Lectures. See particularly the one on the " Scientific Basis of Morals."

rivals (see speeches of André Knox at the Town hall and Grey-friars Church January 1870). It is not the object of this paper to dwell on the changes and improvements in education from 1868 to 1890. Whoever cares to trace them will find them specified in my published reports. I have only to remark here that in introducing the various improvements mentioned into our schools I was met by the bitterest hostility at every step and I was practically fined £400 a year for the efforts I made to preserve and improve our education system—a sum representing roughly about one per cent. on the money I saved to the Government by my recommendations and exertions. But for me to have acted otherwise than I did would have been treachery which I could not have been guilty of. Since my retirement from office I have as an employer of labour in a small way been brought into a closer contact than previously with certain classes of our agricultural population. I have thus been able to see in a clearer light one or two points always more or less evident to me as I have partly indicated. Of the lower classes of the town population I do not now speak for I have little acquaintance with them otherwise than from having had to deal with the children of those classes in the course of my duty as Inspector of Schools. No doubt however that what is applicable to the one is partly applicable to the other also. I think that any one really acquainted with our country population must be more or less aware of the state of ignorance, vice and superstition into which it is plunged. It is true that there exists "a little christianity" which is what one of the most eminent men in this country declared to be the only education necessary for our people. But moral principle seems deficient. Truth, honor and purity if they exist in any form are not evident in the family life. A rude species of honesty is sometimes found and it is true that other good qualities exist but they are usually individual and there is no consensus of opinion in favour of right tendencies. There is in fact no encouragement to the growth or developement of that tribal conscience I have referred to. In a most admirable book[o] published near sixty years ago we read: "no attention to the health and comfort of the working people will be effectual without their own discretion. Intemperance, waste and ignorance will destroy the sources of health and happiness faster than any hand can replenish them. It is in vain to guard against external ills, while in the man himself early corruption is suffered age after age almost to preclude the existence of the moral sense, and gross ignorance leaves him incapable of rational conduct. There is no substitute for early education, not merely directed to the rudiments of learning, but calculated to awaken

---

[o] Woman's Rights and Duties. By a Woman. London MDCCCXL.

the kindly feelings and to form good habits " (Vol. i. page 217). The author proceeds to ask (Vol. i. page 220)," above 200 years the education of the people has been under the control of the church, yet what are the results among the people? Have they been led to sobriety, morality and peacefulness?"

Unfortunately it is not only among the lower classes that we meet with sordid views and aims and the want of a proper appreciation of what is true and right and good. I quote again from the same author as before (page 133), "It is unfortunately but too true that except as to manner, the vices of the highest and the lowest classes have a close resemblance and the state of mind in both, in the one from their power in the other from their numbers, opposes the greatest obstacle to the progress of real civilization."

The book I have quoted from which is one of the finest ever written should rather have been entitled "Directions for the guidance of the conduct of every community as regards social and moral relations." It ought to be known to and read by every woman and every man also. Here is an extract from it which shows the principle on which Education should be based. "When we represent Knowledge as one of the best means of moral Improvement we do not mean the knowledge of trifling facts or insignificant Adventures, however sanctioned by Antiquity; nor a great acquaintance with Fables; nor much learning in exploded opinions and vain hypotheses. We mean the Knowledge of things that are true and which it is important to know because of their applicability to our Feelings or our Conduct. Such are first all great and general Truths the contemplation of which in itself gives growth and expansion to the soul seeming to foster in this world the germ of that nature which shall expand in another. Secondly, the truths of a more confined sort which relate to our social condition and the particular business which it is our lot to follow."— (Vol. I, page 304. See also the seventh book of the Republic of Plato.) If the better educated and more cultivated part of the community could be brought to take higher views, we might be more hopeful for the lower classes. We may hold that to take a fair advantage is right. But to take any and every advantage however unfair and only to aim at one's own aggrandizement and ease without consideration for others is a far-too-prevalent spirit and this spirit our education must be designed to correct. In the existing state of things it is very hard to get at the evil which is of the most serious import. A system of secular education combined with compulsory attendance at school would no doubt if properly carried out effect the object. What we want is a system which will encourage

and promote the development of whatever there is of truth-
fulness and honesty in the human nature, and the experience
of centuries' shows us that this can only be a truly national
and secular system of education. I have said these things
almost daily for years while in office. The first object
of national secular education is the inculcation (not teaching)
of the first Commandment and the second is the inculcation
of the second Commandment. The fundamental basis of
Education must be the Rule of Life. However grand your
education may be, it is nothing without this basis, namely,
the moral Law and this must be inculcated not taught. This
can only be done in secular schools or in such schools as are
practically secular whatever denomination they may assume.
The virtue, happiness and freedom of every individual depends
on education, and it must be the aim of every friend of the
people (using that word in its widest sense), to secure a
thoroughly sound system of education for the people just as it is
the aim of every one hostile to the people, their freedom and
happiness, to prevent if possible such education being given and
when that is impossible to pervert and destroy it or to nullify
its effects and results.

In pursuance of such views I always endeavoured to bring
home to teachers that the inculcation of honesty, industry and
thrift was an essential part of national and secular education.
These virtues indeed flow from the principles already laid down
and it also follows that the object of public education is not the
benefit or aggrandizement of any class or particular set of the
community nor the extension of the power or influence of any
class or set.

Hence in my report for 1885-6-7 I wrote as follows :—
If the Education Department were as autonomous as other
branches of the public service are, and if it had the same power
to make its work effective, its efficiency would be greatly increased. In every other sphere of human activity it is recognized
that business can only be successfully carried on by those, to
whom it is of first importance and not subordinated to any other
function. When this truth is as fully recognised with regard to
education as it now is in regard to all other functions, a very
great amelioration may be expected in this most important and
vital one. Points now looked on as hardly attaching to education, but in reality as necessary as any others to the welfare of
the individual and of the community, will have to be included
within its scope. The business of national education is not alone
the Teaching of the three Rs, but everything that concerns the
life of the individual as citizen and subject. It is certain that

the great aims of national education cannot be achieved until the rightful place of that education is admitted and the fullest powers conferred upon it to enable it to carry out its objects.

In my report for 1881-82, I copied a portion of President Garfield's reference to education in his inaugural speech. I unfortunately omitted to take a note of President Grant's which was even more apposite and I cannot now lay my hand on it. Garfield's was as follows : "There is but one remedy. All the constitutional power of the nation and of the states and all the Volunteer Forces of the people should be summoned to meet this danger* by the saving influence of universal education : it is the high privilege and the sacred duty of those now living to educate their successors and fit them by intelligence and virtue for the inheritance which awaits them. In this beneficent work, sections and races should be forgotten and partizanship should be unknown."

That the principles I have above indicated as lying at the base of public education are widely acknowledged is obvious from the educational policy of many communities. I am now citing the case of the United States which will have none other but secular State Schools. The case with them stands thus When the denominationalists demand that public education should be placed in their hands on the plea (among others) that they can give education cheaper than the State does or can, the reply is "no doubt, but it does not matter how cheap your education is, we do not want it. What we want is really national secular education, and we are willing to pay what it costs." Now some of the denominationalists keep very good schools—in fact some of them spare no pains to achieve success in this as in other directions. They point to these schools and say "compare our schools with the national secular schools, see if they are not at least as good if not better." The State simply replies " We do not care how good your schools are, they do not serve the end of national education and we must have schools that will serve that end."

It would lead me into too intricate a task for my present purpose to attempt an analysis of the education systems of the West Indies. Nearly every petty Colony has a different system and some of them such as for instance, Barbados are though nominally denominational, practically almost exclusively secular. But only one Colony in this part of the world has, so far as I know, a thorough system of avowedly secular schools. That is

---

* The danger referred to is the political Degeneration of the people.

Surinam, and of it Mr. H. C. Ten Brocke wrote in the *West
Indian Quarterly* for April 1886 :—" As in Holland, so in Surinam, the education of the people is the chief care of the Government. Every estate has its school or at least one in its direct
vicinity and all the school-masters are paid by the Government.
It is very rare that one meets in Paramaribo with anybody
belonging to the lower class who does not understand his three
Rs. One thing however, particularly strikes the British visitor to
Suriman namely, the absence of all religious instruction in the
schools." The inculcation of religious ideas is left to the Church.
The result as stated by Mr. Ten Brocke is as follows : "The
statistics of the Magistrate's Court in Surinam will bear a
favourable comparison with those of other places under the same
circumstances. As an instance may be quoted the celebration
of the King's Birthday. From before the dawn of day till long
after midnight there are thousands of people who are keeping up
the anniversary of their beloved Sovereign. But no fight dis-
turbs the harmony of the throng, no abusive language is heard,
very little drunkenness is seen."

To meet the necessities of our case the enactment of a short
and simple law like that proposed by me in 1889 might be a step,
but only a step. And the position of the teacher must be improved by making him a public official appointed and paid in the
same way as all other public officials.

II.—*School Fees.*

In dealing with the subject of school fees I have not to deal
with any abstract or theoretical notions nor with anything
beyond our own experience and the operation of the school fee
system as worked in our own schools. In other countries there
is a maximum limit to the school fee with ample powers of
remitting it and of establishing free schools and in the United
States and elsewhere the common school is absolutely free.
I do not suppose that in any country so pernicious a system as
that in force here could have been devised. The experience of
my last fourteen years of office clearly proved to me that the
exaction of fees under the system then in force was most
detrimental to education. The attendance was greatly injured
thereby, and consequently the efficiency of the schools. I
believe that some modifications have been introduced since my
time, but I cannot believe that a fee system retaining any of the
features of that I left in operation in 1890 can be otherwise
than hurtful. The compulsory exaction of fees in all Government schools was enacted in 1876. Previous to that fees were
not charged in any but the model and borough schools. I say in
Government schools because it is only in Government schools

that the exaction of fees can be really made compulsory. In 1885 at the request of Government I made some special reports on the question of school fees. On Sir A. Havelock's leaving the island, he left these reports to be dealt with by Sir William Robinson, who, on their perusal proposed the abolition of school fees. In these reports I made various suggestions as to ways and means of making up the supposed loss which would result from the abolition of the compulsory exaction of school fees. But a prolonged examination and consideration of the subject clearly showed that not only would the supposed loss be a gain, but that a far larger revenue could be obtained from school fees by the adoption of the principles I laid down, and which had been partially carried into operation under my recommendations, in Port-of-Spain and San Fernando. Notwithstanding that I made these (and indeed several other points), quite clear to Sir William Robinson; this and other obnoxious features of our educational regulations were retained.

To this part of the question I may recur later, but now I propose to show where the injury to the school work by the compulsory exaction of fees in all schools comes in. In the first place the injury to the teacher's work is very great, for in order to collect a matter of one-tenth or even less of the cost of education, he has to devote at least one-half his energies to the task of collecting small sums of money from his scholars. It can readily be seen that this is most harassing to the teacher and injurious to his own proper work, which is teaching and not the collection of and accounting for revenue in petty amounts, which may be and often is tendered at all times, in season and out of season, and which he must receive whenever a scholar may choose to tender it. Further in some parts of the island, the people only have cash at that time of year when they dispose of their produce, and, consequently, at all other times of the year the children are kept at home because there is no money to pay the school fees. The brunt of this difficulty of course, falls upon the Government schools because in them the school fees must actually be collected, for they have to be paid into the treasury, and they must except in rare instances be paid by the relatives of the children, for there is no one else to pay them. In the case of assisted schools, it is different, for the payment of school fees in these, not having to be accounted for to public authority, need not be made a bar to the attendance of children. So the compulsory exaction of fees by law is an incentive to irregular attendance. Monday is often a holiday in this island, but even when it is not, if the cash is not at hand on that morning, the child stays away from school. On Tuesday morning if the cash is at hand, the parent or child says, "O what is the good of paying for a whole

j

week, when one day of it is already gone." So the child misses school for a whole week at least, thereby dropping out of its place in class and school work, and falling into habits of irregular attendance. Not only the individual child's progress hindered but that of the whole class and school, for what teacher can carry out a regular program of instruction where half of his scholars are irregularly present for half their time thus missing their lessons and losing the coherency of the course of instruction they should be following? The injury therefore to the teacher's work from the causes named is far greater than the value of the fees. Further, school fees are in no way either in amount or in effect a substitute for an education rate and as it is the imperative duty of the State to provide for the education of the people so it is the duty of the State to bear the whole cost of making the school efficient. As a matter of fact, the people know that they pay for education by means of taxation, and they do not consider that the public school is a charitable institution. The public school is looked on in the same light as the street hydrant, the street lamp, the public road or bridge, and all such public conveniences as are provided at the common cost for the common use. There is no part of the public taxation so popular among the people as that part of it which is devoted to education. The abolition of school fees will not degrade either parents or children any more than the abolition of turnpike tolls degraded travellers. On the other hand the exaction of a direct contribution in amount one-tenth only of the cost of education in the shape of school fees most certainly tends to the pauperization of the people. If it were possible to imagine that Education were not a public duty and that it was not an absolute necessity for the State to educate its subjects in conformity with the conditions under which they have to live the whole burden of education and not one-tenth of it would have to be borne by parents just as the whole burden of providing for the material existence of every child not a pauper lies on its parents.

III.—*Technical Instruction.*

The foundation of technical instruction is laid in the Kindergarten, where the child is taught the use of his hands and eyes as well as of his reasoning faculties. Sir Philip Magnus, one of the Royal Commissioners, and an acknowledged authority on the subject, agrees with this. He says: "The method of the Kindergarten should be extended to the Elementary School. As regards Technical Education nothing else is needed. All that is wanted follows from the application of this principle" Lord Armstrong in a recent paper observes with reference to the question of providing greater facilities for technical training that "such new facilities should await the demand for them and be supplied gradually and tentatively, for it would be folly to rush into new and costly projects without a certainty of their resulting in adequate benefit."

Hitherto when the child is drafted from the infant class to that for older children the developement of manual training is discontinued. Here is room for improvement. What is wanted is not instruction in any particular handicraft but instruction of a kind equally applicable to all handicrafts such as the use of tools. The Naas Loyd Schools of Sweden are given as examples for imitation in this respect. But there is much difference of opinion as to what is or ought to be included under the head of Technical Education. But all the authorities are agreed on the point that Technical Education of a practical and useful kind cannot be given unless the learner has at his command the elements of general education.

Huxley says " In my judgment the preparatory education of the handicraftsman ought to have nothing of what is ordinarily understood by 'technical' about it. The workshop is the only real school for a handicraft. The education which precedes that of the workshop should be entirely devoted to the strengthening of the body, the elevation of the moral faculties and the cultivation of the intelligence and especially to the imbuing the mind with a broad and clear view of the laws of that natural world with the components of which the handicraftsman will have to deal. And the earlier the period of life at which the handicraftsman has to enter into actual practice of his craft the more important it is that he should devote the precious hours of preliminary education to things of the mind which have no direct and immediate bearing on his branch of industry though they lie at the foundation of all realities." The United States have highly effective technical and agricultural schools the excellence of which is testified to by competent authorities, English and Foreign. From the American reports it appears that as a rule candidates for admission into schools of Mining, Engineering and Agriculture must be well-grounded in Mathematics. There is a noticeable tendency to increase the requirements in English and some acquaintance with French and German is thought desirable. Candidates must have gone through the regular school or academical course before they can enter the industrial schools.

As a type of another class of schools the Workingmans' School in New York may be taken. Children are here received from the Free Kindergarten where the branches of study pursued include Reading, Grammar, History, Geography,

Natural Science, Ethics, Drawing, Modelling, &c. The plan of education consists of a series of exercises so arranged that the different tools and materials of construction employed are successively introduced according to the ages and abilities of the scholars so that the actual practice necessary for the skilful manipulation of tools may be given simultaneously with the education of the mind. The exercises for the lower classes involve the rudiments and principles of geometry and the most useful laws of mechanics and physics. For the eighth and seventh class the exercises introduce the use of paper, pencils, triangles, compasses and rules in the drawing room. In the workroom small toy chisels are employed for carving geometrical forms from pieces of clay.

Turning to European Technical Schools we find that the authorities of the city of Paris in their experiments in the introduction of manual training into ordinary Primary Schools have confined themselves to teaching more advanced drawing from models and the use of ordinary tools without attempting to teach special trades. There are about fifty schools where these experiments are in progress. At the Rue Tournefort School, which may be taken as the type, drawing, modelling, moulding and carving are among the chief technical subjects.

In the Paris Municipal Apprenticeship Schools the subjects of study are similar to those of the American and German Technical Schools including French, English, Mathematics, Mechanics, Drawing, Chemistry, Physics, History and Descriptive Geometry, and of course the use of tools and machines.

The German Technical Schools are of various kinds. In those which promote cottage and village industries modelling and drawing hold an important place.

Of other Technical Schools in Europe a few examples may be cited to show the subjects of study. The time devoted to the workshop varies much and in the Russian Schools they go so far as to construct steam engines. But of these higher Technical Schools there are very few, for instance, only two for the whole Russian Empire. In the Polytecnic Schools of Germany there are only about 2,000 students (though there is accomodation for three times the number) for its population of over 45,000,000, and the cost to the State is about £100 per annum for each student, exclusive of interest and capital. In the Polytecnic School at Dresden the following are the subjects of instruction :— Analytical Geometry, Elementary Mathematics, Optics and Acoustics, Chemistry, Heat, Electricity, Magnetism, Freehand

and Mechanical Drawing, Shading and Colouring, Ornamental Drawing, Differential and Integal Calculus, Architecture, Elasticity and Stability, Machinery, Geology, Astronomy, &c., &c. Such with many variations are the subjects taught in higher Technical Schools. The lower grades of Technical Schools do not go so far, but in all, drawing and modelling hold a prominent place. In the Vienna Trade Schools drawing and modelling in clay claim an equal portion of the students time with basket-weaving. This portion of my statement may be finished with a reference to the conclusions of the Royal Commissioners on Technical Education who strongly insist upon the extension of instruction in drawing and modelling in Elementary Schools as a part of Technical Instruction and preparation for further advance in that branch.

But whatever variation of opinion may be allowed on this subject of Technical Education, on one point I arrived at a definite conclusion, namely that though the State may afford all facilities the cost of special education of any kind should be borne by parents. The State should not assume the cost of the education specially needed to fit persons for gaining a higher rate of pay than others unless indeed in training persons for its own service. And this proposition applies with greater force where the parents are paupers or criminals and who therefore do not merely not contribute to the fund from which the schools are supported but whose maintenance is actually a charge upon that fund. That would be in my opinion only enabling the dishonest and incapable to better himself at the expense of the honest and capable which must needs be a sore discouragement to the latter. Therefore I think that industrial instruction given to the children of paupers and criminals should be of the kinds only that demand the least skill and command the lowest pay. The preceding propositions have laid it down that it may be desirable that Technical Instruction of a general kind be given in schools and in particular kinds of schools it is possible that Industrial Instruction may be given. But while it is admitted that the workshop is the proper school for the mechanic, it would seem also that the cane or corn field is the proper school for the field labourer and that it is questionable whether trades demanding skill should be taught in Reformatories or Industrial Schools maintained at the public expense inasmuch as the persons to whom those trades are taught go to displace the honest artisan who has gained his education at his own expense.

So many delusions and mistakes surround this question of Technical and Industrial Instruction, that I have dealt with the subject at some length to show in particular that such instruc tion is no substitute for, but a complement to the ordinary course of education and that Technical Instruction given in Elementary or other schools, must be of a general and not a special character.

The antipathy to field labor which is alleged, no doubt with reason, to be so prevalent in this country, is the consequence of the degradation of labor, and this is the result of slavery and superstition. This truth may be, and no doubt is, unpleasant, nay, bitter to many—but your Patron told you that the independent man speaks truth—and I, though not independent (as indeed who is), am here to speak truth. The establishment of school gardens if compulsory, would not diminish the distaste for work; but it would, increase the distaste for going to school and the irregularity of attendance already so much complained of. Parents would say, "I have my own garden, when I want my child to work in it, I keep him away from school to do so. I send him to school to learn and not to dig garden." Again in many of the schools especially in towns and populous places, a large number of the scholars do not belong to the class of agricultural labourers, but are the children of clerks, artisans, shopkeepers, domestic servants and others to whom agricultural education would be inappropriate. I say nothing of the waste of money and the utter failure to produce useful results which would follow; for these, though weighty, are of less consequence than the ill effect upon school attendance. School gardens have, from time to time, been tried, and I have in my mind a picture of a very neat one, in which teacher and scholars took much pride. The work was purely optional, and it was done out of school hours. But I cannot imagine that any one can seriously propose to teach work or agriculture by means of school gardens. It is of no use devising remedies until you have removed the cause. The cause in this case, is the degradation of labor and the laborer. The true remedy is to raise labor by raising the laborer, and until you do this, all other remedies will be unavailing. The constant endeavour has been, not to raise but to degrade labor. How often have sugar planters and others said to me, "what do you want to educate little niggers for? put hoes into their hands and send them into the cane piece." Can you wonder that the tree bears the fruit of which you have sown the seed?

In combatting the hydra-headed errors which constantly develop themselves around us, I am obliged to call attention to facts. Those required for my present use are neatly set out in a statement published some time ago in one of our newspapers from which I extract the following: "Our population is 115 to the square mile. Several European countries have a less dense population than this. Only a few of the oldest settled parts of America, such as Massachusetts, Connecticut, and New Jersey, where there are important manufactories and seaports, have such a population. The average for the United States (excluding Territories) is 25 to the square mile, and no other American country has a population anything approaching to this. It was suggested a short time ago that we should take some of the Chinese off the hands of the Cubans. But the population of the island of Cuba does not exceed 36 to the square mile as compared with our 115, and they have in that island an ample area of the most fertile soil to allow of the development of a population ; while at least one half of our country is too sterile to bear a crop, and of the remainder only one-half can be said to be really fertile." *

I think our population is rather denser than stated being over 120† to the square mile. Having traversed and retraversed the Island in every direction year after year and having studied its Geology for more than thirty years I can affirm that the statement above made is not far from the truth. As the writer of it truly remarks "it can do us no good to live in Fool's Paradise" and I may add our good old English saying " Fine words butter no Parsnips."

IV.—*School Organization.*

In the Elementary School it is in the infant class that the foundation and basis of education is laid. This is the most important class in the school and scarcely behind it comes the first standard class. No school is a good school where these classes or departments are not efficiently taught and organised. It was the daily struggle of my life when in office to get this fact recognized. I found a constant tendency on the part of teachers to shirk the instruction of these classes, upon which nevertheless the whole efficiency of their schools depends. Any one who will glance over my printed general reports on education will see with what persistence I called attention to this point. The part of the Government in the matter was of course to provide proper accommodation and efficient teachers for these classes. I can aver that the teaching staff was mostly below requirements but in some schools where it was not so, the teachers could not do their work for want of the proper accommodation. The English

---

* The large extent of poor Soil is faintly indicated in the Geological Report, pages 80, 82 and elsewhere.

† It is stated at 145 in Collens' Almanack for 1898, page 9.

Education Department in its Report for 1889 remarks that
"the methods of instruction for older scholars and infants are
very different, and cannot be efficiently carried on in the same
room. Every school therefore, except the very smallest requires
a separate department for infants." Furthermore, my experience
fully bore out the experience of other countries that the instruction and care of young children, can, as a rule, safely be confided
to women only and that it is only trained women that are really
competent for the work.

The neglect of the most important part of the school work
is partly due to the preference the teacher feels for conducting
the instruction of more advanced scholars. But it is simply
building without any foundation. Many of the teachers who
persisted in this course in spite of advice were simply incompetent
to teach advanced scholars hence their schools exhibited every
year the same dismal failure the cause of which they could
not understand and indeed which they would not admit.
In some cases where by dint of incessant hammering and
better still by stopping the merit grant (called results fees)
I managed to drive the teachers to attend to the point, a constant
and steady improvement followed. But I think that in all such
cases the Inspector should have power to restrict the teaching to
the lower standards so as to avoid the waste of the whole
teaching power of a school upon two or three children who have
passed those standards. In many country schools it is simply a
farce for a teacher to profess to teach fifth or sixth Standards
and the mischief wrought to the school by such pretence is very
great.

In making these observations it will be understood that I
am not criticizing the schools as they now are. I speak of what
I found in my experience and it is possible that some improvements may have been made in these matters. (Highly important suggestions on the points alluded in this and other sections
of this paper will be found in my general report for 1881-82).

Into details of school organization and management, I shall
not enter now. If any one desires to know what ought to be
the routine of school work, I can refer him to the 16th paragraph
of my special report of 7th May, 1889, or the 17th paragraph of
my general report for 1889. This will serve as a model of how
the daily work of a school should be carried under a well-devised
time-table. What is required in the first place, is to establish
a sound system of public education, as the preliminary to any
further improvement. Under such a system you would have
graded schools, such as I partially obtained in Port-of-Spain,

under which the people grade themselves according to their means and necessities, as suggested in my Special Report of 6th May, 1885—" Free instruction for all who choose to avail themselves of it being provided in the Elementary Schools, it may be only fair that those who desire a higher kind of education should pay additionally for it." In the lower grade schools education is free, while in the higher grade schools fees are charged according to the grade of the school. Under this system the fees received amount to a large sum, they are easily collected and regularly paid. They are paid by every scholar on the first day of each month, so as to avoid loss of the teacher's time in keeping accounts. Another advantage of such a system is that the education given in each school is exactly adapted to the class of children using it, the power referred to already of restricting the instruction to the lower standards being exercised where desirable.

V.—*Corporal Punishment.*

As the subject of corporal punishment in schools was rather fully dealt with a few years before I left office it may not be out of place here for me to introduce a summary of the conclusions at which I arrived on the point. These are mostly in accordance with the opinions of the principal educational authorities.

At the beginning of my official life in connection with education I observed many instances of the misuse or abuse of the so-called corporal punishment. Being then inexperienced, I did not at first interfere to the extent I ought perhaps to have done. But as time went on I took a more and more decided stand against what I considered to be mere exhibitions of brutality, and although in this as in most other matters, I often suffered for want of support at the hands of the Government. I managed gradually to effect a very considerable change for the better. The opinion I formed was that corporal punishment was, generally speaking, likely to do more harm than good. The best schools in all respects are those in which it is never used. It may readily be admitted that children often deserve it, but that is not the question, which really is, is it wise or beneficial to employ it. I believe this is very seldom the case. The object of school is to improve children and it is scarcely doubtful that corporal punishment cannot do this. As for indiscriminate strapping in schools, such as I have seen practised, it is most injurious in its effects, both on teacher and scholars. The most disorderly and ill-conducted schools that I have seen were those in which the strap or rod was constantly applied. Punishment should I think, be administered only by the head teacher with only a few witnesses. It should never be administered until

K

some interval after the offence, and it should be confined to two or three strokes on the hand with a small strap. The offences for which corporal punishment is to be inflicted may be stated as serious and repeated misconduct, lying, theft, cruelty, insubordination, bad language, etc.

VI.—*Training of Teachers.*

As regards the training and examination of teachers, I have expressed myself so fully in my general reports, that I can only repeat what I have said in them. On this, as on nearly all points, my experience of twenty-two years at the head of the department, almost exactly coincides with that of the educational authorities of England, the United States and other countries. All rules as to Teachers' Certificates must recognize the principle that approved service as a teacher is of at least as much value as the ability to pass an examination. All certificates must be subject to the condition that the candidate has passed a certain period of probation in actual charge of a school or department of a school. I cannot say what the case now is, but in my time, the examinations for certificates were notwithstanding my efforts to keep things within due bounds crowded by two undesirable classes of candidates. The first of these was the town candidate whose aim in attending the examination, was not to fill the useful but unattractive post of a country teacher, but to flaunt his paper certificate as a kind of diploma. The candidates of this class though useless as members of the general teaching staff of the department having had the advantage of town life and education, usually took good places, sometimes the best in the examination. The other class was chiefly composed of persons who had little chance of ever passing an examination and even less if possible of satisfactorily conducting a school. They were mostly persons who had tried other ways of making a living and failed therein and who took to teaching as a last resort. The candidates forming this class were those for the most part who perpetrated the errors held up to ridicule in the examination reports. It is of the highest importance that admission to examination and the issue of certificates should be confined as strictly as possible to those who are actually likely to become teachers, ready and willing whenever and if required to go through all the grades of the service and to owe their promotion to merit and ability. Upon those who really intend to become teachers and who have the qualifications for the office it is no hardship to be required to undergo a period of probation to prove their fitness for the office. To those young teachers in town schools who do not mind spending a few years at those institu-

tions with a view of improving their own education and at the
same time being paid for doing duty as Assistants and Pupil
Teachers, but who have no real intention of permanently
devoting themselves to the work of teaching or of undertaking
the charge of country schools it is no doubt a hardship not to be
allowed to go up for examination and not to have certificates
issued to them without probation, but the interests of the
Department must be considered before the convenience of such
persons and it must ever be borne in mind that Teachers' Certificates are intended for teachers only and not to serve as a kind
of academical degree.

Some have imagined that the Teacher can gain a sufficient
knowledge of the art of teaching by the study of a Manual of
School Management. But this no more supplies what is required
than a study of Works on Anatomy can take the place of actual
practice in Surgery. This is amply proved by experience ; and
of the two conditions of study and examination on the one hand
and of training and actual service on the other the latter is if
anything more indispensable than the former. In any case it is
a serious error to take the mere ability to pass an examination
as the sole test of the fitness of a person for the office of Teacher.
No person ought to be allowed to have charge of a public school
unless trained and certificated after probation to the satisfaction
of the Educational Authorities.

VII.—Concluding Remarks.

I conclude with a few observations which have occurred to
me on looking over the last two published Reports of our
Education Department. The last year for which I made a
report was 1889. The total cost of Elementary Education in
that year was £23,500 or at the rate of 38/- per scholar in
average attendance. In 1895 the cost was £30,994 or at the
rate of 44/- per scholar in average attendance. In 1896 the cost
was £32,757 or at the rate of 45/- per scholar. The average
attendance in 1889 was 12,215. In 1895 it was 13,890. It
therefore cost £7,494 to obtain the increase of 1,675. In 1896
the average attendance was 14,504. The increase of 2,289
thus cost £9,257. This comparison shows that previously to
1890 a steady increase of attendance (namely from 5,541 in 1881
to 12,215 in 1889) was accompanied by a steady decrease in the
cost per scholar (namely from 49/- in 1881 to 38/- in 1889) since
1889 the increase of attendance (from 12,215 in that year to
14,500 in 1896) has been accompanied by an increased cost per
scholar—this being now 45/-.

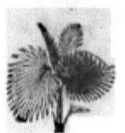

ANNUAL REPORT FOR 1897.

THE Board of Management have the honour to submit the following report of the work done by the Institute during the past year.

At the Annual Meeting held on the 1st April, 1897, the following members were elected, as the Board of Management :—

> Sir JOHN GOLDNEY,
> Professor CARMODY,
> Messrs. R. H. McCARTHY,
>   „   HENRY CARACCIOLO,
>   „   EDGAR TRIPP,
>   „   F. W. URICH,
>   „   T. I. POTTER,

and the following gentlemen were nominated to the Board by His Excellency the Governor:

> The Hon'ble Dr. LOVELL, C.M.G.,
>   „   „   H. C. BOURNE,
> Messrs. SYL. DEVENISH,
>   „   R. J. L. GUPPY,
>   „   J. H. COLLENS.

The Board elected Sir John Goldney, President, and Dr. Lovell, C.M.G., and Mr. Syl. Devenish, Vice-Presidents, Mr. McCarthy, Treasurer, and Mr. Potter, Secretary.

The year 1897 being the 100th year of Trinidad as a British Colony, a public Committee was appointed for the purpose of organizing a suitable celebration of this event. At the request of this Committee, the Board undertook to hold a Centenary Exhibition, during the Centenary week.

The Board with the view of making the Committee appointed by them to organize the Exhibition as representative as possible asked several gentlemen belonging to the old families of the Colony to join the Committee, with the happy result, that the Historical Exhibition was quite the leading feature of the Centenary celebration. An Art and Horticultural Exhibition was held at the same time at which prizes amounting to over £150. were given.

The Exhibition was opened on the 15th, 16th, 17th and 19th of February and on two extra days by special request. Exclusive of Members and Exhibitors upwards of 1,600 persons visited the Exhibition. A very interesting descriptive Catalogue of the Historical Section of the Exhibition was prepared by Mr. L. M. Fraser. Those who wish to possess what is really a brief history of the Colony can obtain copies of this Catalogue at the Institute.

Considerable additions to the Industrial and Commercial Museum have been made during the year; the Board thank the donors of samples for their contributions, a list of which is appended.

If photographs of the cultivation, preparation and manufacture of our staple products could be obtained they would form an interesting addition to the Museum.

At a meeting of the Board held on the 29th of June, 1897, a Special Committee was appointed to draw up a programme of work. This Committee submitted to the Board a report suggesting that there should be a Special Session from October to May with a fixed programme of work. This was agreed to and a copy of the programme is appended. The Governor, Sir Hubert Jerningham, the Patron of the Institute, opened the Session with an inaugural address. The great interest His Excellency has taken in the welfare of the Institute and the influence he has exercised both by his presence and by his advice at the many meetings attended by him largely contributed to the success of the Session. The Board desire also to express their high appreciation of the co-operation of the following gentlemen who prepared papers for the fortnightly meetings :—

Mr. RENE DE VERTEUIL, an experienced planter,
 „ H. S. BIDWELL, Engineer in charge of Harbour Works,
 „ J. H. HART, Supt. Royal Botanic Gardens,
Hon. W. WRIGHTSON, Director Public Works,
Mr. E. W. DICKENSON, Engineer Electric Light and Power Company,
Dr. PRADA,
Mr. F. POGSON, Government Veterinary Surgeon,
 „ BERT DE LAMARRE, Chemist and planter of long experience.

So popular were the meetings and the subjects discussed at them, that it was found necessary to enlarge the lecture room by the addition of one of the rooms at the entrance, to give more accommodation to those who attended the meetings.

The introduction of readings and recitations from the great dramatists was a peculiar feature of this Session, the Board wish to express their thanks to their Honorary Treasurer, Mr. McCarthy, the organiser of these readings, and to gratefully acknowledge the services of the members of the Dramatic Club and the other ladies and gentlemen who took part in them.

A musical competition was held in December, but owing perhaps to its novelty, it did not meet with the success anticipated except among the school choirs.

The Board having decided to include a course of lectures on Ambulance work and Home Nursing, sought the assistance of Dr. Inskip Read, who agreed to deliver the first course of lectures. Towards the end of the year, Sir Vincent K. Barrington, Vice-President of the St. John Ambulance Association, who was then in the island, called a meeting of the local centre of that Association (which had been in existence for many years but had ceased for some time to do any active work) for the purpose of meeting the Board of Management of this Institute. The result of this joint meeting was that, with the consent of the parent Association the Local Committee joined the Board of Management, and the Victoria Institute became the local centre.

It is a matter of congratulation that the Board were able to obtain the services of Dr. Inskip Read as their first lecturer, and of Drs. Knox, Eakin, and Laurence, as examiners for awarding the St. John's certificate.

Lectures on nursing are now being given to a very large number of ladies by Dr. Inskip Read. Eighteen new members and ten associates joined the Institute during the year.

The debt due to the Government on loan account has been reduced to £300.

The Board have again received from the Government a grant of £250 towards the expenses of this year.

A Statement of the Revenue and Expenditure up to the 31st December, 1897, is appended.

Exclusive of those who attended the exhibitions and lectures there were 14,414 visitors to the Institute. The Institute still continues to be the meeting place for various societies and clubs.

The Board in conclusion wish to acknowledge the services of Mrs. Latour, their Assistant Secretary; and the rest of the staff. Much extra work has been thrown upon them during the past year, they have done their duty well and with cheerfulness.

Statement of the Revenue and Expenditure of

RECEIPTS.

	$ ¢	$ ¢
Grant from Col. Government		1,200 00
Subscriptions from Members	219 50	
Receipts from Exhibitions, Lectures, etc. ...	347 90	
Reimbursements in Aid (Rents) ...	190 30	757 70
		1,957 70
Balance to Cr. brought forward from 1896		341 74
		$2,299 44

Balance Sheet.

	$ ¢	$ ¢
Balance on 1st January, 1897	341 73	
Receipts as above	1,957 70	
		$2,299 44

Checked these accounts for 1897 with the vouchers and found them correct.

(Signed) GEO. GOODWILLE.

,, JAS. GRAHAM TAYLOR.

the Victoria Institute for the year 1897.

PAYMENTS.

	$ C	$ C
Salaries and allowances of Staff ...	... 338 00	
Repairs, etc. to Premises ...	... 11 98	
Furniture, Fittings and Apparatus	... 134 34	
Cost of Exhibitions, Lectures, etc.	... 590 58	
Printing and Stationery ...	... 101 31	
Lighting	... 77 50	
Postage and other Petty Expenses	... 43 51	
Repayment of Col. Government of 3rd Instalment of Mortgage Debt ...	... 240 00	1,537 22
Balance in hand on 31st December, 1897		762 22
		$2,299 44

31st December, 1897.

	$ C	$ C
Expenditure as above		1,537 22
Balance to Cr. on 31st December, 1897 ...		
In Colonial Bank ...	... 728 10	
In hand	... 34 12	762 22
		$2,299 44

JOHN T. GOLDNEY,
President.

THOMAS I. POTTER,
Hon. Secretary.

Errata.

Page 138, *N. meleagris* Lam. *not* Linn.

Page 150. The generic caption OSTREA Linn. has been omitted from its place before "O. frons Linn."

Page 183 for Saul read Earl (line 23).

Page 197. After Professor Carmody read "F.I.C."

Page 202. After this Table "read see page 197."

Page 205. 8th line from top read "probable" instead of "probably."

Page 208. At the end of the first paragraph instead of ("read labels") read ("The statements contained in the several different Labels used by manufacturers were here read, and their contradictory character pointed out.")

VICTORIA INSTITUTE—TRINIDAD.

FOUNDED 1887.

PATRON:

His Excellency Sir Hubert E. H. Jerningham, K.C.M.G.

BOARD OF MANAGEMENT:

Sir JOHN GOLDNEY, *President,*

SYLVESTER DEVENISH, M.A., *Vice-President.*

The Hon. FRANCIS HENRY LOVELL, C.M.G., *Vice-President,*

ROBERT JOHN LECHMERE GUPPY,

Professor P. CARMODY.

EDGAR TRIPP.

The Hon. ROBERT HENRY McCARTHY,

The Hon. H. CLARENCE BOURNE,

BRUCE H. STEPHENS, *Treasurer,*

F. W. URICH, *Secretary.*

The Victoria Museum which is the Registered Office of the Institute, contains the Keate collection of Shells (mostly East Indian), the Leotaud collection of Birds and various specimens and objects, given or deposited from time to time. It is open to the Public daily, from 8 a.m. to 5.30 p.m.